SEXUAL GAMES

The Heroes of Silver Springs 8

Tonya Ramagos

EROTIC ROMANCE

Siren Publishing, Inc.
www.SirenPublishing.com

A SIREN PUBLISHING BOOK
IMPRINT: Erotic Romance

SEXUAL GAMES
Copyright © 2012 by Tonya Ramagos

ISBN: 978-1-62241-943-2

First Printing: November 2012

Cover design by Jinger Heaston
All cover art and logo copyright © 2012 by Siren Publishing, Inc.

Printed in the U.S.A.

PUBLISHER
Siren Publishing, Inc.
www.SirenPublishing.com

DEDICATION

To my fans who have contacted me through the years since *Twin Games* was released asking when Jackson and Mallory would get their story. This book is for you.

AUTHOR'S NOTE

Silver Springs, MS is a fictional city existing only in my imagination. Any liberties I have taken or mistakes I have made in regards to fire department, police, FBI, DEA, and military procedures are my own for the sake of the story.

SEXUAL GAMES

The Heroes of Silver Springs 8

TONYA RAMAGOS
Copyright © 2012

Chapter One

The barrel of a gun poked FBI Special Agent Jackson Graham in the small of his back and his mind took a freight train to the past. Instinctively, he started to go for his sidearm, but the memory, coupled with the voice, stopped him.

"Don't."

Don't. Don't move. Don't pull your gun. She's in charge.

Yeah, he'd been here before. Well, not exactly here. The last time he found himself in this particular situation he'd been in the bay of the Silver Springs Fire Department instead of the parking garage at his apartment in Waterston. He hadn't known the woman holding him at gunpoint. He definitely hadn't known how the night would turn out.

"Okay, you have my attention." His attention, his cock, and his heart. Said cock boarded that speeding train and brought it back to the present, hardening to stone in an instant. After all these years, Mallory was finally ready to play.

Thank you, sweet baby Jesus.

And, apparently, not just play. He'd warned her when his tie came off, and he had no doubt it would in his immediate future, he would take more than her delicious body. He wanted her heart, her soul, and tonight was step one in finally wrapping up this case.

"Where to, sweetheart?"

"I, um, right. The blue Impala. Stay by the wall. Walk slowly."

Jackson heard the slight confusion in her softly spoken words and gave himself a mental kick in the ass. He needed to stay in character. They were strangers, one being kidnapped at the gunpoint—most likely a water pistol or banana—by another for a night of bed-burning sex. His sense picked up that it wasn't a water pistol or banana stabbing him in the back. Why use a toy prop when his fellow agent had a sidearm of her own? The safety would be on, of course, and Mallory Stone knew how to use a weapon as well as any man in the bureau.

Okay, so play it right, no endearments, and definitely no calling her by name. He didn't want to ruin this for her.

"Look, lady. I'm an FBI agent," he said, settling into his role as soon-to-be hostage. "Do you know what happens to people who kidnap federal agents?"

She answered him by nudging him harder with the barrel of the gun. Apparently her role in this required her to only give orders in two- or three-word sentences. He turned to his right, spotted the Impala, and lifted a brow. Mallory drove a Lexus. Apparently, she'd decided to make tonight as real as possible by not using her own car to play out this little game. It would have been an instant giveaway. He wasn't supposed to know that, so he didn't ask who she borrowed the Impala from.

Instead, he walked toward it slowly, as ordered, keeping close to the wall. He noted she'd parked in the opposite corner of the garage from him, in the only other spot the security cameras didn't reach. He'd had a conversation with the building manager about the security system in the garage, but since the area was practically a crime-free zone, his warning had fallen on deaf ears. He'd taken to parking in the least secure spot, leaving the safe ones for the not-trained-to-kick-some-ass tenants just in case.

Years as an FBI agent had his gaze flicking to the dealer tag where the license plate should be. "You bought a new car?" Okay, so that ripped him out of character but, come on, what happened to her Lexus? His step faltered at the surprise and confusion, and the gun poked harder into his back. She didn't answer, so he kept walking, stopping at the passenger door of the Impala.

He readied himself, knowing what would come next. *Deep breath in. Deep breath out. Don't think about the dark.* He needed to think about Mallory's sea-blue eyes as she stared at him while she removed his tie and shirt. He needed to think about her pink, glossy lips as they planted soft kisses on the flesh she uncovered. Better yet, he needed to think about her sinfully curvy body finally becoming his playground as he got his hands on her the way he'd been dying to for years.

"Don't move."

The gun shifted and she reached around him, dipped a hand into the inside pocket of his suit jacket, and took out his phone. Okay, this was new. Angelina hadn't patted him down when she'd played this game, unknowingly kidnapping him instead of his identical twin brother, Jason, that day in Silver Springs. He supposed he couldn't expect everything about tonight to be the same, which was a good thing considering he'd ended up sharing Angelina with his brother that night, and no way in hell would he ever share Mallory with anyone. Jason had held onto Angelina the next morning, too, while Jackson walked away. He didn't plan on walking anywhere tomorrow morning except further into Mallory's life.

Her hand went for his sidearm next, pulling it from his shoulder holster. Jackson bit back the protest that sprang to his tongue. Mallory knew there was nothing more debasing to an FBI agent than to be disarmed by an assailant. Could that really be her intention, to humiliate him? He'd started suspecting several months back that the key to winning Mallory was to relinquish control. He'd learned a lot working a case in Silver Springs at Club Vixen, a BDSM club across the water. Those lessons had come from a true dominatrix. He'd played the role of DEA Agent Christa Hutchens's submissive. Christa had never demeaned him in any way, but she'd told him some Doms got off on doing it to their subs.

Did Mallory?

Her hand moved from around him, taking his cell phone and gun with it, and the gun at his back lowered. He steadied his breathing as a strip of black cloth stretched in front of his face next. He fought the urge to grab her wrists, to stop her from tying on the blindfold. Instead, he closed his eyes, for the first time in his life welcoming the dark, easily battling the panic that clenched in his gut because he knew this part of the game. He wasn't supposed to see where she was taking him, couldn't know who held him captive, until they reached their destination.

She tied the blindfold tight then gripped his arm above his elbow, guiding him back and to his left a few steps. He heard the sound of the car door opening and let her gently push him forward.

"Get in. Lay down."

Something else new. Angelina had put him in the passenger seat. "I hope we're not going far. That's going to be pretty uncomfortable." At six-foot-one, he'd have to curl into a ball to get his whole body to fit.

"Trunk?" Though she made the word a question, it sounded more like a threat.

Okay, backseat it is.

Jackson crawled into the car and folded himself on the backseat. He grunted when the door hit his feet as she shut it, and pulled his legs in tighter. Another door opened and the scent of perfume followed her into the car.

Jackson drew his brows together behind the blindfold. Mallory always smelled like strawberries. She never wore perfume. He liked the scent, though. It wasn't too potent or floral like most fragrances.

He made a mental note to ask her what brand it was later, to tell her to wear it more often.

"So where are you taking me?" He could ask, though he knew she wouldn't tell him. He probably should make his voice wobble a bit, too, make it sound like he was frightened, just to heighten the intent of the game. After all, he was being kidnapped by a total stranger.

As he expected, she didn't answer him. He heard the engine come to life, heard the click as she put the car in gear, and felt them start to move. In the cramped space of the backseat and with the blindfold over his eyes, he could do little more than listen. He focused on the sounds around him. He heard cars passing by, heard the tires screech faintly on the pavement when she didn't slow enough for a turn, but it was her audible, labored breathing that caught him by surprise.

Mallory Stone didn't get rattled, at least not to the point that she let it physically show. Her training coupled with self-discipline and a smart head kept her steady and outwardly unfazed in sticky situations. He'd watched her come straight out of the academy and hit the club scene on assignments that sent other rookies running. She collected the intel, solved the cases, and moved on to the next assignment without blinking a beautiful sea-blue eye. She had proved herself a mover and a shaker in the bureau. She could handle herself in the line of duty better than some of the male agents he knew.

She could handle her own heart, too, masterfully keeping it under lock and key. He should know. He'd been waiting for that lock to bust for years. It was happening now and it was obviously scaring the shit out of her.

Please, don't get so scared that you put an end to this. Follow it through, Mal, and let me take care of the rest.

Anticipation pumped with hope through his veins. What would she do when they reached wherever she planned to take him? The memory of his previous "kidnapping" resurfaced and he let it come, replacing Angelina with Mallory in the vision as he'd often done in his dreams since that night. He felt Mallory's hands on him, skimming down his torso to the waistband of his slacks. She freed the button, lowered the zipper, and sank to her knees in front of him, taking his pants and briefs down with her. His balls tightened as her nails lightly grazed over his nut sac before palming it and rolling his balls between her fingers. He felt the moan rumble in his chest and fought not to let it out as she closed her pink glossy lips around his cock head.

Jesus, he had to stop the image or he'd end up blowing his wad in his pants before she even touched him. He attempted to shift, to relieve some of the pressure behind his zipper, but the backseat didn't afford him enough room. He wanted to say something, anything to ease the nervousness he heard in her breathing, but he didn't want to ruin it. If he said too much, said the wrong thing, she would run. He knew that as well as he did his own name. Mallory Stone's only fear was losing her heart. She'd come this far. She had to know she was putting that on the line. He'd spelled it out for her and left her no room for doubt about that. It was his job to continue to let her make the moves tonight. If he could pull it off, he'd finally have what he wanted.

Her.

What felt like hours to his tortured cock, but probably only amounted to fifteen minutes tops, passed before she finally slowed the car to a stop. She shut off the engine, got out, and opened the door at his feet.

"Get out."

Jackson had heard her give orders before. Okay, so those orders had been on an assignment and not in the middle of a sex game. Still, her tone was different. It didn't drip sex like it always did when she spoke to him. Then again, maybe it was his desire for her that made him hear that constant you-know-you-want-to-fuck-me in her tone because, hell, yes, he did want to fuck her. Every time he looked at her he had to work not to envision her bronze flesh naked and writhing beneath him as he thrust his aching cock into her sopping pussy.

He uncurled his legs, the move giving his rock-solid cock the necessary space to stretch further, and slid ungracefully out of the car. A gentle breeze greeted him as he straightened. He turned his head, not trying to see because that would be futile, but listening for new sounds, indications that would clue him in on where they were. Outside, obviously. *The lake, perhaps?* Desire looped through him like a ribbon of silk. The idea of making love to Mallory beneath the stars tied that ribbon securely around his stiffened cock.

"This way." She took his arm above the elbow again and led the way.

"Where are we?" Fallen limbs and leaves crunched under his feet. Something brushed his cheek. *A low branch of a tree?* Crickets chirped in the distance. His mind reeled as possibilities of their location created a list he couldn't check off without the ability to see. *Damn it*, he wanted this blindfold gone.

"You'll see."

The first dart of alarm shot through Jackson's system. She'd stopped whispering, apparently no longer afraid of being overheard, and suddenly she didn't sound like Mallory. She didn't feel like Mallory, either. He'd been trained to notice everything, and now the mental notes he'd been subconsciously making started to take the shape of puzzle pieces looking for a fit. The hand on his arm wasn't just soft and warm. It was covered in some sort of glove. Even through the material, he realized she wore a ring on the third finger. Mallory never wore rings. The breasts that had brushed his bicep when she'd taken hold of him and steered him the direction she wanted weren't as pliant or large as Mallory's.

Christ! If he'd been thinking with his head and not his cock, he would've realized the obvious in an instant. This was *not* Mallory Stone.

The toes of his right foot connected with something hard on the ground and he stumbled, stopped, and started to turn. The sound of her pulling back the slide on likely his own M9 Beretta followed by the feel of the barrel as it returned to the small of his back sent an icy chill through his soul. She held the gun with her left hand, something else that should've immediately set off his internal alarm bells, and—*holy shit*—she apparently knew how to use that gun, too. Shock she might actually shoot him propelled him forward.

"Who the hell are you?" Just like that the anticipation in his veins morphed to adrenaline. Forget where they were. Getting away from here alive suddenly became his top priority. He could take her. He didn't doubt that. They taught him more in Quantico than how to shoot a gun. A quick, low sweep of his leg to hers as he spun, coupled with a blow to her gun arm, and she would go down, sending the gun flying.

Hopefully before she gets off a shot.

"Someone who needs your help." Her voice still wobbled with nerves. That could be both good and bad. A nervous person with a gun could find herself too scared to shoot or too trigger-happy to realize what she'd done until it was too late.

Jackson prayed for the first outcome because the second would lead to his certain death. Then again, if she really wanted his help, he couldn't very well do that from a grave. "I don't suppose it crossed your mind to ask?"

"Too risky. Stop here."

Jackson gave a half-humorless laugh and stopped walking. "As opposed to kidnapping a federal agent?"

"No one saw. No one followed. You made it easy enough. Thank you for that."

Yeah, no need to remind him how he'd willingly walked, hard-dick and full of hope, to her car. He'd let her take his cell phone, allowed her to freaking *disarm* him, and gotten into that car with a head full of images and a system surging with need for Mallory.

Fuck! That woman might quite literally be the death of him.

"You can thank me by taking off this blindfold." *And by not shooting me.* "I'm claustrophobic. All this darkness is freaking me out worse than that gun you're holding to my back."

"You're handling well."

"I'm a trained agent. We handle lots of things well."

"That's why I need you."

Need. Jackson knew all about need, though he strongly suspected her definition of the word and his fit in totally different dictionaries.

"You're in the middle of a wooded field on the wrong side of town. I suggest you don't stay here too long after I'm gone."

Jackson felt the gun in his back lower once more, felt her other hand reach around him, and realized she was returning his cell phone to his pocket and his sidearm to his shoulder holster as she talked.

"You're just going to leave me out here?"

"You're a trained agent. You'll handle it well."

Touché. "Do I know you? Because you sure as shit seem to know a lot about me."

She ignored that. "Don't try to follow me. Don't take off the blindfold until you can't hear my car anymore. The club through the trees to your left is where you want to focus. Start with Lexie Stratus. Find her, Agent Graham. No one else will."

"Who is she? What can you tell me about her? Who else is looking for her?" His questions fell unanswered in the night air, followed by a brief silence and then the sounds of twigs and leaves crunching as she left him where he stood.

He turned toward the sound of the car cranking. The black cloth covering his eyes turned a dark gray as the headlights hit him. He didn't take off the blindfold, knowing she was still watching him, knowing one wrong move could still spell death or, at the very least, an exchange of gunfire he'd rather avoid. He waited until the cloth turned stark black again, until the sound of the car's engine started to fade, and yanked the blindfold from his eyes.

He found himself in a wooded field just like she'd said. His gaze landed first through a group of trees in front of him where he saw a path barely wide enough for the Impala she'd been driving. He spun to his left, his attention latching onto the trees where she'd told him to focus. Though them, he saw the flickering neon lights that spelled out *Stardust* above a building that had surely seen better days.

He knew the club, a strip joint that catered to the slime balls and lowlifes of the area with more drugs going in and out the doors than a Rite Aid Pharmacy. The Waterston PD had an undercover task force that frequented the premises of Stardust and other clubs in the area, following up on leads to drug pushers and pimps. As far as he knew, none of those leads had turned over anything at Stardust beyond minor infractions of the law, and nothing that even remotely suggested anyone who hung around the place might be involved in a missing person's case.

Start with Lexie Stratus. Find her, Agent Graham. No one else will.

Apparently his good-Samaritan kidnapper believed otherwise.

* * * *

Mallory Stone looked around at the midthigh skirts, low-cut shirts, and faces with heavily applied makeup and felt decidedly out of place. Six months ago, she could've come straight from the office to the club and fit right in. Then again, until six months ago she'd been on constant assignment. She'd worked undercover and frequented the clubs at all hours of the day and night, following leads and checking out the validity of tips. She still did, though lately her work had been done in the office, thumbing through intel that may or may not be pertinent to her team's ongoing Operation Water Down.

These days, she'd scaled down her dress code, wearing more conservative attire around FBI HQ. She dressed like an agent in slacks or longer skirts, dress shirts and jackets. Today, she'd gone for a black skirt that fell just above her knees with a button-down solid white shirt and a black jacket tapered at the waist. Three-inch black heels completed her outfit and carried her confidently and surely toward the bar.

"What can I get for you?" The bartender was new, male, thirtyish, with no defining features to make a girl swoon, and greeted her with a too-wide toothy grin.

"Vodka and tonic." Mallory settled on a barstool, saw his gaze move over her, and knew when he made the mental decision that she was old enough to be in the club. He might have carded her in her club clothes.

She curled her fingers around the glass he set in front of her and turned on her stool to take in the club behind her. Cinderella's was a middle-class establishment in the middle-class part of town. It stayed off the bureau radar by maintaining a good reputation, with few fights and even fewer drug busts on the premises. Not much trouble broke out in Cinderella's, which made it her favorite place to unwind after a long day at HQ.

Dimmed track lighting illuminated an open floor plan with a close scattering of tables surrounding an LED disco-style dance floor. At seven p.m., the crowd was still thin, the techno music playing from the raised DJ booth soft enough to talk over but loud enough to dance to. Cocktail waitresses dressed in uniforms that were both sexy and classy wove their way through the people holding trays of Jell-O shots and test tubes of the night's special. In little more than an hour, those trays would be close to empty, the music blaring, and the dance floor packed with hot, sweaty bodies grinding to the beat.

She wouldn't be here that long.

"My first instinct is to ask what an amazing-looking woman like you is doing here all alone."

Mallory turned at the voice and met a set of eyes so bright green they stood out even in the dimness of the club. Well-honed observations skills had her taking him in with a glance—mid to late twenties, naturally tousled chestnut hair, and baby-face complexion. He had the build of a swimmer and the tan to go with it, clad in a dark Polo shirt and black jeans. He was handsome, but something in those eyes set off her internal danger alarm. It was probably the way he'd obviously taken her in, like one of the test tubes the waitresses carried around, and decided she would be fun to fuck for the night. The danger came in knowing she'd gobbled him down just as quickly and deduced the same, though she knew she wouldn't follow through with the lusty urge.

"I'm Jim." He looked more like a Nathan, as in Bartell, or a Jeff, as in Bosley, and those eyes were seriously potent.

"Jacqueline." Caution had her giving him the name she used on undercover assignments as she put her hand in his extended one. The contact sent that lusty urge sizzling up her arm right along with the warning of danger she knew she'd do well to heed.

"Are you waiting for someone?" His voice moved over her like whipped cream, smooth and thick, like a politician with the skill to turn anything he said into a conviction.

"No." It didn't occur to her to lie. Years of training and experience, coupled with the sidearm concealed securely in her shoulder holster beneath her jacket, made her feel safe enough to enter any establishment alone.

He smiled, a slow unfolding of shapely lips that promised a fuck, if she were to go for it, would be a damn good one. "In that case, can I buy you a drink?"

Mallory glanced at her glass, lifted it, and took the first sip. "I won't be staying beyond this one." And she wouldn't allow him to buy her another if she decided to stay. If working the club scene had taught her anything, it was to never let a stranger buy her a drink, even in a reputable establishment like Cinderella's. An imperceptible sleight of a hand hiding the hottest date-rape drug on the market was the fastest and far too easiest way to spell a girl's doom.

"Sounds like I'm on borrowed time to convince you to change your mind." He settled on the barstool next to her, flagged the bartender, and ordered a Heineken. "Do you come here often?"

He didn't wince at the obvious pick-up line. Confidence and control pumped off him in waves. In that way, he reminded her of Jackson, always cool and collected. She ought to know. She'd been trying to ruffle Jackson's feathers for years.

One day this tie is going to come off, and you and I are going to play.

Jackson told her that once, just before leaving for an assignment in Silver Springs. She'd finally broken him, if only a little. She had finally gotten him to admit aloud he wanted her. But that admission had come with a threat. The promise and desire in his tone stayed with her even now, shooting through every erogenous zone in her body like a heat-seeking missile. It was his parting words that day that doused the icy water on the flames.

When that happens, it will be more than this delicious body I take.

"Now and then." She pushed the recollection aside, knowing it wouldn't stay from the forefront of her mind for long. Every time she looked at Jackson, every time she thought of him, those words reverberated in her memory. He wanted more than she was willing to give him, more than she *could* give him. Why couldn't no-strings-attached sex be enough?

"It's a cool place. Great crowd," Jim commented. "You know, you'll have to stay long enough to give me at least one dance."

Dance. Yeah, that's what she and Jackson had been doing almost since the day she grew into a woman. They'd been dancing around each other, around the mutual attraction, and the intense desire to be bare skin to bare skin. Because Jackson didn't do flings, or at least he hadn't until she'd goaded him into one with another woman. Or was it two? She still wasn't sure if he'd indulged on his last trip to Silver Springs. She knew he had more than two years before, and with his twin brother and now sister-in-law at that.

You're much too uptight lately, Jackson. Get laid while you're gone. Have a quick fling. Maybe it will do us both some good.

How many times had she told him that very thing? He'd listened, too, at least once, and it had done them some good, though not enough to land him in her bed.

Mallory let her attention slide over Jim and didn't try to hide her attraction in her gaze. Should she take her own advice? She'd been so focused on breaking through Jackson's stuffy shell for so long that she hadn't allowed herself to indulge in... Wow, she couldn't remember how long it had been since she had kept a night of company with anything other than her vibrator.

Because she knew no other man would satisfy the bone-deep, hormone-capturing need that churned through her for Jackson Graham.

"I'll think about it," she told Jim and lifted her glass for another sip. Maybe a little liquid courage would set her on a different track. It might not be the right one, but it might be time for her tie to come off, too.

* * * *

"He's not home." Thaddeus Carter glanced at Terri Vega and bit back a grin at the *duh* expression on her face. Considering he'd knocked on Jackson Graham's apartment door three times, waiting a full minute between each, and he'd yet to hear so much as a rustle from inside, he supposed he deserved the look.

Terri set her duffel bag on the floor at her feet. "Maybe he forgot we were coming."

Thaddeus shook his head. "I confirmed our visit this afternoon before we left the station."

Terri shrugged, her shoulders reaching the tips of her chin-length, blonde ringlets and sending them swinging. "He could've gotten held up at the bureau."

"He must have." Thaddeus put down his own duffel bag and pulled his cell phone from the pocket of his navy blue cargo pants.

Terri folded her arm beneath her breasts and rested a shoulder on the wall beside the door, watching him through eyes that were partly amused and definitely exhausted. The drive from Silver Springs to Waterston had been a three-hour nothing, but hours spent on a structure fire followed by gear cleanup and debriefing had preceded that. "So what now, Vegister?"

He slid Terri a quick look as he thumbed through his contacts. She'd taken to calling him Vegister because he stayed on her case about eating healthier. The woman was a junk-food junkie. How she sustained her amazing figure with the way she consumed cheeseburgers and sweets all the time was beyond him. He might be a chocoholic himself, but he made up for it with a high-vitamin, low-carbohydrate diet and plenty of exercise.

Thaddeus found the contact labeled *MIB – cell* in his phone, slid his thumb over the green receiver icon, and brought the phone to his ear. "I'm calling his cell, see if you're right." Four rings connected him with Jackson's voice mail. He waited for the beep then left a message. "Jackson, it's Thad. Terri and I are in town, standing outside your apartment, actually, where you don't seem to be. We'll hang here a while. Call me back, sweetie."

"Sweetie." Terri grinned. "Oh, he'll love that."

Thaddeus winced. "It slipped, okay?" The endearment slipped a lot these days, and every time it did, it reminded him of Adrien.

He shook off the thought of the other man before it could fully form and moved to the contact labeled *MIB – work*. He listened to three rings this time before a male voice that was decidedly not Jackson Graham answered the phone.

"Agent Graham's office."

"Um, hi," Thaddeus stammered. "I was actually trying to reach Agent Graham. Is he available?"

"He's already left for the day. This is Agent Cameron Stone. Can I help you with something?"

The name rang a bell, though Thaddeus had never met the man. Adrien—who was never far from his mind no matter how much he wished he would be—had mentioned him many times when the Silver Springs DEA had teamed with the Waterston branch of the FBI to catch a notorious Cambodian drug lord who'd wreaked havoc along the coastline.

"No. Maybe. I don't know." Thaddeus's mind ping-ponged around information he'd picked up in conversations with Adrien, too-far-between, way-not-long-enough conversations with Adrien. Aw, man, would he ever get over his obsession with the dude?

The voice on the other end of the cellular waves chuckled. "Let's see if I can help you pick one. Whom am I speaking to?"

"Thaddeus Carter. I—"

"Work with Jackson's brother, Jason, at the SSFD," Cameron finished for him. "Somehow we've never managed to actually meet, but I know who you are."

That's right. It clicked. Cameron Stone was one of Jackson's closest friends. "Terri, she's also on the department, and I are supposed to stay with Jackson for a few days."

"Yeah, you're in town for the Firefighter Challenge, right?"

Waterston was the city host for this year's annual Firefighter Challenge—a competition that sought to encourage firefighter fitness and demonstrate the profession's rigors to the public. Teams of firefighters from around the state would compete wearing full bunker gear and SCOTT Air-Pak breathing apparatuses while racing head-to-head as they simulated the physical demands of real-life firefighting. A linked series of events including climbing a five-story tower, hoisting, chopping, dragging hoses, and rescuing a life-sized, one-hundred-seventy-five pound "victim" would put the firefighters in a race against themselves, their opponents, and the clock.

Thaddeus's rank as engineer of Engine Company 1 and Terri's status as Firefighter/EMT made them the least likely two on the SSFD to accept the challenge. Hence the reason both were immediately gung-ho to do it. Individually and together, their mission was to prove every member of a fire department's crew was as invaluable and competent as the next, even those who spent more time operating a fire truck or attending to the injured than actually fighting the fires.

"Right," Thaddeus answered Cameron. "Thing is, well, we're standing outside Jackson's apartment right now, have been for a while, actually, and he doesn't seem to be home. I thought he might have gotten held up at work."

"He left here over an hour ago. Did you try his cell? Do you have that number?"

"I tried that first and got his voice mail." *And called him sweetie.* What a way to start off a friendship. Thaddeus had never met Jackson face-to-face either. He'd talked to the man on the phone but knew him only by association with his twin brother. One thing he knew with absolute certainty was the other man was not gay. Jason had assured him that his brother didn't have a problem with Thaddeus's sexual preference. Of course, that didn't leave Thaddeus open to hit on the guy, for Pete's sake.

Not that he'd been hitting on Jackson in the message he'd left. The word had simply slipped, just like he'd told Terri. He hoped Jackson would realize that, too, or he might be booking a hotel room for this little trip after all because no way in hell would he and Terri bunk at his parents' for the week.

"Tell you what. Hang tight. It'll take me about ten minutes to get there. I've got a key to Jackson's place. I'll let you two in and then we'll see if we can track him down."

* * * *

I suggest you don't stay here too long after I'm gone.

Jackson's good-Samaritan kidnapper had been right on the money with that one. He needed to get out of this field. Street gangs, thugs, and drugs ruled this part of town. Even in his position hidden in the wooded field, he could see evidence of that all around him. Slivers of moonlight landed on graffiti-painted tree trunks, on broken bottles and used syringes cluttering the ground at his feet. Obviously, those gangs and thugs had taken refuge in these woods a time or twelve dozen. His kidnapper might have returned his cell phone and gun, but neither of those would do him any good if a full crew of violent, Fed-hating men found him.

He mentally tossed around his options as he pulled his cell from his inside coat pocket. Strutting into Stardust, which happened to be the closest establishment, dressed in clothes that screamed *federal agent* wouldn't be so wise. Calling a cab would likely keep him waiting far longer than wise, too. He needed to get back to FBI HQ across town. Cameron had still been there when he left. So had his boss. And wasn't that going to be fun? He could imagine himself calling Adam Cooper, team leader and all-around head badass in the bureau for a ride. Explaining why he needed that ride would be the icing on the cake.

He'd have to, though. As humiliating as it would be, he'd have to tell his boss and teammates everything about tonight because his good-Samaritan kidnapper had gone after him for a reason. She'd known he was an FBI agent.

Still, calling Cameron or the boss would leave him standing here for close to an hour. He knew of only one person who should be closer, one person who could get here sooner, and he really, *really* didn't want to call her.

"Suck it up, Graham," he muttered to himself and looked at his phone. The screen displayed two missed calls, the first from Thaddeus Carter and the second from Cameron. *Shit.* He punched the speed dial for Mallory, making a mental note to return both calls once he knew she was on her way to get him.

He didn't sweat asking her to come to this part of town where reports of carjacking and rape came with bone-chilling frequency. The time when he'd coddled her, kept her under his wing, and watched her every move had long ago passed. Well, okay, he still watched her every move, but not to protect her. The only thing Mallory Stone needed protection from was herself.

Jackson listened to three and a half rings before Mallory's sex-kitten voice filled the line.

"Hello?"

He closed his eyes as that single word sent an excess of testosterone straight to his cock. The woman's voice dripped sex, even when she didn't intend for it to. One word, *any* word, brought vivid images to his mind of supreme out-of-this-world fucking that he knew would leave him bleeding and still wanting more.

"Are you there?" she asked when he didn't answer. "I can't hear you."

It clicked then, both that she was apparently in a club somewhere and she didn't want anyone around her to know who was on the phone. The high techno beat of music nearly drowned out the purr of her voice, and the fact that she'd answered with a simple *hello* rather than her usual clipped and businesslike Stone told him as much. She didn't use his name either, another sign she wasn't alone.

Is she on a date?

Jackson shut off that question before any semblance of an answer started to form. No way did he need to think about her being with another man right now, especially not after what he'd first thought was a sex game between her and him had turned into a total, mortifying disaster.

"Mal, where are you?"

"Cinderella's. Where are you, Slick?"

Slick. Of all the names for her to pick up calling him. Christa Hutchens had called him Slick during the assignment he'd worked with her in Silver Springs.

You're supposed to invite me in, Slick.

Oh, that had been a bad idea.

Does it feel good, Slick?

Oh, yes, it had. Hence the reason inviting her in had been a bad idea.

Don't look so surprised, Slick.

That one had come after she'd blown his mind by telling him she already knew he wasn't the man for her, that she knew his heart belonged to someone else.

"In the woods next to Stardust," he told Mallory. "You know the place?"

"What are you doing there?"

Jackson took a deep breath and let it out slow. "I'll explain later. Are you in a position where you can come get me?"

Mallory laughed, low and hot, and the sound burned a path from his ear straight to his cock. "Now what kind of position do you think I'm in, handsome?"

Oh, no, he was so not going to answer that one. He wasn't going to think about it either. The woman was a pro at turning every thought in his head into pure, carnal, provocative explosions.

Jackson sighed. "Just come get me, Mallory."

"Why is it that you finally say the words I've been waiting to hear and I still don't feel like I'm getting anywhere?"

The blaring music started to fade and he knew she was already headed for her car. "Because you know that's not the way I meant them." *Not unless you plan on giving me what I want in return.*

"Yeah." Her disappointed sigh filled the line and he heard the beep of her car alarm as she disarmed it. "I know. I'm on my way."

"Mal, be careful."

"I always am," she sing-songed and cut the connection.

Yeah, she was, even when she didn't need to be.

* * * *

Cameron Stone stepped off the elevator on the third floor of Jackson's apartment building and immediately spotted the firefighters planted outside Jackson's door. Both turned to look at him as the elevator doors swooshed closed behind him. He took Terri Vega in with a glance as he walked toward them. Her trim, muscular body, deep bronze flesh and short bob of blonde ringlets gave him an unexpected stir in his groin. His step faltered, though, when his attention shifted to Thaddeus Carter, when the man's thin, pink lips unfolded in a dazzling smile that affected Cameron from his head straight to his suddenly stiffening cock.

Sweet Jesus.

Cameron's gaze dropped to the man's feet and did a slow climb back up strong legs encased in navy cargo pants that led to narrow hips, a trim waist, and a mouthwatering torso. The SSFD T-shirt he wore defined every rip of his hard-tone abs and put his impressive set of pectorals on a delicious display. Cameron's attention skipped over the wide expanse of the man's shoulders, over the man's square jaw, over those damnable lips, and collided with a set of Hershey chocolate eyes that made his stomach growl.

"You must be Agent Stone." Thaddeus extended his hand when Cameron reached them, his smile widening to reach his eyes.

Cameron's insides started a milk-chocolate meltdown. "Call me Cameron." He took the man's hand, registered the warmth of his palm, the firm grip of his handshake, and realized he was staring into the man's eyes as if they were lovers.

Christ. What had gotten into him? Cameron liked men. He liked women. He liked sex, in any variation of the act. In truth, he was a playboy and he liked it that way. Few people realized his attraction to other men. He didn't attempt to hide it. He simply kept it on the down-low. Openly flirting with a man he barely knew beyond his name was so not keeping it cool.

"I'm Thaddeus, but you can call me Thad." The man lifted a nonchalant shoulder. "Most people do."

Cameron eased his hand from Thaddeus's grip and broke eye contact because, *holy cow*, the swirls in the man's eyes were telling him he would far more prefer to be called honey or baby over Thad any day of the week. And, yes, that was one other thing he knew about this man besides his name. Thaddeus Carter was openly, undeniably gay and, if that even glide in his rich, deep baritone was any indication, he was openly and undeniably flirting with Cameron.

You started flirting with him first, dumb shit.

"You must be Terri." He turned his attention to the woman, needing a distraction before he did something crazy like back Thaddeus against the wall, capture his way-too-kissable lips, and send both their hormones flying to get-it-on-ville. *Jesus, Mary, and Joseph.* He hadn't had this kind of reaction to a man since meeting Adrien. Even then, he'd been able to control the intense lust coursing through his system. So much so, he'd kept Adrien wondering for well over a year if Cameron even swung to his side of the plate.

"Yep." Terri gave him a smile and a quick nod that had her ringlets bouncing.

Cameron shook her hand and didn't feel more than an ounce of desire wind through him at the contact. She was beautiful, obviously spunky, and smelled of roses and aloe, and she did absolutely nothing for him.

"It's nice to meet you, Cam." She lifted one perfectly plucked blonde eyebrow, the corner of her lips twitching in a knowing grin as she released his hand and let her gaze fall down his front. "So, what, are you protesting the whole MIB look?"

Cameron chuckled and made a mental note to thank her later. Her vivaciousness broke the sexual tension floating in the hallway and gave him the ability to think again. He shot a glance down the pale blue button-down shirt he wore untucked with a pair of khaki cargo shorts and worn tennis shoes.

Rather than answer her because, *hello, testosterone*, he could literally feel Thaddeus's gaze moving slowly down his body inch by cock-teasing inch, he changed the subject. "I talked to Jackson on my way over. He, uh, had a sudden change in plans for the night."

Cameron hadn't been able to get his buddy to tell him exactly what went down tonight. He knew only that Jackson had ended up on the wrong side of town and his car had stayed behind at his apartment. Cameron had parked next to it in the parking garage when he'd arrived.

"He called a few minutes before you showed up. He said he'd be working late," Thaddeus said. "I guess that means you're headed back to the office, too."

Cameron blinked. The way Thaddeus was looking at him left him no doubt the other man wanted him to stay. Funny thing was Cameron suddenly found himself wishing he could, too. "I, well, yeah," he finally stammered.

"Then let us in, if you will, and you can be on your way. Terri and I can get settled in ourselves."

Cameron unlocked the door to Jackson's apartment, pushed it open, and stepped aside. Terri went in first, moving at a brisk walk as if the blazes of hell were after her ankles.

She must have to pee.

But, no, he realized in the next nanosecond when Thaddeus positioned himself between the doorframe and Cameron. She'd hightailed it inside to purposely leave him and Thaddeus alone. He squashed all ideas of thanking her later as he drew in a deep breath and started to say good-bye. The deep breath proved to be a mistake.

Damn, he smells good.

"We'll be in town for a few days." Thaddeus's cheeks turned a truly charming shade of red, yet he still didn't let up. "Maybe I'll see you around again."

Holy heaven.

Cameron held the other man's gaze inappropriately long. His heart pounded against his ribcage. Every response that came to mind rang a warning bell, but for the life of him, he didn't know why. He licked his lips, watched as Thaddeus's gaze dropped to follow the path of his tongue, and his cock pulsed in sheer agony.

"I'm sure you will," Cameron dared to say, then turned and walked swiftly back to the elevator, feeling Thaddeus's heated gaze on him with every retreating step.

Chapter Two

Mallory kept her speed to the posted limit, driving through the Waterston streets with one hand on the wheel and the other on the console gearshift. She hoped she painted the picture for laid-back cool even though everything inside her was tied in knots. A tension-filled silence tainted the air inside her Lexus. Jackson hadn't said much since getting into the car. She'd noticed him scoping the area as she'd pulled away from the woods where she'd found him and could almost see the wheels turning in his head in full FBI mode.

"What happened tonight?" She glanced at him and desire tightened another knot in her core. He looked the same as he had when their paths had crossed earlier that day at HQ. He had the same effect on her now, too. Everything from his shiny black shoes with a black Armani suit and tie over a crisp white button-down shirt to his utilitarian-cut brown hair screamed agent-licious. The man was sexy as sin and dangerously yummy. Okay, so she was guessing on the yummy part. In all her years of chasing after him, he'd never allowed his control to slip even for a kiss.

He'd held her, though. In a moment of apparent weakness after she'd finally pushed him too far, he'd drawn her against him and short-circuited every sense in her body. She'd fit against him like a long-lost puzzle piece, her pliant curves to his solid frame, and she'd known he felt it, too. When he held her, he couldn't hide his attraction to her, couldn't hide the need she so often saw brewing in his stormy gray eyes. That had been the first and only time he'd admitted aloud that he wanted her.

Then he'd made the threat that stayed with her till this day, released her, and walked away.

Beside her, Jackson shook his head and continued staring out the passenger-door window. "I'd prefer to only tell the story once, at the office when we get everyone rounded up."

"Were you hurt?" She started to slow for a stale yellow then gauged the distance too close to stop. She punched the gas, gliding the car beneath the traffic light just as it turned red. She glanced at him. The fleeting red glow illuminated the muscle ticking in his jaw.

"Not physically," he answered dryly, not looking at her. "My ego took a hell of a blow, though."

Mallory knew what it cost him to admit that. Tough as nails, stuffy, and often a pompous ass, Jackson Graham didn't let much penetrate his steely shell, especially on the job. He was a robot, or at least that's what he preferred people to believe. He kept his emotions hidden, on and off assignment.

Except for that one time.

Yeah, and that one time had scared her to the tips of her toes.

"I apologize for pulling you away from Cinderella's."

He made the conversational shift before she could prod for more answers. She let it go, finding a string of patience within herself to latch onto until they reached HQ.

"It's no big deal. I was considering leaving when you called anyway." That was a half-truth, but she went with it. She'd really been debating on another drink, a dance with Jim, possibly more.

"Considering?" Jackson finally looked at her, his expression blank, guarded. "Was there something that might have kept you there if I hadn't called?"

Should she tell him? Would it help her mission or hinder it? Making Jackson jealous had never worked for her before. That was if she'd ever managed to make him jealous in the past. If she had, he damn sure never let it show.

"I thought about staying for another drink, maybe a dance or two." As she said it, she felt herself slip into you-want-to-fuck-me mode. She'd been playing the game with Jackson for years, laying it on thick, not attempting to hide an ounce of her attraction to him. That, too, hadn't worked yet, but hope sprung eternal. "What's the matter, handsome? Does the thought of me on a dance floor make that conservative brain of yours think provocative thoughts?"

"I've seen you on a dance floor. You're idea of dancing makes Patrick Swayze and Jennifer Grey's interpretation fit for a Disney special."

Mallory threw her head back and laughed. "You should try it sometime. A couple of hot, sweaty bodies bumping and grinding to the beat of the music, a little alcohol to numb the senses..." She trailed off as her words created an image in her head that made her panties wet. She saw Jackson on a dance floor, his tie gone and shirt half unbuttoned to reveal a rock-solid chest speckled with dark springy hair. She saw his stormy gaze lock with hers as he crooked a finger, beckoning her closer. She could almost feel one corded, muscular arm as it slid around her waist and yanked her close. Then he started to move, grinding his thickening cock against her belly and sending slivers of erotic heat straight to her pussy.

"I should try it with you, I suppose."

His words ripped her from the quickly accelerating porn flick taking form in her mind. She shifted in her seat and felt more juices escape her slick folds as she pulled the car into the parking lot of FBI HQ. She looked at him as she put the car in park and shut off the engine.

"It would be a place to start." She slid her gaze from his face to his chest, her hands burning to touch. She wanted to push off his jacket, rip open his shirt and flatten her palms on his tanned flesh. She wanted to feel his dense muscles flex under her hands. She dared to lean closer to him, to reach for his tie, and let the silk glide through her fingers. "You're still wearing this tie far too tight, Agent Graham."

His hand closed around her wrist and she suddenly felt dizzy, intoxicated. It was as if his fingers came equipped with tiny needles that penetrated her flesh and injected her with a heavy dose of erotic desire. His stormy gaze locked with hers and the intensity in his stare took her breath away. Challenge, promise, and hope twisted in an expression that was starkly sexual and dangerous as hell.

"Take it off, Mallory. You know what you'll get."

Sanity teetered as need urged her to do things her mind screamed she shouldn't. Yeah, she knew what she would get, exactly what she'd wanted for more years than she could count. Knowledge of what it would cost her in return had her slowly dropping her hand and easing back into her own seat.

A flash of disappointment moved through his handsome face. "You still aren't ready to play."

The passenger door closed with a finality that sent a shudder down her spine. Anger and a fear she could no longer ignore kept her planted in her seat as she watched him walk into the building, saw him stop just inside the door to wait for her. He'd taken over the game, changed the rules.

"Not by a long shot," she muttered as she got out of the car and slammed the door behind her. She was Mallory Stone, and she didn't stand placidly by while anyone attempted to take control of anything she possessed. Jackson wanted to play. Well, then, she'd just have to stage a game he'd never forget.

* * * *

"Oh my God, did you see how he looked at you?" Terri plopped down on the end of the sofa in Jackson's apartment and folded her legs Indian style as she reached for a slice of pizza from the open box on the coffee table. She had taken a quick shower and changed into a pair of barely there shorts and a cut-off T-shirt that had seen better days.

Thaddeus considered a shower himself, but his grumbling stomach demanded he eat first. They'd decided to call for a pizza, finding a flyer for a local pizzeria under a magnet on the fridge. Terri had danced around the apartment as if they had hit a gold mine. Jackson's kitchen was stocked with better, healthier options that Thaddeus could have whipped up in a jiffy, but everything was meticulously organized and seeming to scream *mess me up and you die*.

When Jackson had called, he'd told them to make themselves at home. One look around his apartment and they'd both been afraid they might cross a line. Absolutely nothing appeared to be out of place. A buttery leather sofa and recliner with brown marble end tables and a coffee table decorated the main room. Bookshelves laden with nonfiction novels, crime thrillers, and framed photos flanked a big-screen television. Two barstools sat at the bar separating the kitchen and living room. Thaddeus had taken a peek into the bedrooms to discover both were furnished with king-size beds, a wooden dresser, and matching nightstands. Everything was in neutral colors and probably came straight from IKEA.

"Of course you saw," Terri said around a mouthful of pizza, "because you, my fruity friend, were looking right back at him."

"What did you expect me to do, ignore the guy?" Thaddeus handed her one of the canned sodas he'd taken from the fridge, put a slice of pizza on a saucer, and settled on the opposite end of the sofa.

Terri laughed, a quick burst of thoroughly amused air. "Honey, you couldn't have ignored that man if you'd tried. Hell, I couldn't have. He was H-O-T."

Tell me about it. Wicked hot would've been Thaddeus's description. He still felt the heat of Cameron Stone's presence and the man had been gone for over an hour. The FBI agent oozed sex from every pore, and the way he'd looked at Thaddeus nearly made him come in his cargo pants. Thaddeus had never found the grunge, surfer-boy look appealing, until today. Who knew when you put a pair of tennis shoes and khaki cargo shorts with an untucked shirt on a strongly defined, muscled body like Cameron's, you'd get six feet of pure temptation wrapped in carnal sex appeal? And his eyes, sweet baby Jesus, those blue eyes had taken Thaddeus on a dive headfirst into the want-to-fuck-you sea.

Terri frowned as she took another bite. "I've really about had it with all the super scrumptious guys being gay. First Adrien, then you, and now Cameron Stone. I mean, aren't there any hunk-a-licious, doable, *straight* men anymore?"

Thaddeus's lips twitched. "Sure there are. That's why this trip should be like a treasure hunt for you. Think of it, Ter, a whole city full of men you've yet to explore."

"Mmm hmm, and who starts exploring with the first guy we meet?" She leaned over and patted his thigh. "I'm proud of you, Vegister. You flirted first. I've never seen you do that."

Thaddeus couldn't believe he'd done it himself. He'd glanced down the hall when he'd heard the elevator doors slide open, and his hormones had overloaded his brain. When was the last time that had happened?

When you looked at Adrien Bingham.

Yeah, he'd boarded the same flight to Happy Hormonal Land the first time he'd set his gaze on Adrien, too.

And look how that turned out.

"It was good, you know, to see you let yourself be attracted to another man. You've been holding out for Adrien for so long and, well, it's probably a good thing that you're finally moving on."

Thaddeus didn't want to move on. He wanted Adrien. He'd had the man, too, in an afternoon of amazingly explosive sex right in the middle of his own kitchen. God, he still dreamed about that day. He wished he could turn back the clock and do it all over again. His attraction to Adrien wasn't one-sided. Adrien wanted him, but someone else stood in the way, someone Thaddeus had never met.

Or had he?

Thaddeus's gaze landed on a framed photo on top of the bookshelf across the room. In the picture, Cameron and Jackson stood on either side of a beautiful autumn-haired woman. Their arms were entwined around each other's shoulders, the woman's head resting on Jackson's chest, and Cameron smiling down at her. That smile pulled at something in Thaddeus's gut.

"I think he's the one." He didn't realize he'd put voice to the thought until Terri responded.

"Aw, honey, I know you did, but you can't wait around for him to make his choice forever."

Thaddeus shook his head. "I meant Cameron."

Terri's eyes widened. "Now hold up, Road Runner. You talked to the guy for, what, all of five minutes, with me standing there, might I add? I've heard of love at first sight and all that jazz, but you can't really believe that."

Thaddeus sighed and set his saucer holding his untouched slice of pizza on the coffee table, his appetite suddenly gone. "You're not getting it. Cameron knows Adrien. They were both a part of the operation that brought down Ving Kim Phay's cartel."

Terri's jaw dropped. "Oh my God. You think?"

Thaddeus shrugged. "It fits. Adrien talked about the man a lot. Sure, it was all related to the case and stuff, but…"

It did fit, far more than Thaddeus wanted it to. The DEA and FBI had worked closely for over four years before they'd finally taken out the notorious Cambodian drug lord. Thaddeus had met Adrien in the midst of it all, and Adrien, though single, had already been hung up on another guy.

I don't really believe he's an issue, but I need to know for sure before I go any further.

Adrien had said that after laying a kiss on Thaddeus in the middle of a movie wrap-up party Thaddeus had never been able to push far from his mind. Unable to give up on the man, Thaddeus had stood on the sidelines, quietly going crazy while he waited for Adrien to figure things out.

"What are you going to do?"

"I don't know." What could he do? He could make sure the next time he saw Cameron he kept his happy little flirt bunny in check, for starters. Yeah, that would definitely be a good idea.

"You could ask him." She giggled when Thaddeus slanted her a disbelieving look. "Oh, come on, you're not as chickenshit as you think. Remember how you staged that meeting at the gym so you'd purposely run into Adrien? Remember how you admitted to it over drinks at the Paradise Lounge? A confession, might I remind you, that led to a sensual walk on the beach and several days later—"

"Yeah," Thaddeus cut her off. "I remember." *Far too well.* That several days later was when he and Adrien pushed all caution to the wind and had their wild bout of monkey sex in his kitchen.

"Okay," Terri said slowly. "I can see how you wouldn't want to come right out and ask Cameron, considering you just met the guy. So call Adrien. Ask him."

Sure. Thaddeus could just hear that conversation. *Hey, baby, you know that guy you said you didn't believe was an issue? The one who's kept you from closing in on me for years? The one you said wasn't an issue any longer the last time we talked, but then suddenly you were backing away again? His name wouldn't happen to be Cameron Stone, would it?*

"No." Thaddeus pushed himself off the sofa and raked a hand through his hair. "I'm not calling either of them. I'm not asking either of them. What I am going to do is take a shower, then go to bed."

And lie there awake half the night thinking about both men because, *fuck*, he suddenly had a feeling fate had dropped him into a game of three-man chess he hadn't known was already in progress.

* * * *

Jackson sat in a chair in front of his boss's desk and held the other man's gaze. Most agents squirmed when they found themselves subject to that inscrutable stare. He would not make that basic blunder. He kept his posture relaxed, his expression blank, and simply waited.

Adam Cooper sat behind his desk, his posture relaxed in his dark Italian suit. Everything about the man screamed badass agent, from his muscular build to the rough features of his face. Power and control pumped off him in waves. Speculation had been flying around the bureau for years as to whether the man was even mortal.

He held a pen in his left hand but, like usual, didn't make any agitated or nervous movements. A pad was on his desk with notes scribbled across it in handwriting worse than any doctor's. He'd taken notes of Jackson's account of the night, not commenting once on anything Jackson had said.

Jackson saw the muscle jumping in the man's stern jaw, though. Cooper was likely grinding his teeth so hard it was a wonder he didn't have little bits of enamel shooting out of his ass. Then again, he was sitting on said ass.

A heavy silence filled the office. Jackson knew what Cooper was doing. Mallory, Cameron, and Marcus Kell would know, too. The four of them had worked under Cooper's lead long enough to know the man could outwait the dead. In turn, Cooper should know neither of them would jump in with excuses, even when they'd fucked up as badly as Jackson had tonight.

"Since no one else seems to have the balls to ask, I'm going to." Cameron broke the silence, his tone half amused as he flattened a hand on the wall closest to the boss's desk. "What the hell were you thinking, Graham?"

Yeah, Jackson had left that much out. He had recounted every second of the night from the point that he'd gotten out of his car in the apartment garage to the moment he had called Mallory for a lift. Everything, that is, except for the thoughts that had been going through his head.

"She obviously knew you." Cooper put down the pen, propped his elbows on the desk, and steepled his fingers, his stare on Jackson unwavering. At times like this, Jackson felt like the man could peel him like an onion, layer by layer. "Instinctively, a part of you thought you knew her. Otherwise you wouldn't have gone with her so easily. What was it about her that made you think that?"

Absolutely nothing. Everything she'd done, everything she'd said, his mind had twisted around, putting Mallory in the starring role.

"Was it something about her voice, something she said?" Cooper's own voice sounded hard, restrained. The man was holding back, no doubt waiting for the moment when he could ream Jackson's ass in private. "What about her scent, the feel of her hand?"

Jackson shook his head once. Those were all things he'd noted were different when he'd finally started thinking with the brain in the head on his shoulders rather than the one between his legs. "The only thing I saw before she blindfolded me was the car, a blue Impala with dealer tags."

"That should be easy enough to trace," Mallory said from her place on the leather sofa against the sidewall of the office. "Dealer tags are good for thirty days. We'll pull up a list of all the blue Impalas sold in the last month, then start narrowing it down."

Cooper looked at Mallory. "Do it." His attention switched back to Jackson. "What about the name, Lexie Stratus?"

"It doesn't mean a thing to me, boss. My hunch is she works, or has worked, at Stardust. I wouldn't think she'd be a customer considering the vast majority of the club's clientele are men." Then again, his hunch could be way off. It sure as shit had been all night long.

Cooper's gaze flicked over Jackson's shoulder. "Pull her up, Kell. Get me everything you can find on this woman. I want to know who she is down to her fucking shoe size. And check with our guys at the PD. They've had a task force working the clubs in that vicinity for months. See what they've turned up." He picked up a soda can near his keyboard and leaned back in his chair, studying Jackson as he took a sip.

Here it comes. Everyone had ignored the question when Cameron put voice to it first, but Jackson could see it now in his boss's vivid blue eyes. The man was a stickler for perfection and details. He wouldn't rest until he knew everything.

"Go through it again. Just the parts about the woman, what you picked up about her, what made you comfortable enough to go with her without question."

"I thought she was Mallory." Jackson didn't flinch, didn't sigh, didn't let his gaze waver from his boss's eyes. He heard Mallory's quick intake of breath across the office, but he didn't look at her. It took every ounce of training, skill, and willpower he possessed to come across calm, cool, and collected, knowing those five simple words had just revealed more to his team leader and colleagues than he'd ever wanted to admit.

Cooper put the soda can quietly back on the desk. For a moment, Jackson swore his gaze lessened in intensity. He let a full ten seconds pass before he spoke again. "You judged her to be the same height as Mallory."

He didn't ask the obvious. Why would Jackson think Mallory would pull a gun on him, kidnap him from his parking garage, take him to a secluded place in the woods, more than likely because he'd already guessed. The man hadn't made it to his high-level position in the FBI by being stupid. He didn't miss anything when it came to the job or the members of his team. The man's extensive observational skills had already uncovered the powerful effect Mallory had on

Jackson's senses, the way her mere presence could cloud his better judgment.

His judgment had gotten clouded tonight, all right, and it hadn't even taken her presence to do it. The simple thought of her had been enough.

"Yes, sir, same height and close to the same build. Her breasts brushed against my arm. They were smaller, firmer than Mallory's." *And please don't ask me how I know that.* Jackson continued speaking before his boss had the chance to ask. "She was left handed and wore a ring on the third finger of her right hand. She wore perfume. I didn't recognize the fragrance. It had a soft scent, not too potent or floral."

"What about her voice?" Cooper asked. "Did she sound like Mallory?"

"She spoke in whispers, or close to it at least. I didn't really get a good bead on her voice until we were in the woods, but yes, she sounded a lot like Mallory, at first, in any case."

"What else?"

As in what else had he left out? What else could he tell his team that would not only lead them to catching his good-Samaritan kidnapper but would also humiliate him further?

"She was wearing thin gloves. Not latex. Something soft. I doubt it will do any good to dust my Beretta and cell for fingerprints, but I'll turn them over to the lab anyway."

"Good enough. Have you had any dealings with any women in your apartment building, anyone who might fit the sense description you've come up with?"

Dealings? As in any women in his apartment building he'd had sex with? Jackson shook his head. "Most of the tenants are older couples. There are three who I can think of offhand who aren't, but I've never done more than share a passing glance and a curt hello with them."

"Check them out, as well as any other woman you've been in contact with recently. Whoever she is, she knows you by some association, well enough to know you're an agent, possibly better than that. She knows where you live and where you park. She knows that building well enough to know the areas the security cameras reach and where they don't. She's got the inside track on us right now. I want to know how." Cooper paused and flicked a glance to his left. "Cameron, get with the manager of the apartment building. I want the security footage. This woman obviously knew how to stay off camera, but she had to get into that garage. Maybe the lighting was good enough to catch her behind the wheel of the Impala when she pulled in." He waited a beat then added, "Go."

Cameron and Kell moved for the door.

Jackson started to push himself to his feet, noting in his peripheral vision that Mallory did the same, when Cooper stopped them.

"You two, stay."

Shit. Jackson knew he should have seen this coming. The boss didn't do heart-to-hearts often but, when he did, watch out.

Cooper got to his feet, walked to the window behind his desk, and waited for the click of the door as it closed behind the other agents. "Fraternizing is not forbidden in the bureau. Some team leaders frown upon it. However, you both know there are several agents in this office alone who are romantically involved or even married. I'm your team leader, not your babysitter or your sex therapist. If you two have something going on, I'm not going to say a word about it. But you can both bet your badges I will say something when it causes one of my two best agents to lose his head and forget everything he's trained for."

He turned around, looked from Jackson to Mallory and back again. "I don't know what kind of games the two of you are playing. Apparently, some pretty steamy ones, if what happened tonight is any clue. Get your head right. Next time, it might not be just your life you put on the line, Graham."

"Yes, sir." Jackson got to his feet, waited for Mallory to walk out the office door in front of him, and followed her out, closing the door quietly behind him.

"Why do I feel like I was just dismissed from the principal's office?" Mallory asked softly, a slight trace of amusement in her tone.

Jackson fell into step beside her. "You weren't. I was." He probably owed her an apology, too. After all, it wasn't her fault he'd immediately assumed she was playing a sex game with him tonight.

Except, damn it, it was her fault. She'd been the one to start chasing after him years ago. Sure, he'd been attracted to her. Hell, he'd wanted her with every ounce of his being. But he'd refused to act on it, to even *think* about it because she was both a coworker and his best friend's little sister. She had been the one who couldn't leave well enough alone.

"You really thought it was me tonight?"

And she still can't.

"Wow." She laughed, a quick burst of air that sounded half disbelieving and half flattered. "Talk about giving me credit for creativity. I don't know whether to thank you, handsome, or laugh my ass off."

"I'm glad you find it so amusing," Jackson said dryly and pushed the door open to his office down the hall from Cooper's. He flicked on the overhead light and headed for his desk.

"You didn't answer Cameron's question, you know?" Mallory, of course, followed him inside, closing the door behind her and proving for the second time in as many minutes that she couldn't leave well enough alone.

"I believe I answered it plainly enough when I told Cooper I thought the woman was you."

"But why?"

Jackson sat down behind his desk and bumped the mouse to his computer to pull it from sleep mode. He didn't look at Mallory. He didn't need to. Her shapely, golden legs had carried her into his office, bringing with them the scent of strawberries and pheromones that radiated straight to his cock enough times that he didn't need a refresher image.

"Remember my fling in Silver Springs?" His fingers flew over the keyboard as he pulled up a list of every tenant with an address in his apartment building.

"The first or the second?" She walked around his desk and perched her delectable ass on the edge a mere half inch from where his right arm rested.

His grip on the mouse tightened as the heat from her closeness wrapped around him like an erotic blanket. He slid her a look out of her corner of his eye. "There was only one." Only one that led to penetration sex, in any case, and the only one that had any pertinence to this conversation.

"With Angelina, your brother's wife."

Jackson returned his attention to the computer screen, to the list of names he'd pulled up. "I'm not going to ask how you figured that out, and she wasn't his wife at the time but, yes, with Angelina."

"What does she have to do with tonight?"

"That night with her started the same way tonight did," he answered her absently as he scanned the list. Bob and Nancy Smith, George and Marsha Timmons, Jean Cooley, Deborah Forsythe…all men and women above the age of fifty except for the last. He made a mental note on Deborah Forsythe, though the picture in his memory of the woman was as far from his good-Samaritan kidnapper as a woman could get. Short, overly plump, and the raspy voice of a three-pack-a-day smoker, she definitely didn't fit his sensed profile of his kidnapper. Could his senses really have been that far off?

No, not possible. Still, he'd have to check her out.

"She kidnapped you?" Surprise and sheer amusement laced Mallory's tone.

"She got the wrong twin, but yes, she kidnapped me."

Bert Alcove, Sarah Sweeney, Mitch and Allison Brinkley...not all over the age of fifty but either married, male, or not fitting to the profile. He added Sarah Sweeney and Allison Brinkley to his mental list. If his memory served, Sarah was too tall and not overly plump but built heavier than his kidnapper. Allison, on the other hand, just might fit.

He thought about the ring, distinctly knew it had been on the kidnapper's middle finger of her right hand. Had she touched him with her left hand at all? No. Her left hand had been otherwise preoccupied with the gun she'd been holding.

"What a way to spice up a relationship." Mallory's hand brushed his arm as she put her own arms behind her and leaned back on the desk. She made a sultry *hmm* sound and whips of arousal slashed at his cock. "Very creative. Apparently, it worked and got her more than she bargained for."

"She got the idea from a book, *Sex Games*, or something to that effect." He pretended ignorance, though he knew damn well all about the book. Angelina had sent him a copy as a gift. The book now sat on a shelf in his living room.

Mallory leaned in, angling her head until she blocked his view of the computer screen. She was so close he felt her breath fan his lips, smelled the remnants of the drink she'd had at Cinderella's. If he shifted a fraction of an inch he'd be kissing her.

Christ, he wanted to kiss her. He wanted to push everything on his desk to the floor, lay her back, and ravage her.

"Is that what you want, Jackson?" she asked softly, her tone dripping with ecstasy and promises of so much more. "Are those the kind of games you want to play?"

Jackson stared into her eyes, drowning in their deep blue sea, and he almost did it. Fuck niceties. Fuck what would happen come morning. Fuck the control that had kept him from taking what he wanted, what she blatantly offered him for so very long.

He reached for her, tunneled his fingers through her satiny autumn-leaf colored hair, and cupped her nape. Victory sparked in her eyes, igniting the challenge that was never far away.

"Do it," she whispered. "Kiss me. I dare you."

Desire stole the oxygen between them, making it hard to breathe, even harder to think. Sanity teetered on the brink of explosion. If he kissed her, he wouldn't stop with her lips. His mouth watered to taste so much more. His tongue pulsed with the need to lick his way down her neck, her throat, to delve beneath the material of her blouse and find the swell of her ample breasts. He wanted to taste every inch of her, to feel her writhe beneath his tongue as he painted a path down her body that would lead him to her pussy.

"You're wet, Mallory." Need made his voice husky, dark, thick. Surprise flashed though her expression. He'd never spoken to her so bluntly. "I can smell you."

"I'm always wet around you." She tried to close the distance between their mouths, but he'd tightened his hold on her hair, preventing her from moving. Calculation swirled with frustration in her eyes. "Touch me, Jack. Taste me."

"Not at the office." He brushed his lips to the tip of her nose and forced himself to pull back before he took it any further. "And not tonight." He released his hold on her hair and pushed away from his desk. She didn't reach for him, didn't try to stop him, but he saw a flash of anger move through her angelic face.

"You're a pompous ass, Jack." She slid off the desk and straightened her skirt, her movements jerky.

Yes, I am. Calling on that part of him was the only thing that kept his head straight around her. "It's been a long night, Mal. Are you going to give me a ride home or do I need to call a cab?"

"Kick you out at the curb is what I should do." Her heels clacked angrily on the tiled floor as she headed for the door.

"At least I'll be that much closer to home."

Chapter Three

"We've officially lost our minds." Thaddeus's gaze climbed the five-story tower where the firefighter challenge would take place for the next three days, and his gut did a funky little dance. He remembered watching the firefighter challenge as a kid, the intense longing that had overcome him to be out there, to be a part of it. It had taken him twenty years to get here, but tomorrow that dream would come true.

"Aw, come on." Terri gave his shoulder a playful slap. "You're not intimidated, are you?"

Thaddeus slid her a look. She'd dressed in a pair of short denim shorts, tennis shoes, and a pink and black polka-dot blouse. With her short bob of blonde ringlets, she looked like a sixteen-year-old school girl rather than a twenty-eight-year-old kick-ass firefighter/EMT.

"And you aren't?" He watched as her attention did the same slow climb up the tower his had done seconds before.

She pursed her lips when her gaze reached the top and slowly nodded. "Yeah, okay, maybe a little. Good thing neither of us is afraid of heights."

"Nah, can't say it wouldn't be more fun to jump from the top, though. You know, as long as there's a safety net waiting on the ground to catch us."

Terri barked a laugh. "You can be such an adrenaline junky sometimes."

Thaddeus lifted a brow. "Aren't most firefighters?"

"Well, yeah." She stabbed a finger into his bicep. "What you have to remember, Road Runner, is to hit each and every step on your way back down that thing."

"Details, details." Thaddeus grinned, but he knew she was right. The tower consisted of six sets of stairs, each with ten steps. The rules stated he could take those steps two at a time while carrying the forty-two pound, one-hundred feet of coiled hose on the way up, but he had to hit each tread while holding onto both handrails on either side on his way down or he would be penalized. During practice, he'd often gotten ahead of himself, especially when he neared the bottom. The instinct to jump over the final few steps to the ground took over without thought.

That simply meant he had to think. *Okay, no biggie there.*

"Details that will cause us to lose precious seconds, Vegister."

Thaddeus saw her gaze move over the rest of the course. The Firefighter Combat Challenge course had been set up on the grounds of the Waterston Coliseum, cordoned off from the spectator stands on either side. Food and memorabilia booths were scattered about the perimeter, waiting to serve the crowd.

"We've trained for this, all of it. We're awesome. You know we're ready. We've got this licked, my fruity partner."

Her confidence was inspiring. Thaddeus would give her that. She was right, too. They had trained for it. They'd worked their asses off for close to four months preparing for the rigorous challenges they would face tomorrow and Sunday. And they were awesome. They'd registered for the challenge individually and as a coed tandem team. They would both compete in the individual divisions the next day. Sunday, when they competed as a tandem team, he would start off the course, knocking out the first half consisting of the high-rise pack-carry, hose-hoist, and forcible-entry events. Terri would complete the course with the hose advance and victim rescue.

"My time is still off. The record to beat is a minute and nineteen seconds." He puffed out a hard breath. "The best I've done so far is a minute thirty."

"You're just saving the speed for when it matters."

"If that's the case, then you should skunk the female record." He'd timed Terri and watched her complete the course seconds below the current minute-and-forty-eight time for the female division.

"Let's hope so."

"The current coed tandem team record is a minute and twenty-six seconds." He knew he didn't need to tell her that. They had studied the challenge's website, as well as the course layout they'd been provided upon their online registrations. They had talked about strategies and carefully decided which of them would be best at completing each of the five events. Despite their differences in gender, they were pretty evenly matched in strength and endurance.

"We did it in Billings in a minute twenty," Terri reminded him.

"Once." Thaddeus turned and hooked his thumbs in the pockets of his cargo pants.

"In an enclosed stairwell," Terri pointed out. "Climbing that tower will be different. It's open, brighter, wider."

"And exposed to all the elements. The building we used for practice in Billings was also only four stories, not five."

Terri shrugged and pushed a blonde ringlet out of her eyes. "So you have five seconds to make the extra flight. Look at it this way, if we don't win, at least we tried. That's the whole point, right?"

"Absolutely." Winning wasn't the only goal on his mind. Sure, he wanted them to come out on top in all three divisions. He had no doubt they'd come damn close, too. But as far as he was concerned, he'd know the sweet taste of victory the moment he stepped onto the course tomorrow.

"Will your parents be here? Have you talked to them yet, let them know you're in town?"

Thaddeus nodded. "They'll be here, them and any other member of the Carter clan they can round up. I talked to them this morning. Mom is still giving me shit because I didn't want to stay at the estate instead of bunking with Jackson."

"We could have, you know? Stayed with them, I mean. I wouldn't have minded."

Thaddeus would have. Spending close to a week in the family home with his parents and Terri would have been a bad, *bad* idea. He glanced at his wristwatch. "I'm thinking it's time to find some lunch. What about you?"

"I'm game. I could go for a big, thick, juicy cheeseburger right about now."

"Uh uh, you got pizza last night. Today we eat healthy."

Terri wrinkled her nose and feigned a pout. The combination of the expression sent him into a fit of laughter.

"I talked to Jackson before he dashed out of the apartment this morning. There's a place called the High Noon Café a few streets over from here. I've never been there. He said it opened a few months ago. He recommended it highly, said it has fantastic blue plate specials every day."

Terri groaned dramatically. "Something tells me I don't want to know what a blue plate special is."

"Well, I do. Besides, the last thing you need is to tank up on carbs before you tackle that thing tomorrow." He tossed a look behind him at the challenge course and started walking.

"You know, Vegister. You really have your priorities screwed up. Carbs are supposed to be good for active people."

"Carbs loaded with nutrients, yes. The stuff you shovel into your body, no." He shot her a grin as he reached the car. "And vegetables have carbs. Some just have less than others."

"Does Jackson eat at this place a lot?"

"It sounded like he does from the way he talked. Why?"

"Just curious."

Thaddeus narrowed his eyes. Terri Vega was rarely *just curious* about anything. "Spill it." He waited a beat and a thought formed in his mind that had him spinning in front of the car to look at her. "Interested?" He knew he didn't need to say more. Sure enough, her eyes widened and she stammered so fast he couldn't help but grin.

"In Jackson Graham? Are you kidding! He's hot, yeah. I'll admit that. Hell, I already knew *that*. I mean, Jason's hot and we've worked with him for years. Kind of hard not to notice. And Jackson *is* his identical twin, so it stands to reason that…"

Her babbling trailed off as Thaddeus let his grin spread. She puffed a hard breath up her face, causing her ringlets to flutter wildly.

"No. I'm not the least bit interested in him. He's too…straight-laced. Yeah, that's the perfect description for him, straight-laced and stuffy. Too serious, too."

"You got all of that from talking with him for all of ten minutes last night when he finally made it home?"

"And how much did you get out of your less-than-five-minute conversation with Cameron Stone last night in the hallway, my fruity friend?"

Hell, walked right into that one, didn't I?

"Let's not go there." He rounded the front of the car, opened the driver door, and slid in behind the wheel.

"Touchy, touchy." Terri got in the passenger seat beside him and fastened her seatbelt. "I asked if Jackson ate at this place he told you about a lot because I figured if he does, well, he and Cameron are close friends."

"And you figured we might run into them there." Thaddeus stabbed the keys in the ignition and started the car with a jerk of his wrist.

"It's a possibility."

Yeah, it is. A good enough possibility that Thaddeus almost considered letting her have that cheeseburger she wanted instead of taking the chance.

She turned slightly in her seat so she could look at him. "Have you decided what you're going to do?"

"Yeah, I'm going to eat lunch, let my food settle, then hit that gym in Jackson's apartment building he mentioned to me this morning." He didn't need to look at Terri to know she rolled her eyes at that. The low-throated growl she made always came complete with an eye roll.

"I meant about Cameron, numbskull."

"Absolutely nothing."

"But...but—"

"We were exhausted last night." He cut her off as he pulled the car away from the sidewalk. "He was friendly. Friendly does not equal gay. I was probably wrong about the whole thing, including him being the guy Adrien is hung up on. And if I wasn't, that is not a situation I need to be mixed up in."

He was messed up enough already. Pining for a guy who couldn't make up his mind, instantly attracted to another man who probably wasn't even gay. He didn't need a calculator to know that equaled supremely fucked up.

The memory of Cameron's sea-blue eyes surfaced in his mind, the heat he'd felt from the other man's gaze, his quietly spoken words laden with the promise Thaddeus would see him again. In the blink of his eyes, the image transformed, taking on the shape of Adrien's too-handsome face.

Terrible thing about it was he *wanted* to be mixed up in that situation, really, *really* bad.

* * * *

"That's the car." Jackson put his hand on the back of Cameron's chair and leaned over the man's shoulder, tapping the television screen as the blue Impala came into view. He watched as the car drove past several open parking spots and disappeared from the screen.

"She knew exactly where to park to stay off camera," Cameron commented as he let the footage play. "And apparently what time you usually get home."

Yeah, Jackson already noted that. The clock in the lower right corner of the screen showed the time to be six forty-seven p.m., less than fifteen minutes before he had arrived.

Cameron sped up the footage and slowed it to normal speed when Jackson's car pulled into the garage.

"Of all the nights for you to play the considerate agent," Cameron muttered as Jackson's car moved off the screen.

"That's something else she apparently knew." Jackson watched the time pass. One minute, two, five, then two shadows fell on the pavement at the top of the screen.

"Can't tell a damn thing from those shadows." Cameron shot a glance up at him and lifted a questioning brow. "I don't suppose it occurred to you to walk a little more to your left?"

Jackson kept his attention locked on the screen. "She told me to stay close to the wall. She knew the layout of that garage as well as I do, knew the camera's blind areas."

"Which means she must be a tenant or a close friend of one," Cameron deduced.

That had been the initial assumption of everyone on the team, and the most obvious conclusion. Except, Jackson would bet a year's salary over half of the people who lived in his building didn't know jack about the security. Sure, they knew it was there, but they didn't know how it worked, what areas were really caught on tape and which weren't.

"Not necessarily." He had thought about it through the night and come to a conclusion that didn't make their job of identifying his good-Samaritan kidnapper any easier. "It could've been maintenance personnel, past or present. There was a major overhaul done on the building less than a year ago when the new owner bought the place. All sorts of contractors were brought in to do the work. Any of them could've spotted the security cameras and figured out their range. Hell, it could've been someone connected to the previous owner."

On the screen, the Impala returned to view as it exited the garage.

"The lighting sucks ass. Can't see a thing beyond shadows and silhouettes even through the windshield." Cameron rewound the footage, stopped it when the Impala first entered the garage, then replayed it in slow motion. "That could be friggin' Santa Claus in that driver seat from all we can tell here."

Jackson straightened and shoved his hands in the pockets of his slacks. "Did Mal tell you she ran the check on the dealer tag? It turns out it belonged to a Chevrolet Equinox sold to a husband and wife and their four kids in Meridian two weeks ago. They reported the dealer tag stolen three days after the purchase. It was apparently taken off their vehicle while it sat in their driveway in the middle of the night. Of course, no one saw a thing."

"Of course," Cameron said sardonically. "That would've been too easy."

"So far we've been unable to pull up any sort of connection between them and anyone close to Waterston."

"What about you?" Cameron let the security tape roll as he leaned back in his seat and looked up quizzically at Jackson. "You got any connections in Meridian I don't know about?"

Jackson sighed and raked a hand through his hair. "If I do, I don't know about them any more than you."

Cameron pinched the bridge of his nose between his thumb and forefinger, a gesture he did often when his brain was working ninety-to-nothing. "And I'm guessing this Lexie Stratus doesn't either."

"Kell's still working that angle, digging up what he can find on her. She was an employee at Stardust, worked as a stripper. According to employee records, the Waterston PD's files, and the people he's been able to talk to associated with the place so far, she quit between sets almost a month ago and hasn't been seen or heard from since."

"Somebody must have pissed her off."

"Maybe." Jackson shrugged. "From what Kell found out from one of the cocktail waitresses on shift that night, she didn't make a scene, didn't say a word to anyone. She danced her first set, walked off the stage, and apparently out the back door."

"Meridian isn't but, what, two hours from here?"

"More like an hour and a half." Jackson rolled with the conversational shift, knowing Cameron was playing out all the angles, his mind following his friend down the path.

"Easy enough to make the trip, snag the tag, come back here, and devise her next move. One thing is certain, this wasn't a spur-of-the-moment thing. It was definitely premeditated. This chick had it all planned out to the smallest detail."

Jackson pushed a hard breath from his lungs and turned, paced to Cameron's desk, turned again, and paced back to where he'd started. "Tell me something I don't know."

Cameron's office mirrored his own down to the drab-but-utilitarian furnishings and neutral paint, save for the extra table set along the far wall that held the video and audio equipment.

Cameron sat at that table now, turned in his swivel chair, and nodded once. His expression was as starkly serious as it had been all morning. "Okay, how about I tell you that I don't give a shit if you've got a thing going with my sister."

"I don't have a thing going with her." Jackson didn't miss a beat, though this time Cameron's conversational shift caught him off guard.

"You want to." Cameron propped his elbows on the chair arms, laced his fingers together, and regarded Jackson with a look that told Jackson he couldn't deny anything. "Hell, man, I see the way you look at her, the way you've *always* looked at her. If our friendship is what's holding you back, stop letting it. A big brother rarely thinks any man is good enough for his little sister. I got lucky. You're a damn good man. She couldn't do much better. You have my permission, my blessing. Shit, you've got whatever you need from me."

"Mallory is what's holding me back." Sure, he'd been concerned how Cameron would react if he and Mallory hooked up. He and Cameron had been friends over half their lives, they'd gone through the academy together, worked together, and shared a bond he considered unbreakable. Knowing and believing in the strength of that bond was what had lessened his worries where his best friend was concerned.

Cameron nodded, acute understand swirling his eyes. "Because you want it all and she wants sex." He didn't guess. His tone made the statement a certainty.

Jackson sighed and backed against Cameron's desk. He leaned on the edge, folded his arms, and crossed his ankles. "Got it in one."

"Yeah, I figured as much. Mal and I come from the same mold. We've got the same hang-ups."

"Is that what's holding you back from Adrien Bingham?"

Cameron blinked at him, the only sign of surprise the man allowed to show. Then his lips unfolded in a half-sardonic smile. "Tit for tat, I suppose. When did you figure that one out?"

"During the assignment in Silver Springs, the one where we took down Veng Kim Phay. I spent a lot of time with Adrien on that assignment. Things he said, expressions he made when your name would come up"—Jackson lifted a shoulder—"it wasn't hard to put it together."

Cameron looked at the ceiling, waited a beat, then met Jackson's gaze. "Were you ticked?"

"You mean because you've been holding out on me? We've been friends most our lives and you've never once hinted that you're bi-sexual."

"I'm not the man you thought I was." Apology rang in Cameron's voice.

"Yes, you are. Hints weren't necessary."

Cameron gave a half laugh, but there wasn't much humor in the tone. "Guess I didn't keep that part of me under wraps as much as I thought."

"I noticed the glances now and then, picked up on a few comments here and there. It was enough."

"Not directed at you," Cameron said quickly.

"They never were. Christ, man, does everybody think I'm a stuffy, pompous ass?"

Cameron laughed again and this time the sound rang with amusement. "Naw, that's just Mal's description." He sobered, his expression serious once more. "I just, well, I never wanted to make you uncomfortable and shit, man."

"It's not the kind of thing men talk about, even when they're as close as we are. Yeah, I get it. Want to know a truth? I've been hoping that playing on the other side of the fence would help you figure shit out, because playing on my team hasn't seemed to do it for you."

Cameron bowed his head. "Switching only made it worse."

"Adrien." Jackson made the name more statement than question.

Cameron's gaze slammed back into his and he saw turmoil in his friend's eyes he'd never seen before. "Got it in one."

"Touché." Jackson smiled. "He's got it for you, bad. I didn't need my FBI decoder ring to figure that one out."

"I know." Cameron sighed and rubbed the back of his neck. "I, um, hurt him, pretty badly I think, too."

"Why did you do it?"

Cameron took a deep breath and let it out slowly. "He wants more than I'm ready for. He deserves more than I'm ready to give him."

"I can relate." Jackson nodded, all he'd been through with Mallory instantly coming to the forefront of his mind. "To Adrien, I mean."

"Yeah, I guessed Mal was giving you the same runaround." Cameron turned back to the television, stopping the surveillance footage as he continued, "I told you, dude, we're from the same mold."

Jackson studied his friend for a long moment and noted the tension that had settled in the man's shoulders, the way he no longer sat so relaxed in his chair. He should probably drop the subject. Deep conversations like this were not something they got into often. He could probably count the ones they'd had in the past on the fingers of one hand and still have a few digits left over.

He didn't drop it, though, deciding this was one time when his buddy needed to open up. "What would it take for Adrien to break that mold?"

Cameron didn't look away from the television. "You're asking because, if I've got an answer, you're thinking you can use the same approach with Mal."

Actually, it hadn't occurred to him, but… "It's worked in the past in other situations."

"Sorry, bro." Cameron shook his head and spun back to face him. "I can't help you this time. I don't even know if I want Adrien to break the mold. I like who I am. Single and fancy-free, so to speak."

Jackson's lips twitched. "Fancy-free? That might be the gayest thing I've ever heard you say."

"Better than admitting I'm scared." Cameron's voice was as stone-cold serious as his expression.

"You just did," Jackson pointed out.

Cameron aimed a finger at him. "Only to you." He let the finger drop to his thigh. "That's Mal's problem, you know? She wants you. Hell, I know my little sister better than I know myself. She's fucking in love with you, and it terrifies her right down to the tip of her stiletto heels."

Jackson frowned even as a sultry image of Mallory in red heels and absolutely nothing else stirred his cock. "She's learned to run like hell in those stilettos, too."

"One thing about it, the women is a professional female. There isn't much she can't do in heels."

Jackson pushed the image of Mallory aside and glanced at his friend's feet. "I often wondered why you stuck with Reeboks. Now I know. They make the best running shoes."

"You think I'm running from Adrien?"

Jackson didn't think. He knew. He didn't see the need to point it out, so he asked a question of his own. "What did you think of my temporary roommates last night?"

Cameron grinned. "Are you wondering if I'm going to make a play for Terri?"

"Actually, given our current conversation, I was thinking of Thaddeus."

"Shit, you really do know me, don't you?" Cameron pulled the surveillance disc from the player and snapped it inside its case.

"So what did you think?" Jackson asked again.

Cameron slanted him a look full of skepticism. "You really want to know?"

Jackson nodded. "I really want to know."

Cameron barked a laugh. "He's fucking hot."

Okay, so this is new. He'd heard Cameron talk about scores of women in the lives but never another man, at least not so blatantly.

You asked.

Yeah, he had. It didn't bother him, either. It just sounded…weird.

"Are you going to make a play for him?" Forget weird. This was his best friend and he accepted the man for who he was, bisexual or not.

"I kind of already did." Cameron didn't blush. He never did. But if a blush could be heard, Jackson would've sworn it was there in his voice. "It wasn't intentional, but he started flirting—not right out flaming flirting or anything, just nonchalantly coming on to me—and I couldn't help myself. I couldn't *not* flirt back."

Jackson could relate. It took every ounce of willpower he possessed not to flirt back with Mallory when she laid on her you-know-you-want-to-fuck-me act. He failed often enough lately, too. "Did you ask him out?"

"No, I just sort of made it clear I wanted to see him again before he left town."

"You should. Maybe it would do you some good." The advice spilled from Jackson's mouth before he could think to stop it. Was he crazy? How many times had Mallory suggested he have a fling with someone else? How many times had she told him it would do them both some good?

From Mallory's viewpoint, she thought it would help to loosen his tie, make him more apt to go for no-strings sex. Jackson didn't think that was the case with Cameron. The man was the king of flings. Yet, those flings had become next to nonexistent the last few years. When Jackson did the math, he pretty much settled on the pivotal moment being somewhere shortly after Cameron met Adrien Bingham. Maybe what his buddy needed was a night in another man's company to make him realize what he truly wanted was the man he ran from in Silver Springs.

"In other words, get my mind off Adrien for a while."

"Something like that." Jackson nodded. "I'd be careful, though. Thaddeus is from Silver Springs, too. I don't know if it's still happening, but when I was there, the DEA office was crossing paths with the SSFD quite frequently."

"Think Thaddeus would be one to go home and gossip to the town?"

"No, but there's a good chance he and Adrien are acquaintances. Until you decide what it is you truly want, you may not want word getting back to Adrien that you're moving on."

Cameron looked away and Jackson saw a memory move through the man's expression. "He wouldn't be surprised."

Jackson pushed off the desk and moved to the closed office door. "Then I guess you don't have anything to worry about."

"No, I guess I don't." Cameron got to his feet and walked behind his desk. "Where are you headed?"

"Cooper's office. I'll let him know we didn't get shit from the surveillance disc. Then I'm going to the apartment. I've got a list in my head of tenants to talk to, none that actually fit the profile, but ones to check off before I move on."

"You should take Mallory with you. These are women you're going to talk to, and correct me if I'm wrong, but a few of them are married. It might be good to have a female agent at your side."

Yeah, it probably would be a good idea. Though spending time alone with Mallory after all that had transpired last night probably wouldn't be.

* * * *

Mallory looked around Cooper's office, noted the partially opened door to his private closet, and walked toward it. "Do you mind if I hang this here for now, sir?"

"Go ahead," Cooper answered absently, his attention focused on his computer. "Kell hasn't been able to pick up a morsel on Lexie Stratus, nothing beyond background information anyway." He sighed, his frustration evident in his tone. "We can trace her from birth through last month and then nothing. She disappeared."

"You and I both know that's not the case." Mallory moved to one of the two chairs in front of his desk and perched on the edge.

He flicked his vivid blue eyes her way as she sat. "Of course we do."

Mallory studied her boss. Dressed as he always did in a well-tailored dark suit, sans the jacket hanging over the back of his chair, with a crisp white shirt, she could easily detect every rigid muscle in his sculpted biceps. Broad shoulders and a well-defined chest strained the material of his shirt. Dark hair and chiseled facial features added to the power of his eyes. No doubt about it, for a man in his midforties, her team leader was yummy to the max. Yet, she'd never seen him with a woman, never even heard gossip about him keeping company with a one. *What is up with that?* She wouldn't dare ask, so she went with a more relevant question instead.

"She's been missing for a month and no one reported it?"

"Apparently, there wasn't anyone to report it, unless you count Graham's kidnapper last night."

"What about her family, friends, coworkers?"

"Her coworkers thought she simply quit. We're assuming Jackson's kidnapper is someone close to her, but she appears to be the only one. The girl's father is serving a life sentence in the ADOC— the Alabama Department of Corrections—for killing her mother when she was two years old. She became a ward of the state after that and was bounced around in the foster system until she did a stint in juvy herself. They released her at eighteen and she hit the streets."

"A prostitute?"

"If she was, she managed to keep it off the books. Her adult record is clean. Employment records put her working at a number of restaurants and bars in Alabama and Mississippi, none of them for very long at a time."

"Running from something or someone?" If so and they could determine what or who, they may have their first clue as to what happened to the girl.

Cooper shook his head and finally gave Mallory his full attention. "More like trying to find herself would be my guess. She settled in Waterston about a year ago, landed a job here and there at fairly respectable diners and a few clubs, and enrolled in the community college at the start of this term."

"Enrolled but never attended a class," Mallory concluded, immediately picking up on the distinction.

"It doesn't look like she got the chance."

"You might be right. She seemed to be attempting to get her life together. Always having a legit job, keeping her nose clean, and signing up for college… That leads me to think she was working toward making something decent out of a screwed-up life."

"The worst strike we've turned up against her so far is her job at Stardust."

"I'm gathering she was a stripper, not a cocktail waitress."

Cooper nodded, pulled a paper from a file on his desk, and slid it across the desktop.

Mallory leaned forward, her heart aching for the girl who stared back at her in the enlarged driver's-license photo. The girl wore her blonde hair long and brushed to the left. A few tendrils hung over her left cheek and drew attention to blue eyes that obviously wanted to be happy but still held the haunted secret of a tough past. She had pushed the rest of her long hair behind her left ear for the photo, exposing a thin scar at her temple.

"She's beautiful." Mallory eased back and met her boss's gaze. "I know I don't have to tell you this, but you realize what we're likely up against here? A twenty-three-year-old beautiful woman working as a stripper in a seedy club with no family ties, no friends save one, and no one to miss her if she's suddenly gone."

Cooper's expression turned grimmer than she'd ever seen it. "Another part to Operation Water Down. Human trafficking and likely sexual slavery." He tapped the photo of Lexie Stratus. "Given her history, profession, and appearance."

Mallory ran her fingers through her hair, thinking. "Our office, along with the WPD, have been keeping tabs on all missing-person cases in the area since we busted the last known ring in Waterston." A bust in which she'd herself been taken out of a local nightclub by a lowlife looking to break into human trafficking. The guy had been an armature with the intent of auctioning her and a dozen other young women and girls to the highest terrorist bidder and transporting them overseas. "Nothing suspicious has turned up to substantiate our belief that there is another local ring kicking into action."

"You just said the key word, Stone. *Known. Known* ring. *Known* missing-person cases." Cooper picked up the photo of Lexie Stratus and replaced it in the file. "We didn't know she was missing until last night. Who knows how many other girls are out there we don't yet know about."

"I would say it's time we find out." Adrenaline and determination pumped through Mallory's veins. It had been too long since she'd gotten the chance to sink her teeth into a good assignment. She wouldn't rest until they found Lexie Stratus and knew everything down to the millisecond of what happened to her in the last month.

"Lexie is not the only Stardust employee to quit suddenly."

Well, now. That was news to Mallory. She stiffened and sat up straighter.

"Kell is checking out the others now," Cooper continued. "There have been four in the last six months."

"Why didn't we know about this? Waterston PD has had a team frequenting that place for over a year."

"Quitting a job isn't against the law, nor is it uncommon in a club like Stardust."

"But if those four have vanished without a trace as well..."

"Then we have more than a missing Lexie Stratus on our hands and possible substantiation of a trafficking ring," Cooper finished. His gaze flicked to the uniform she'd hung on his closet door when she'd first entered his office. He lifted both brows. "Those are some clothes. Looks like there's barely enough material to fit on the hanger."

Mallory bit back a smile. "I've worn less on the job."

"You're in, then."

He made it more statement than question, but she answered anyway. "I start tonight at seven."

"Cocktail waitress?"

The underlining hope in Cooper's tone almost made her let the smile come. "The woman who interviewed me, Betty—who coincidentally reminded me a lot of Betty Boop—offered me a stripper position, but I declined. She left the offer on the table, stressing how much more money I would make, and told me if I changed my mind to let her know."

She chewed her bottom lip and waited a beat. "It might be necessary. If we are uncovering a trafficking ring, the ringleader might be focusing on strippers in the club. If that's the case, I won't get far as a cocktail waitress."

Cooper nodded once. "Let's hope it doesn't become necessary."

Yes, yes, please, let's hope. Mallory would do anything for the job, anything to catch bastards who were taking women as hostage, turning them into sex slaves, and auctioning them off to the highest bidder. If it meant taking off her clothes in front of a bar of drooling, disgusting, lowlifes, she'd do it, but she really, *really* hoped she wouldn't have to.

"I'm sending Tarantino in with you. He'll be playing the role of a customer. I don't want you going in there alone. You okay with that?"

"Absolutely," Mallory answered quickly. She'd worked assignments with Nick Tarantino before. He was a good agent and a valuable stand-in on their team. Tall, impressively built, and blond with olive-hazel eyes and a naturally dark complexion, he ranked quite high on the bureau stud-o-meter. He was also a keen observer. Practically nothing got past the man.

Cooper opened his mouth to go on, shut it again, and frowned when a knock at his office door cut him off. "Enter," he bellowed curtly.

Mallory shot a glance over her shoulder as the door opened and Jackson walked into the office. Powerful thighs encased in dark slacks carried him closer to the desk, closer to her. Sweaty nights and tangled sheets sprang to her thoughts as her gaze slid up his hard, muscular body. He was raw power and masculinity in one incredible package, and she knew he would be tasty and immensely satisfying if she could ever get him between her legs.

Jackson stopped mere steps away from her and addressed Cooper. "Am I interrupting something, sir?"

Cooper shook his head. "Have a seat, Graham."

Three long strides brought Jackson to the seat next to her. He put a hand on the armrest of the chair, the muscles in his bicep flexing as he sat.

Heat ignited in Mallory's core. His biceps and big, strong hands were made to hold a woman as he brought her to orgasm after orgasm. *Christ*, she wanted his hands on her, wanted to feel that power between her legs as he slid his cock in and out of her pussy.

"Are you allowed to accessorize the uniform, or do we need to come up with another option?" Cooper picked up their conversation where he'd left off before Jackson interrupted them.

Mallory tamped down her lusty thoughts about Jackson and looked back at Cooper, realizing his attention was fully focused on her once more. "Jewelry is not a problem. I was told it's actually encouraged."

"Good. We'll use the anklet and earrings." Cooper glanced at the uniform again. "They should match rather well."

Toshie—whose real name was something she could rarely pronounce and get it right—was the bureau's all-around tech guy. He designed gadgets that they found invaluable on the job. He had created a studded-leather anklet for her on a previous assignment that hid a high-tech tracking device along with a signal scrambler and tiny USB tool to use when she needed it. The earrings were a pair of silver oval-shaped studs with silver and black dangling chain tassels. She only had to push firmly on the stud twice to call in the team if an undercover assignment went bad.

Both accessories had already proven to be priceless. She had used them in the last trafficking undercover assignment, leading the team straight to her and the eight other women who'd been taken from local clubs with the intent to be sold at auction.

Beside her, Jackson cleared his throat. "Match what, if you don't mind my asking, sir."

"Mallory's uniform." Cooper looked at her quizzically. "Or should I say Jacqueline? I assume you used the same alias this time."

"Yes, sir." Jacqueline Monroe was safe, solid, an alias with absolutely no strings to her real life. They had created Jacqueline with a concrete background in the club industry and the spotty past of a runaway teen who had sometimes gotten mixed up with the wrong crowd. Jacqueline didn't have anyone in her life, no parents, no friends to speak of, no one to truly care for her. She was easy bait for slime balls operating a sex-trafficking ring. Mallory had used the name only during her sparse ventures into Cinderella's and on two previous cases. Neither had blown the cover or stemmed connections to what she would be going into tonight.

"Jacqueline's uniform, then." Cooper angled his chin toward the closet, indicating the clothing hanging on the outside. "She's going undercover as a cocktail waitress at Stardust. Tarantino will be her partner for this assignment."

Mallory saw a muscle tick in Jackson's jaw, the only sign that he didn't like the idea. It wasn't personal. It wasn't jealousy or even fear for her safety, though they all felt that bone-chilling fear anytime one of their own went undercover on a potentially dangerous assignment. They all rolled with it, knowing it was part of a job they all did supremely well.

No, that ticking was because he wanted to be the one there with her and he knew damn well he couldn't be. Someone with some connection to Stardust knew what he looked like and knew he was a federal agent. If he stepped foot inside the place, pretending to be a patron, flags could be raised in bright neon red.

She watched as his gaze moved to the uniform and the ticking turned into a time bomb he skillfully prevented from detonating. *That* was personal. It was jealously. That was the look of a man who felt the effects of the outfit in his cock.

It took a skill of her own not to allow her gaze to drop to his lap, to see if his cock was hardening inside his slacks. She knew she didn't have to be wearing the uniform for him to see what it would cover and what it wouldn't. The barely there black spandex skirt fit her snug and stretched to just below crotch level. The blue metallic bustier had a jeweled choker with thin straps connecting to a V bodice that dipped way low between her breasts and stopped just before her belly. The design would expose the swells of her breasts as well as the silver bellybutton ring she always wore beneath her clothes.

Jackson glanced at her, his expression now masterfully guarded and completely unreadable, then settled his focus on Cooper. "The surveillance disc didn't turn up anything. I'm going to the apartment to talk with the tenants. I honestly don't believe the woman who kidnapped me last night lives in the building. I've been through the list of tenants, my memory of their appearances, and none of them fit my mental profile of her. I'm hoping a voice would trigger more."

"Do you want to take someone with you?" Cooper asked.

"I was going to take Mallory. This is all females I need to talk to and a few of them have husbands. I thought a female presence with me would help to prevent ruffling any feathers." He shook his head. "But if Mallory is going undercover, she doesn't need to be seen with me. Nor does she need to be seen anywhere connected with the assignment outside of Stardust."

"Good call." Cooper picked up a pen from the desktop and toyed with it between his fingers as he leaned back in his chair. "You're instincts are good, Graham. Keep your head clear and focus on what you remember. If you talk to this woman again, you'll know it."

Keep his head clear. As in keep Mallory out of his thoughts.

Nice way to discreetly imply what you really mean, sir.

"If there's nothing more, I'm going to wrap up a few things in my office then head home to get ready for my new job." She had some paperwork to complete from another assignment and she needed a shower as well as some time to get into what she thought of as her club mode before seven o'clock.

"You're both free to leave." Cooper straightened, replaced the pen on his desk, and returned to whatever he'd been working with on the computer when she'd interrupted him.

Mallory snagged the uniform and walked out the door, hearing Jackson's soft footfalls directly behind her. She let him close Cooper's door and didn't look back as she made her way down the hall to her own office.

"Mal."

Her step faltered when he softly said her name. She took a deep breath as she turned, readying herself for the detonation. He stopped close enough to her that his familiar, musky scent surrounded her. It seeped into her flesh, wound through her system, and teased every erogenous zone in her body. *Sweet hormones,* she wanted to play scratch and sniff with this man.

"Be careful tonight." His hand brushed hers so gently she might have imagined the touch. No way could she imagine the electric fingers of sensation that sizzled up her arm. "And use those earrings at the first sign of trouble."

She knew he was thinking about her last club assignment, how she'd confessed to the team that she had allowed herself to be taken from the club, had waited until the ringleader exposed his hideout before she had alerted the team.

"You be careful, too." Emotion tightened her throat as she gazed up at him and saw things in his eyes she didn't want to see. He was the only man who'd ever awakened a desire in her she had to fight so hard to control. The only way to fight it, the only way to control it, lay in her continued ploy to get him where she wanted him...beneath her, against a wall, in the backseat of a car. Who the hell cared as long as his cock was buried deep inside her sopping pussy. Only then would she be able to get him out of her system.

She flatted her hand on his chest and let it slide down, absorbing the feel of his rock-hard body beneath her palm. "I'd hate for something to happen to this body before I finally get to play."

He closed his eyes, sighed, and slowly shook his head. When he looked at her again, the frustration and pain twisting with something she didn't dare define in his eyes took her breath away. He held her gaze a moment longer, took a step back, and walked down the hall.

She winced as the door to his office closed with a loud thud. It was past time to stop this dance, to change the game. It needed to happen soon or they were both going to wind up hurt.

Chapter Four

"To call or not to call," Cameron said aloud in his best Shakespearean-era imitation as he stared at the number in his recent call log. "That, my friends, is the million dollar question of the night."

He shouldn't make the call. Every fiber of his being screamed for him not to do it.

Every testosterone-driven cell in his body screamed exactly the opposite.

Call Adrien instead, a voice in his head whispered.

Yeah, like that would help. Except, it might. He'd tried calling Adrien last night, but the man hadn't answered. As a matter of fact, Adrien's number was right there on the screen in his recent call log above Thaddeus's. Talking with Adrien always put him in a better frame of mind as long as he didn't dwell on how badly he wanted to fuck the other man. Which was exactly why he hadn't been able to walk away like he told Adrien he was going to do the last time he had seen him.

Right, it had nothing to do with your feelings for him.

Cameron cursed the persistent voice in his head that obviously didn't have a clue about shit and touched the icon to call Adrien without looking at the screen. Two rings and a voice that stopped his heart answered.

"Hello?"

Shit, fuck! Cameron pulled the phone from his ear, his eyes widening as he stared at the display. The screen didn't say Bingham, A. with the number below it. It showed only a Silver Springs number. Thaddeus's Silver Springs number. *Double shit, fuck.*

"Hell-*o*?" Thaddeus said again slowly as Cameron put the phone back to his ear. "Silence can be great sometimes, but it gets a bit awkward on a telephone, especially when I don't know who I'm supposed to be talking to."

"It's Cameron." He closed his eyes and rested his forehead in his hand, pressing at his temples with his thumb and forefinger.

"Wow. Well, hello there," Thaddeus said on a half laugh of surprise. "What can I do for you?"

Hang up on me. Stop me from making a huge mistake. Tell me to fuck off.

He didn't say any of that, though. Instead, he said the first thing that came to mind.

"I was wondering if you had already made plans for dinner tonight." He was?

Oh, hell.

"I, um, no, I haven't." Thaddeus sounded flabbergasted.

Cameron could relate. He felt pretty stunned himself. Jesus, what the fuck was he doing?

"Actually, I just got out of the shower," Thaddeus went on, and Cameron so didn't need to hear that.

Images of Thaddeus's rock-solid body, naked with remnants of his shower beading on his tanned flesh, flipped through Cameron's mind like an X-rated slideshow.

"You weren't headed to bed, were you?" Oh, yeah, and thinking about that was really going to help him turn off the personal porno starting to play in his head. "Your first competition in the firefighter challenge is tomorrow, isn't it?"

"It is," Thaddeus confirmed. "Nine a.m. I've been in the gym. You know, trying to keep up my stamina and all that?"

And the mental pictures just keep on coming.

Cameron's porn flick rewound to before Thaddeus's shower. He saw the other man flat on his back on a weight bench, shirtless with beads of sweat scattered over the hard planes of his pecs and abs. The muscles in his arms grew taut as he lifted the weight bar, brought it down within an inch of that mouthwatering chest, and pushed it up again.

"What did you have in mind?"

Thaddeus's question snapped Cameron from his reverie.

Honey, you so don't want to know. "I'm not sure exactly." He ran through the restaurants he knew of near Jackson's apartment. "Do you like Chinese? There's a great little Chinese restaurant about two blocks from where you are. It's within walking distance, or I could swing by and pick you up."

"Or you could park here and we could walk together," Thaddeus countered.

"Or I could park there and we can walk together," Cameron repeated, already hearing the nails being hammered into his coffin. He shouldn't do this. He *knew* he shouldn't, but he couldn't seem to stop himself. Suddenly, a thought popped into his head that just might provide a safety net for the evening. "Why don't you ask Terri to come, too. There's no sense in her sitting around Jackson's apartment alone."

"She has her own date." Thaddeus laughed, and Cameron's hopes for protection plummeted to his gut. "The girl works fast. She met this guy at lunch today, another firefighter at that. We went to the High Noon Cafe Jackson told us about. Anyway, we were walking out and she plowed into this guy who was walking in. Instant attraction. Since she'd already eaten lunch, he asked her out to dinner. They left here about an hour ago."

"Then I guess it's just you and me." Lord save him, because it damn sure looked like no one else was going to.

"Great. I'll meet you downstairs in, what, a half an hour, or do you need more time?"

"Half an hour is good. See you then." Cameron ended the call and slouched in his chair. "What the fuck did I just do?"

He'd asked a guy on a date. That's what he'd done.

His phone vibrated in his hand. He glanced at the screen and closed his eyes on a sigh. And fate, being the naughty bitch that she was, chose that moment for Adrien to return last night's phone call.

He ignored it, raked a hand through is hair, and got to his feet. There was nothing left for him to do here at the office tonight. Mallory was undercover at Stardust with Tarantino watching her back, Cooper was doing whatever it was Cooper did, Jackson was tracking down leads, and he'd taken the surveillance footage to their analyst in hopes the agent could turn the darkness to bright and pull out some sort of photo of the woman driving the Impala. That left him with nothing to do except wait.

And go on a date.

"I'm so fucked." Any other time, that's exactly what he'd be looking for. And maybe it was tonight. Maybe Jackson was right.

Yeah, and maybe a cosmic blast of energy would destroy the earth before he got to Thaddeus and end all his indecision and misery. Hey, it could happen.

* * * *

The beat of the music pulsed through Mallory's body as she wove her way through the tables of Stardust. Smells of alcohol, colognes, and arousal permeated the air. She walked confidently in her five-inch stilettos, adding an extra sway to her hips for the benefit of the men watching. She had applied her makeup thicker than usual, purposely accenting what she had been told were her best features, her eyes and cheekbones. She had left her hair down, allowing it to flow freely around her face and down her back. The uniform hugged her every curve like a second skin. The bodice left enough of her breasts exposed for a tantalizing view. The skirt rode so high, if she bent her knees, she was in danger of showing off the thin, black, satin-and-lace thong she wore beneath.

She knew she looked hot. She might be on an assignment with seedy, testosterone-crazed men eyeing her every move, but a small part of her that was all female enjoyed the attention. She smiled as heads turned when she walked by their table. It was good for business, good for her character, employment security for Jacqueline. It was, after all, the first step in infiltrating the club and finding out what went on behind closed doors.

She took several drink orders as she made her way to her destination, her attention on constant alert, observing every customer, every action, picking up on tidbits of conversations. Years of training, coupled with a keen innate instinct, told her approximately how many people were in the bar, who she needed to watch out for, and the best route to the front and back exits. She filed it all away in her memory as she settled into her role.

A plump and balding man at the table by the stage where she stopped grabbed her ass as she attempted to hand him his drink order. She had been expecting it, time number three in the last hour, definitely someone to watch out for.

Three strikes and you're out, bud.

She tightened her grip on the tray in her left hand and held his drink in front of him. "Why don't you wrap your hand around this instead of my ass, darlin'." She put a butt load of sweetness in her voice with a dash of flirtation and accented it with a heavy Southern drawl.

"But your ass feels much better," he said in a drunken slur and squeezed her right cheek.

A warm breeze caressed the bottom curve of one bare cheek and she knew her skirt had hiked up far more than she wanted it to. She shifted her stance, but the skirt stuck where it had positioned itself like glue.

"I bet it does, but we have a rule here at Stardust, no touching the staff," she reminded the man sweetly. Sasha, the barmaid, had told her the man was a regular patron of the club when he had first walked in. He knew the rules but, hey, why not push it with the new help?

"Now, wouldn't you rather sit here and watch the next beautiful woman hit the stage instead of having our bouncer over there toss you out the front door on your nose?" She flicked a pointed glance at Bruno, a fitting name for a bouncer in her opinion, then smiled at the man.

"It wouldn't be the first time." He squeezed her ass again before taking his drink from her hand.

Mission accomplished, at least for now. "Well, now, we don't want it to be the last, though, do we?" The volume of the music increased as the next stripper sashayed onto the stage behind her. She raised her voice. "Now, behave yourself and enjoy the show." She gave him a flirtatious wink and moved away from the table, discreetly pulling down her skirt with her free hand as she walked back to the bar.

"Nicely played," Sasha said, evidently impressed. She was a petite woman in her late twenties with an hourglass figure, chin-length golden blonde hair, wide green eyes, and a silver bar with black balls on each end through one brow. "I couldn't hear what you said, but it was obviously firm yet polite. It appeared to work, too. A couple of waitresses have gotten fired for decking that dickhead."

Had they been fired or disappeared like Lexie Stratus? Out of the corner of her eye, Mallory saw Tarantino lift his beer to his lips. He sat on the barstool closest to the waitress station, turned toward the stage, his posture relaxed. Inside, she knew he was in full alert mode, cataloguing everything he saw and heard as he watched her back.

She didn't ask any questions about the other waitresses. Tonight was all about getting her feet wet, getting to know the current employees and the people who frequented the club. It was about watching the back rooms to get a bead on the office and how she could get inside to copy the hard drive from the computer to the USB device hidden in her anklet. It was about making everyone comfortable with Jacqueline so that maybe, just maybe, she would find herself in one of their confidences enough for them to spill a portion of the proverbial beans.

"And he's still allowed in here?" Mallory widened her eyes for effect. "Wow!"

Sasha shrugged. "He's been banned a couple of times, raised a stink about it, and the boss man let him back in. The slime ball is connected, if you can believe that."

Mallory actually felt her ears perk up. "Really? How?" She didn't hesitate to ask, hoping what Sasha likely deemed as general Stardust gossip would reveal far more.

Sasha rolled her eyes. "He's got an uncle or brother or cousin or some shit on the ABC."

The Alcoholic Beverage Control board. Yeah, Mallory could see why the boss man wouldn't want to piss off a skuz-bucket like that. She could also see how a man like that could be involved in a trafficking ring.

"Who is he, anyway? You know, so next time he gets out of hand I can scold him by name."

"Ha. If you do, make sure the music is low so I can hear it this time. His name is as classy as the man. Leroy Platt."

Mallory's lips twitched as she filed the name in her mind with a neon tab to pull up everything she could find on him when she hit her office tomorrow morning. If Tarantino didn't beat her to it.

* * * *

Thaddeus didn't know what Cameron drove, but he figured it out easily enough when a silver Corvette with a black racing stripe down the center of the hood pulled into the parking garage of Jackson's apartment building and eased into a guest slot. Cameron looked his way, a smile unfolding on his lips that sent Thaddeus's heart through a repetition of hard-core calisthenics. The purr of the Corvette engine died as Cameron shut off the car and got out.

Damn, he looks good.

He wore a solid black T-shirt with worn jeans and equally worn tennis shoes. He looked more excitedly appealing than Thaddeus remembered, his clothes defining every well-cut muscle to pristine perfection. Potent sexuality radiated from him as he walked toward Thaddeus, and the effect went straight to Thaddeus's cock.

Thaddeus shifted his stance, attempting to alleviate some of the tightness pressing against his zipper. He felt Cameron's gaze move over him the same way he was allowing his own gaze to do to Cameron, and prickles of heat sizzled over every ounce of his flesh. Cameron's shoulders were broader than he'd realized, his arms and chest wider and bunched with raw power. Thaddeus raked his gaze down the man's biceps, thick forearms, and strong wrists, instantly imagining what it would feel like to have those arms locked around him in a lover's embrace.

"You look good." Cameron put to voice the thought ping-ponging in Thaddeus's head. His attention dropped to Thaddeus's mouth and Thaddeus swallowed, his lips tingling as if he'd just been kissed. He had dressed for comfort and casual class, deciding on a green-and-brown striped polo shirt tucked into a pair of tight-fitting jeans and brown loafers.

"So do you." He flicked a pointed glance at the Corvette. "Hot car."

Cameron grinned in a boyish way Thaddeus understood. "I like toys. I have an SUV I use for practical purposes, but when I'm off duty, I like to play."

"So do I." Independently wealthy thanks to a family of old money, Thaddeus's garage back home was chocked full of boy toys.

Cameron lifted both brows. "Something we have in common." He shoved his keys in the front pocket of his jeans and turned, motioning with his head toward the exit of the parking garage. "Come on. You can tell me about them while we walk."

Thaddeus didn't start talking immediately. A gentle breeze moved the air as they stepped onto the sidewalk and rounded the apartment building. Nerves rocked his insides, twisted his gut, and sent a cacophony of thoughts bouncing into one another in his mind. He remembered the last time he had taken a walk with a man on a starry, moonlit night. Adrien had been the man. The location had been the Silver Springs beach. He had fallen for Adrien that night, really and truly fallen.

And spent the next year waiting for him to come back.

Thaddeus shut off that thought and concentrated on the man walking beside him tonight. He refused to dwell on the past, on the suspicion probing his gut that Cameron was the reason Adrien continued to keep his distance. If it turned out to be true, at least after tonight he figured he would have a better understanding of why.

"Tell me about your toys." Cameron broke the silence, angled his head, and looked at Thaddeus with an expression of genuine interest.

"I just bought a BMW 650i convertible, vermillion red, black interior."

Cameron gave a low whistle. "Sweet. Stick or automatic?"

"Stick, twin-turbo charged, V-8."

"Nice. Took it cruising down the Billings strip yet?"

Thaddeus shot Cameron a boyish grin of his own. "The second I drove it off the lot."

Cameron chuckled. "Yeah, I would have, too. So what else you got?"

Thaddeus scanned the storefronts that came into view as they rounded another corner and stepped onto a busier, nonresidential street. He recognized some of them, saw others in places where older business had obviously closed down. Waterston had changed a lot in the years since he had moved away.

He lifted a shoulder. "Remote-control gadgets, things that go bang, things that go boom, that sort of stuff."

"Sounds like I should've asked you out to Toys"R"Us instead of a Chinese restaurant."

Thaddeus laughed. "Now there's an idea, put a Chinese restaurant inside a Toys"R"Us. I'd probably never leave."

Silence fell between them, but this time it felt more comfortable, easy. Thaddeus's gut settled, his nerves calmed, and he found himself relaxing in Cameron's presence.

"This is the place." Cameron stopped in front of the restaurant, one of the newer ones Thaddeus didn't recognize, and pulled the door open for Thaddeus to enter first.

"Thank you." Thaddeus stepped inside, his gaze quickly sweeping the room as the hostess greeted them and led them to a secluded table in a darkened corner. Like many Chinese restaurants, the place was dimly lit and immaculately decorated, with instrumental music playing softly in the background. The romanticism struck him as he took the seat across from Cameron and caught the intensity swirling in the man's sea-blue eyes through the flickering candlelight between them.

Cameron held his gaze for several breath-taking heartbeats and Thaddeus's arousal shot through the roof. *Christ on a pogo stick.* When Cameron looked at him like that, he wanted to climb over the table and attack the man.

"Maybe we should have gone for takeout," Cameron said softly, as if he had read Thaddeus's mind.

Thaddeus dropped his gaze to the table, shook his head, and felt his cheeks heat. "Am I being that obvious?" he asked on a half laugh and lifted his head.

Cameron leaned forward, resting his forearms on the tabletop. "No more than I am, I'm sure. I—" He broke off as the waitress approached the table to take their drink orders. "I'm thinking wine"—

he told the waitress, then turned his attention to Thaddeus—"but I honestly don't know what goes well with Chinese food."

Thaddeus pursed his lips, wondering what Cameron had been about to say before the waitress interrupted. "That depends on your main course. Do you have a particular entree you usually go for?"

"Twice-cooked pork."

Thaddeus nodded and addressed the waitress. "We'll have a bottle of your best pinot noir, please." He saw surprise move through Cameron's handsome face as the waitress left the table, and he smiled, a little embarrassed. "I'm sorry. I didn't mean to take over there."

"No, I'm glad you did," Cameron said quickly. "I don't know what the hell I'm doing. I'm glad you do."

Do I? Thaddeus wasn't so sure, but he had made up his mind before leaving Jackson's apartment that he would simply see where tonight would lead.

"My family owns a couple of wine vineyards. All the Carter children learned at a very young age how to pair wine with food, even though we weren't allowed to drink more than a sip with each course."

"I gather your family is rich."

Thaddeus rolled his eyes. "Ridiculously. Carter family reunions have been known to make magazine headlines."

"Son of bitch," Cameron whispered, and Thaddeus saw when realization took hold. "Carter. As in Carter Industries and a crap load of other stuff. You're a local boy."

"It's been years since I lived here. The city has changed a lot since I left. But, yeah, my family is from Waterston."

"How did I miss that? I didn't make the connection until now." Cameron grimaced. "I'm not sure I would like that much, being in that kind of spotlight, trying to live up to those kinds of expectations."

"The pressure can be pretty daunting at times," Thaddeus admitted. "But you learn to deal with it."

"Is that why you're staying with Jackson instead of with your parents at the Carter family mansion while you're in town?"

"That's part of it." Thaddeus waited a beat. "Terri is the other reason."

"You don't think your family would like her." Cameron made it sound like more statement than question, but Thaddeus answered anyway because he knew the other man didn't quite yet get it.

"Just the opposite. She's classy in her own way, beautiful, fantastic, with a personality that doesn't stop. My family would absolutely adore her."

"Ah, and wonder why you aren't *with* her, with her. I get it now."

"Exactly. I mean, they know I'm gay, and they stopped trying to change it a long time ago, but, well, I don't want to give them any encouragement to start again."

The waitress returned with their wine, poured a splash into Thaddeus's glass, and waited. Thaddeus nudged the glass toward Cameron, who eyed him as he lifted the glass and sipped.

"That's good." He licked his lips and Thaddeus watched the path his tongue took, his own tongue burning to follow, to taste and tangle.

"Wait until you taste it with the twice-cooked pork."

Cameron placed their order and filled their glasses.

Thaddeus studied the man for a long moment over the rim of his wine glass as he drank, then set it back on the table. "What about you? I know you have a sister here. Is the rest of your family here, too?" He had put it together that the woman in the photo with Cameron and Jackson he had seen on Jackson's bookshelf was Cameron's sister, Mallory.

"There isn't anyone else besides my mother. She lives in town. My father was killed in nineteen eighty-three in Operation Urgent Fury."

"Wow, I'm sorry." Thaddeus remembered by the end of the invasion of Granada, codenamed Operation Urgent Fury, the United

States armed forces had sustained eighteen causalities and as many as one-hundred-sixteen wounded soldiers.

"He died serving his country, doing what he loved. Being a Marine was the most important thing in his life, outside of my mother, Mal, and me, of course."

"I can't imagine losing one of my parents. I know it will happen someday, but..." Thaddeus let the sentence trail off and shook his head.

"It's hard to lose someone you love, even harder to watch someone else you love try to learn to live without them. Seeing my mother, the way she's been since my father was killed, it shows me I never want to go through something like that, you know? I was five when he died, and Mal was barely a year old. We grew up without him. Mom did a fabulous job, but she never remarried, never met anyone who could take my father's place. The whole experience made Mal and I loners to a point."

It made you afraid to love, Thaddeus suspected but didn't voice the thought. "Your dad was a Marine, yet you and your sister landed in the FBI." He changed the subject. "How did that happen?"

Cameron chuckled. "Jackson started it. His family lived here when we were growing up. His father and brother moved to Silver Springs. Jackson stayed. I can't really remember what set the whole career goal in his head, but the more he talked about growing up and joining the FBI, the more I wanted to do it, too. Mallory stuck to us like glue and inevitably followed us."

Cameron picked up his glass, took a long swallow, and asked, "What about you, rich boy? You're family owns more companies than I can count and you become a firefighter. What's up with that?"

Thaddeus told him the story, starting all the way back with Thaddeus Leopold Carter II and the man's dream of being a firefighter engineer for the Waterston FD. The waitress returned with their entrees and they settled into conversations that jumped from one subject to the next. Three hours passed with the feeling of mere minutes. They likely would've talked longer if the restaurant hadn't started to close around them.

"I guess that's our cue to leave." Cameron grinned as he tossed enough cash to cover the check and tip onto the table and got to his feet.

Thaddeus glanced at his wristwatch. "It's eleven o'clock. Holy cow," he said on a laugh as he followed Cameron out of the restaurant.

"I'm sorry. I didn't mean to keep you out so late."

"Did you hear me complaining?"

"No."

They walked in a companionable silence back to the parking garage, the time passing far more quickly than Thaddeus wanted it to. He followed Cameron to his car.

"Do you want me to walk you up?"

"No, it's late. You probably have an earlier day at it tomorrow than I've got scheduled. You should get out of here, but if you get a chance to break away tomorrow, I'd like it if you could stop by the challenge."

"I'll see what I can do."

Thaddeus gazed into Cameron's eyes and knew he wasn't getting a brush-off line. The man really would stop by if he could find the time.

Cameron reached for his hand, and the contact sent electric sensations speeding through his system. His heart pounded against his ribcage. Anticipation with a trace of trepidation tightened his throat and cock.

"Thanks for, you know, asking me out tonight," Thaddeus managed to say as he fell, not for the first time that night, into the blue sea of swirling promises and desires in Cameron's eyes.

"Thanks for accepting." Cameron's gaze dropped to his mouth, intent igniting that sea of desire, and Thaddeus felt his lips part. "I had a great time."

Thaddeus started to say he did, too, when Cameron kissed him. His lips were soft, moist, and he took Thaddeus's parted lips for the invitation Thaddeus hadn't realized he was issuing, but thank God he had. Cameron pushed his tongue into Thaddeus's mouth and a world of sensations exploded through his mind and body.

Aw, God, he tastes good.

Thaddeus met Cameron's tongue stroke for stroke, reveling in the remnants of the pinot noir that lingered in his mouth to mix with an innate flavor he suspected he would forever remember as belonging only to Cameron.

Cameron put a hand on his hip and drew him against his body, hard plane to hard plane. Thaddeus wrapped an arm around the man's neck, angling his head and allowing Cameron to deepen the kiss. The man blew his mind, dancing his tongue over his, licking his teeth, pulling back ever so slightly to nip his bottom lip before plunging inside again. The kiss was hot, full of desire and lust, and Thaddeus knew it wouldn't stop there if they had been anywhere besides a public parking garage.

It did stop, though. Slowly, Cameron drew back, and the look of utter torment in his now-darkened eyes took Thaddeus's breath away.

"You're right," Cameron whispered. "I should get out of here."

Unable to find his voice, Thaddeus nodded and stepped back.

"I'll see you again soon, okay?"

Thaddeus swallowed hard. Emotions too intense to define clogged his throat, but he managed to speak around them. "I'd like that."

Cameron's lips unfolded in a sinfully sexy smile as he slid into the Corvette and started the engine.

Thaddeus turned and walked to the elevator. For the first time in hours, Adrien popped into his mind and he realized he knew all he needed to. If Cameron was that other man, he understood more than he wanted to why Adrien hadn't been able to walk away. He'd been on only one date with Cameron, shared four glorious hours and a single mind-blowing kiss, and he already suspected leaving when the time came was going to be harder than hell.

* * * *

Mallory pulled her trench coat tighter around her body and called Jackson on her cell as she walked to the elevator in his parking garage. It surprised her when he answered at two thirty-eight in the morning sounding completely alert.

"What's wrong?"

Her step faltered at the sound of his voice, the urgency in his tone, and trepidation clashed into the anticipation pumping through her veins. "Good, you're awake."

"Yes, where are you?"

"About to step onto the elevator downstairs."

"Here?" His voice rose an octave. "Mallory, you shouldn't be here. What if someone sees you?"

She glanced behind her at the deserted parking garage, then up at the security cameras. Yeah, she had taken a risk by coming here tonight after ending her shift at Stardust. She planned to make damn sure that risk was worth every second.

"No one will see me as long as you open your door, handsome. I'll be up in a jiffy." She ended the call before he could say anything more just as the doors to the elevator opened. She didn't give herself time to think or time to reconsider her plan. She stepped onto the elevator, pushed the button for the third floor, and let out a heavy breath. Tonight, it was time to play. Jackson wanted games, and she had the perfect one in mind to keep him from talking either of them out of it.

The elevator stopped at the third floor and the doors opened with a soft swoosh. "Game on," she whispered and walked on legs that wanted to shake, straight to his still-closed apartment door. Her knuckles barely hit the wood before the door swung open and her breath caught in her throat.

Sweet God of hormones.

Jackson stood before her wearing only a pair of pajama pants that rode low on his hips, his cell phone in one hand, and an expression fierce enough she almost turned tail and ran. He shifted to his right, giving her space to enter. Inspired, she trailed the tip of one fingernail from his right bicep across his chest to his left bicep as she walked passed him into his apartment. She didn't go far, stopping close enough she could still feel the heat of him behind her.

She spotted a sleeping figure on his couch. Perfect! They weren't alone. She hadn't expected them to be, knowing he had two firefighters from Silver Springs staying with him for a few days. It fell exquisitely into her plan.

She heard a soft click as he shut the door behind her and she turned to face him. A sliver of moonlight peeked through the curtains on the living room window, affording her just enough light to see and be seen.

"Mallory, what—"

She lifted a finger to his lips, silencing him as she rose to her tiptoes and whispered in his ear. "Shush, you don't want to wake your guests. It's time to play the silent game, slick. Are you in?" She licked his earlobe between her teeth and gently nipped it before stepping back a fraction of an inch. Before he had a chance to answer, she shrugged off her trench coat and let it fall in a pool of leather at her feet.

* * * *

Holy Mother of God.

Jackson dropped his cell phone and didn't spare it a glance when he heard it shatter on the tiled foyer floor. He heard Thaddeus stir on the living room sofa and he waited a beat, silently thanking the good Lord above when the other man didn't wake.

Jackson's gaze fell down Mallory's body—her very naked, very spectacular body—and every ounce of sanity he possessed plummeted to his cock. He had seen her practically naked before in the club outfits she'd worn on assignments but never all the way there. The view was incredible. His attention swept over smooth, bronzed flesh silvered by the moonlight, her full, voluptuous breasts, her flat stomach with that damnable bellybutton ring that always drove him out of his mind, and down to the V between her legs. He found smooth-looking flesh there, too, hairless and beckoning for him to discover exactly how silky that part of her truly felt.

Was he in?

Hell, yes! And so far over his head he couldn't remember how to swim for the surface.

She didn't give him even a nanosecond to respond. Gaze locked with his, she backed him against the door, flattened her amazing body against his, and every thought in his head of putting an end to her little silent game flew out the living room window.

Jackson had held her before but never skin-to-skin, never like this. She was all soft curves and heated flesh, and when she licked her lips, his gaze was instantly there. The sight of her moist, pink tongue grazing softly, sultrily over her lips made his cock dance in hopes of equal attention. Hopes he couldn't find the strength to tamp down.

She drew out the moment. Her soft breaths moved hot and seductive over his lips, seeped through his skin, and took possession of his control. She'd had enough. He saw the evidence of that in her gaze. No more waiting. No more dancing around. She intended to put an end to it all tonight. But had she had enough to let him in all the way?

The question got lost in the sexual fog clouding his brain as she closed the distance between their mouths. Her lips brushed his in a kiss so light, so tender he might have imagined it, except she barely pulled back before she did it again.

Something inside him snapped. He wound his arms around her, flattening one hand on the small of her back and delving the other beneath her hair to cup her nape, and yanked her harder against him. He tasted the victory in her kiss as she swept her tongue into his mouth. She laced her fingers through his hair and held his head firmly in place.

The snap morphed to an explosion in his mind, his body, his very soul. He could no more stop it than he could stop his own heart from beating. Her kiss hardened, quickened. Her tongue danced over his in a brisk pace of control and heady need.

He let her have the control, let her feed her need, and knew he would damn himself for it later. She moved one hand from his head, covered his on her nape, and guided it down between their bodies to her breast, showing him where she wanted to be touched.

He covered her breast with his hand, squeezed, and felt her sigh into his mouth. She left his hand there, skimmed the backs of her fingers down his side, leaving a sizzling trail in their wake on her destination to the elastic waistband of his pajama pants.

She moaned, a barely audible sound, as she drew back, nipped his bottom lip and licked her way over his jaw and down his neck. Her fingers dipped beneath the elastic of his pants, danced between the material and his flesh, and splinters of anticipation stabbed in his cock. Her mouth continued its downward exploration, planting wicked kisses on his neck, her teeth grazing over his collarbone, her tongue licking a path over his left pec. Her other hand left his head to curl over his right shoulder, her palm caressing his flesh as it slid down his bicep.

Momentarily distracted by that hand, he sucked in a startled, utterly tortured breath when her other hand pushed into his pants and her fingers curled around his shaft. His head fell back against the door behind him, his eyes closing as she lifted his cock out of his pants and stroked his length. He squeezed her breast harder and her grip on his cock tightened in turn. A primal, animalistic growl rumbled in his throat. He nearly let it slip when he felt her body start to slide down his.

He lifted his head, his gaze landing first on Thaddeus's sleeping form on the sofa barely fifteen feet away. He caught her shoulders and she looked up at him from beneath lashes over eyes darkened by desire and naughty intentions. Remembering her game, both unable to stop it and determined to let her play it through, he shook his head. The last thing he wanted was for Thaddeus to wake up right now and see this.

He shoved his throbbing cock back inside his pants, swept her into his arms, and carried her to his bedroom, not bothering with the light. Her arms wound around his neck and she held on tight, taking him down with her when he laid her on his bed. Realization struck him like a physical blow. He eased back, putting his weight on his hands as he lifted his upper body and stared down at her. Moonlight spilled through the opened curtains on his window, and he knew she could see him as clearly as he could see her. He couldn't hide even a smidgen of the emotions wreaking havoc on his mind, his body, or his heart. They were all there in his expression and in his eyes for her to see.

This was Mallory gazing up at him, her long, autumn hair fanning the sheet on his bed. This was Mallory with her arms locked around him, her naked flesh pressed to his, her legs spread on either side of his hips.

Christ, how many nights had he laid in this very bed dreaming of this, aching for this so badly he thought it might kill him? He swallowed, his throat tight with words he wanted to say, pleas he wanted to make.

You're so beautiful.

The expression on her angelic face, so full of desire, heat, arousal, and eagerness, made her more arresting than ever. He let his attention move down her body, over her breasts, pausing at the bellybutton ring he wanted to circle with his tongue, then stopping at where their bodies pressed together. The scent of her pussy drifted up to tease his senses. He felt her wetness through his thin pajama pants, knew he would find a slick, creamy treat if he touched her there.

She moved one hand to the juncture of his neck and shoulder and his gaze slid back to hers.

I love you.

He knew he did. He always had. He wasn't scared to admit it, but it would sure as shit scare the hell out of her if he did right now.

Please, don't fuck this up, Mal.

He knew she wanted this to end with sex, knew she would walk out come morning if he didn't do something to take away her fears. The trouble came in realizing long ago that he didn't have a clue what to do to help her.

The look on her face softened, and he thought he caught a glimmer of tears in her eyes as she shook her head, then blinked. A band constricted around his heart, one he feared would squeeze the life out of him far too soon.

A devious grin slowly unfolded on her sensuous lips, and her thighs clamped his hips tightly between them. She flattened her hands on his chest and flipped him over, rolling on top of him. The move startled a soundless chuckle from him. The woman might be smaller than him, but as the saying went, dynamite came in small packages. She had always been able to take him down when he wasn't on his guard. Every second of tonight from the instant he had answered the phone was laying heavy proof to that.

She slithered down his body, dragging her palms down his chest in her descent. His need to finally have her hands on him this way had destroyed his common sense. He wanted his pajama pants off, wanted to fully feel her perfect body and vixen hands on every inch of his bare flesh. He wanted to be inside her, damnit, wanted to feel her pussy convulse around his cock as she came apart in his arms.

Fuck this silent game. He was on the verge of saying it when her fingers latched onto the waistband of his pants and tugged them down. He lifted his hips off the mattress, his cock screaming hallelujah as it sprang free once again. He saw her hungered gaze settle on his cock, saw that tormenting pink tongue of hers glide across her lips, and a whip of anticipation slashed at his balls.

She dipped her head, licked the head of his cock, and his eyes rolled back in his head. She ran the tip of her tongue around his girth just below the foreskin then closed her lips around his cockhead, and a brutal pleasure tore through his system. Her mouth was hot, tight, drawing on his cockhead, her tongue rasping the ultrasensitive flesh beneath it. His balls drew up painfully tight as she cupped them in her fingers and massaged his taut sac.

He fought to breathe even as he lifted his head, opened his eyes, and gazed down at her. She looked at him from beneath her lashes, a temptress's smile curving the corners of her lips around his cock. Her delicate fingers gripped his shaft, worked it slow and easy as she drew on his pleasure-tortured crest, then swallowed his length.

Christ.

He let his head fall back again, and he fought for control. Every muscle in his body tensed as the pressure mounted in his cock and balls. No, he would not come this way. He wouldn't let go until he was buried deep inside her sodden pussy.

She fucked him with her mouth, her head bobbing, her teeth lightly grazing the flesh, her throat expanding to take every inch of his cock. She worked the hardened flesh, milked it until he teetered on the edge of a loss in control more ferocious than he had ever experienced.

He bucked his hips, using movement rather than words to warn her. He reached for her, fisted the hair that spilled over his abdomen, and tugged.

She pulled back so slowly it nearly did him in, releasing his cock from the capture of her lips with an audible pop. Lightning bolts of pure deviousness flashed in her eyes as she crawled on her knees up his body and settled herself over his cock.

As badly as his cock ached to be inside her, he wanted to stop her, to slow this down. He wanted her beneath him again, wanted to touch her, to taste her, to make her writhe and beg, to make sweet love to her.

She didn't allow any of that. She closed her fingers around his wrists, pinned his arms to the bed on either side of his head, and lifted a curious brow as she bent her head to brush her lips to his.

He smelled himself on her breath and he realized she'd wondered if he would be one of those men who would turn away from her kiss now that she'd had her mouth on his cock. *Not a fucking chance.* If anything, that scent acted as an aphrodisiac to his already-colossal desire simply because he knew, and could still feel, where her mouth had been.

Her gaze imprisoned his as she shifted her hips slightly and then, *sweet heaven*, sank down on his cock. All thoughts of touching her fled as the sensations of feeling her body joining with his overwhelmed him. Her eyes closed and he thought he saw a flash of pain move over her face as her body took its time accepting his cock despite her quick descent. Her pussy was drenched, the entrance tight, almost as if she hadn't had sex in years.

The possibility stunned him. Mallory was the fling queen. She went for sex whenever she wanted it with whomever she believed would give it to her without expecting anything in return. Didn't she? Holy shit, when had that changed? Was it possible she'd been holding out for him?

He tried to reach for her, wanting to comfort her, to slow her down, but her grip on his hands remained firm. Her eyes opened and that devious glint was back, swirling with a primitive possession that sent rapturous chills through his bloodstream. She was in control here. He might be burning to touch her, but he could only do so if she let him. Permission to do so was apparently no longer in tonight's rule book.

She rocked her hips forward, grinding her pussy on his cock, and he forgot all about his attempts to get free. Her inner muscles gripped at his shaft as she started to ride, picking up momentum with each grinding thrust. Raking fingers of pleasure clawed through his body as he watched her fuck him. If he'd thought she was beautiful before, she was beyond gorgeous now.

She laced her fingers with his and lifted his hands, turning them over and pinning them at his sides just above her knees as she sat up on top of him. Her hair fell over her shoulders, parting around her breasts. She gyrated her hips on his cock, using the flesh of his pelvis to caress her clit, then lifted her body and fell again, taking his cock deeper and sending him on a spiraling trip to ecstasy. Her head fell back on her shoulders, and his mouth watered to sink into the column of her throat she exposed. Her breasts bounced, her engorged nipples taunting him because he couldn't feel them, couldn't wrap his lips around them and suck her to oblivion.

He shifted his gaze down and watched as his slick, glistening shaft powered in and out of the flattened curves of her pussy. The erotic sight drove him straight to the edge.

She shifted her hold on his hands again, this time guiding them up to her breasts. Finally, he got to touch her. He took her breasts in his palms gratefully, molding the mounds with his fingers and squeezing tightly. Her lips formed an *O* of pleasure, her expression one of sheer erotic passion. He flicked his thumbs over her hardened nipples, saw her draw her bottom lip between her teeth, and knew she teetered right there on the edge with him. He felt her inner muscles turn to vises around his cock and struggled not to let go until she came.

He caught her nipples between his thumbs and forefingers, pinched, pulled, and watched in absolute fascination as she thrashed on top of him. Her delectable body shook from the force of her orgasm as it tore through her, spilled out of her, covering his cock and balls with her juices. Her pussy convulsed around his cock and she collapsed onto his chest, her breathing ragged, her heart pounding so hard he could feel it.

He couldn't hold back his own release a second longer if he'd tried. With a growl that totally blew her silent game to hell, he came inside her. Boneless, breathless, every muscle in his body relaxed. He wrapped his arms around her, loving the arch at the small of her back, the way her ass fit so perfectly in the palm of his other hand. Her head rested beneath his chin and he felt a drop of wetness hit his chest.

Sweat? Both their bodies were slick with it. But, no. He knew with a certainty that ripped through his soul that wasn't sweat he felt. It was a teardrop. He lifted his head, tried to look down, but saw only the top of her head. He kissed it softly, glided his hand up her spine and down again, caressing, hoping to soothe.

"Mal," he dared to whisper because, *Jesus God*, the woman he loved was crying in his arms after making love to him for the first time. Sure, it hadn't been the lovemaking he'd had in mind. Most people would call what they had just done pure, carnal fucking. He knew why she had all but insisted it to be that way, too. She hadn't wanted to think, hadn't want to feel.

She was feeling now, though, and if that teardrop was any indication at all, the emotions were shattering her.

"The silent game doesn't end until morning," she said softly, her voice steady despite the raggedness of her breathing, the quivers he felt moving through her.

Jackson laid his head back and closed his eyes. He would let her have her way tonight. The next time they played, and there would be a next time, it would be by his rules.

Chapter Five

A persistent vibration pulled Jackson from his favorite dream. The semi-conscious part of his mind realized it wasn't all a dream. Mallory lay beneath him, her bronzed skin heated with desire, her gaze on him beckoning, pleading as he spread her legs wide and took his time studying her glistening folds.

Touch me.

Her whispered request moved over him like warm velvet, but he resisted, drawing out the moment, heightening her anticipation.

Yeah, he knew that part was definitely the dream. The silent game was gone. So was the wall she had kept so firmly in place guarding her needs and her heart.

I want your hands on me. I want to know what it feels like to have you inside me.

Reality splintered into his dreamland on that one. She hadn't let him touch her, but she knew what his being inside her felt like now.

The vibration kicked up again, bringing with it another fragment of realism. There was no place for vibrators in his dream world because, in a shift of the fantasy that stole his chance to touch, he pushed his cock inside her sopping pussy, and the phone rang.

Jackson bolted upright and muttered a curse when the sharp movement jarred his rock-hard cock with enough force to break the damn thing off. He looked beside him as he reached for the phone on the bedside table and sighed as disillusionment morphed into a pain in his chest more acute than anything he had ever felt.

"Graham," he said by way of greeting as he brought the cordless phone to his ear and raked his free hand through his hair. She was gone. He should be used to waking this way, alone with a cock so hard it could split rocks, and an emptiness inside that made him want to do nothing more than slip back into his dreamland.

Except, this morning should have been different. He should have awoke with Mallory in his bed, in his arms the way she had been when he had drifted off to sleep. Had he really thought she would stay the night?

He sighed, closed his eyes, and silently admitted the truth. No. He had prayed she would, but deep down, he had been expecting to wake exactly like this.

"We think we found her," the caller informed him, short and to the point.

Jackson opened his eyes, instantly recognizing Cooper's voice, understanding the implications of his words. "Which one?" His kidnapper or the woman missing?

"Lexie Stratus."

"When? Where?"

"About an hour ago in an abandoned warehouse on the west side, about as far from Stardust as you can get and still be in city limits."

Jackson glanced at the bedside clock. It was barely six a.m.

"We won't know for sure until we get the results back from the autopsy." A heavy sigh followed Cooper's words through the line. "The body is barely identifiable as human, let alone our missing girl. She hadn't been dead long, maybe an hour, two tops."

Grief for a woman he had never met, never even seen beyond a driver's-license photo, washed through Jackson. "How did you find her?"

"An anonymous tip called into the bureau."

Jackson froze as he started to climb out of bed. "My kidnapper?"

"We don't know. The voice was disguised. Well enough we can't even tell from the tape if it was male or female. The trace on the call led us to a disposable cell found in a dumpster five miles from the warehouse. Forensics is seeing what they can pull from it now."

"I doubt it will be much, if anything." If the caller knew enough to disguise his or her voice so well, he certainly knew how to wipe a phone clean of any trace, physical or technical.

"So do I, but I'm calling everyone in. I've already got a team of agents going through that warehouse with a fine-toothed comb. I want that entire area searched. I want any morsel we can find. I want to catch these bastards before I have another unidentifiable girl on my hands. And I want to find out who is playing games with this bureau."

Jackson did, too. Especially when he had been at the head of what apparently started this game. "Mallory?" he asked, then added quickly, "Cameron and Kell?"

"Stone and Kell are already in. Mallory is on her way."

Jackson nodded as he straightened. At least he knew Mallory was physically okay. Mentally, he figured she would be in a far different state. "I'll be there in twenty," he told his boss and cut the connection. He paused as he set the cordless back on the bedside table, his gaze landing on his cell phone.

He had dropped his cell phone and heard it shatter when Mallory took off her trench coat at his front door at two a.m. The light on the screen faded in and out, indicating a missed call. Apparently, it hadn't shattered beyond repair. She must have found it on her way out, put it back together, rebooted it, and placed it on the table for him to find when he woke.

Considerate since you didn't even bother to say good-bye.

Fury made his steps heavy as he walked to the master bathroom. He showered quickly, washing away the scent of sex, the only thing that remained besides the memories to convince him everything about last night had not been part of the dream. He dressed and walked out of the bedroom in less than ten minutes, finding his houseguests sitting at the bar separating the kitchen from the living room.

"Good morning." Terri greeted him with a smile and a tone far too bubbly for his current mood.

He forced himself to return the smile. No need to take out his foulness on a woman who had done nothing wrong. "Morning. You two are up early." He stepped into the kitchen, snagged his keys off the counter where he had left them last night, and pulled a bottle of vitaminwater from the fridge.

"We could say the same about you. I snagged one of those, by the way. I hope you don't mind." Thaddeus lifted his own bottle of vitaminwater to his lips and took a swig.

"Of course not. I told you guys to make yourselves at home." Jackson twisted off the cap and tossed it in the nearby trashcan.

"It looked like you had a later night last night than we did. Is everything okay this morning?"

Jackson considered Thaddeus for a long moment. Had the man been awake when Mallory showed up? He was pretty sure the answer was no. But Thaddeus could've waken when Mallory slipped out, at whatever the hell time that had been.

"Got a break in a case we're working on," he said, deciding it best not to question. "I've got to get to the office."

"So you'll be working all day, then. No chance of breaking away to come to the challenge for a while?"

The disappointment Jackson heard in the other man's tone puzzled him. He hadn't had much time to talk with Thaddeus and Terri since they'd arrived, but in the few conversations they'd managed, he hadn't gotten the sense either of them was really counting on him showing up at their firefighter challenge. Not that he wouldn't like to go. It had been years since he'd watched firefighters in action, even if it was only a staged competition. He had enjoyed the few times he had gotten to tag along on calls with Jason when he had first joined the fire department.

"Sorry, but probably not. You two kick some ass, though." Jackson started for the front door. "Hopefully before you leave we'll get a few hours to hang together, and I want to hear all about it."

"You bet," Terri said. "Be careful out there, MIB."

Her spunkiness made Jackson smile as he walked out the door. MIB, man in black. Angelina's sister, Tess, had called him that before, still did when the occasion arose.

The elevator at the end of the hall slid open and a woman about Mallory's height and build stepped off. He knew in an instant it wasn't Mallory. The woman's hair was long like Mal's but stark black and didn't fit with her milky, freckled complexion.

He met her brown-eyed gaze as he headed to the elevator, keeping to one side of the hall to allow her room to pass by him. He didn't recognize her as one of his neighbors. There were five other apartments on the third floor, each of them occupied by older, married couples except for one. He hadn't crossed paths with the single redhead who lived two doors down from him in several months.

"Agent Graham." She gave him a slight nod and averted her gaze as she passed him.

Jackson stopped in his tracks. The voice. He knew that voice.

Son of a bitch. It's her.

He whirled around and found her stopping at the redhead's apartment. She stuck a key in the lock of the apartment door and slid a nervous look his way.

"You?" Shock made his eyes wide. Instinct made him start to go for his sidearm beneath his suit jacket, but a gut feeling stopped him.

"Not here," she said softly, firmly. Her eyes pleaded with him to listen, not to make a move. "You trusted me before. Trust me again."

Trusted her? He had thought she was Mallory. "I should take you in." Protocol demanded it. They had spent countless hours looking for this woman, following up on the information she had provided, wondering what more she knew about Lexie Stratus's disappearance that she hadn't yet revealed. She was also a criminal. Hell, she had kidnapped him, for Pete's sake.

She shook her head. "If I'm seen with you they'll know I've gone to the FBI."

"They who?" Jackson cast a cursory glance up and down the empty hallway. A security camera hung in the far corner, videotaping their every movement. Did she think someone with access to the building's security was behind Lexie's disappearance?

"Whoever took Lexie." She unlocked the apartment and pushed the door open a half inch. "Give me one hour, Agent Graham. Please. I'll come to your office and tell you everything I know. You can do what you want from there, take me into custody, whatever you have to do."

Could he trust her? Her gaze pleaded with him to do this her way. What was it with the women in his life insisting they be in charge lately?

"You aren't worried someone will see you coming to the bureau?"

She shook her head again. "I know how to make sure I'm not followed."

"And what if you don't show?" Did she really think he would walk away from a key witness and offender?

"You wouldn't know anything if I hadn't come to you. I want her found, Agent Graham. I also want to keep myself alive. I'll be there. One hour." She pushed the door open and walked inside the apartment, closing and locking the door behind her.

* * * *

"You let her go." Cooper made it more statement than question. Not an ounce of derision or anger sounded in his tone.

Mallory crossed her legs and watched the byplay between her boss and Jackson. Cooper sat behind his desk, a perfect picture of laid-back cool. Jackson paced the floor, hands shoved in the pockets of his slacks, head bowed and eyes on his feet. His posture might have screamed defeat, but she knew better. Jackson didn't lose. He conquered. Right now, he would be replaying the scene he had told them about in the hallway, plugging in the missing details to the kidnapping two nights ago, and calculating his next move.

Good for him.

It was all she could do to keep her mind from replaying every second of last night when he had been naked beneath her, inside of her. She swore she felt his body heat even though his pacing took him farther away from her. It made it hard to think, much less concentrate on anything beyond a plan to get him right back in bed again.

"I went with my instincts." Jackson lifted his head and confidently met Cooper's unwavering gaze. "She'll show."

Cooper nodded once. An excellent team leader, he trusted all of them to make their own calls, follow their own guts, and never bashed them for it even if they turned out to be wrong. "She could be our informant from this morning, the one who called in with the tip about the body."

"If she is, we'll know in less than an hour. Has the medical examiner identified the body?"

Cooper shook his head. "Nothing yet. You said the woman from this morning, your kidnapper, is named Jennifer Moss. What else do we know about this woman?"

As if on cue, a sharp rap sounded at the partially open door, and Cameron walked in with Marcus Kell at his heels, not waiting for an invitation. "She's an open book, boss. Twenty-eight years old, bachelor's in psychology, currently enrolled at Waterston University to turn that into a master's. She also holds a certificate from a local bartending school, which she is currently utilizing in her job as a bartender at Cinderella's."

That bit of information got though the sexual cloud in Mallory's mind. She sat straighter. "I know her. Not well, but I've talked to her a time or ten at Cinderella's. She's about my height and build with a head full of fireball red hair and brown eyes. She's sweet, seems to have a great personality and a quick wit."

Jackson looked at her, his expression neutral, his eyes focused and intense. "Her hair is black now, but yeah, that's her."

She had already been in Cooper's office when Jackson arrived. He had greeted her as he always did and had gotten straight down to business. She had expected him to be angry, hurt. If he was, he certainly didn't let it show. All morning, he had been acting as if last night never happened.

Wasn't that what you wanted?

Yes. She had gone to him last night hoping to exorcise her lust for him once and for all. One night, a few hours in his arms, a few moments with him inside her, and all the sexual tension that had been building between them for so very long would be broken, diminished.

It hadn't worked. He couldn't know the willpower it had taken her to crawl out of his bed and leave after he had fallen asleep. She had wanted to stay, wanted to wake in his arms this morning. The mere thought of leaving him had torn through her soul, propelled her out of his bed and out of his apartment.

Out of his life?

No, if anything, her little game last night had backfired to hell. She still wanted him. Dammit, she wanted him even more now than before. Worse, last night had made her acutely aware of things she didn't want to face, emotions she wasn't ready to deal with.

"The degree in psychology doesn't surprise me," Mallory went on, pushing everything else aside. "She's empathetic and a great listener."

"What does she know about you?" Cooper asked.

Mallory instantly saw where he was going with his question. "Not much. Not even my real name. I've always used Jacqueline when I've introduced myself to anyone in that club." She had talked to Jennifer about Jackson, though. She hadn't revealed his name or even a description, nothing that would have clued Jennifer in on the fact that Mallory had been talking about her neighbor.

"She will recognize you," Jackson pointed out.

Mallory nodded. "Yeah, she will, but she isn't the one we need to worry about, right? I mean, she's our informant not our bad guy."

"I think the jury is still deliberating on that one," Kell muttered.

"When was the last time you saw her?" Jackson asked. "She obviously wasn't working two nights ago when you were at the club."

No, she was too busy kidnapping you. "It's been a while, at least a week or more."

"According to the owner of the club, she hasn't worked in a couple of weeks." Cameron moved behind her and rested his hands on the back of her chair. "She told her boss she needed some time to concentrate on her studies. She took a leave of absence shortly after Lexie disappeared and hasn't been back. He said he's called her a couple of times to check on her, make sure she didn't intend to quit, to ask when she might be back, but she hasn't given him a specific date."

"She's lucky he hasn't fired her," Kell added. "Most bosses wouldn't put up with that."

"He said she's too good of an employee to lose," Cameron said.

"Has she still been attending classes?" Cooper asked.

"Every one of them. Her records at the college are exemplary."

"It would've set off an alarm if she dropped from sight completely. She thinks she's being watched." Jackson raked a hand through his hair and continued to pace. "That's why she wanted to come in on her own, why she said coming to us in any normal way would've been too risky. She's afraid for her life."

"Her brother was Waterston PD. Did you know that?" Cameron asked.

Jackson nodded. "Narcotics detective. We crossed paths a few times. He was killed in a drug bust gone wrong last year."

"Which would explain how she knows to spot a tail and how to lose one." Brothers looked out for their little sisters. Mallory knew that from firsthand experience. Cameron had taught her how to defend herself, how to shoot a gun, and how to follow her gut when something didn't feel right long before she joined the bureau.

"Her apartment is leased under her parents' names. They lived there with her until her brother's funeral, moved out, and bought a place in Meridian."

"Son of a bitch." Kell let out a disbelieving laugh. "That's how she got the dealer tag."

Jackson shot a look Kell's direction. "Mal is right. Jennifer is a smart woman. She's being cautious. She's taken risks—stealing, kidnapping—that have put her own freedom in jeopardy."

"Obviously something she knows has made her feel the need to break the law to stay safe," Mallory cut in. "She's scared. Why and of whom are the questions we still need answered."

The intercom on Cooper's desk phone beeped and his administrative assistant's voice filled the office. "There's a Jennifer Moss at the front desk asking to see Agent Graham."

"Have her escorted to interrogation room two, Glenda." Cooper flicked a look at Jackson and said, "Agent Graham will be with her shortly."

"Yes, sir."

Cooper got to his feet, snatched his suit jacket off the back of his chair, and shrugged it on. "Let's go get those answers."

* * * *

Jackson smelled her the instant he opened the door to interrogation room two. He recognized the scent as the one she had worn the night she had kidnapped him. He remembered making note of the fragrance and had thought to tell Mallory to wear it more often. That, of course, had been when he had thought Jennifer was Mallory. He fixed his gaze on her as he preceded the rest of the team into the room and took a moment to introduce each one in turn. He sat in the seat across from her. Cameron and Kell stood behind him, leaning against the wall at their backs.

Jennifer stared at Mallory, realization and recognition plain on her face. "I know you. But I thought your name was Jacqueline, not Mallory."

Mallory took the seat adjacent to Jennifer and smiled warmly. "That's the name I use sometimes when I'm in clubs. It's nice to see you again. The new guy they have working your shift at Cinderella's is kind of cute, but he doesn't make a vodka and tonic the way you do."

Jennifer gave a nervous laugh at that and appeared to relax, albeit marginally. "I miss my shift." Her brown eyes clouded. "I know it probably sounds stupid, but I love being a bartender."

"There's nothing stupid about enjoying your job," Mallory said. "And you're good at what you do."

"Kyle keeps telling me that. He's called me several times asking when I'll be back." Jennifer looked down at her hands folded on the table. "I hope I can go back soon."

"What makes you feel like you can't?" Cooper took the seat at the head of the rectangular table, rested his forearms on the edge, and steepled his fingers.

Jackson watched his boss study Jennifer. His expression revealed nothing of his thoughts or first impression of the woman.

Jennifer took a deep breath and let it out slowly. She didn't look at Cooper when she lifted her head. She settled her gaze on Jackson, instead. "The night before Lexie disappeared, she came into Cinderella's during my shift. She did that sometimes when she had the night off and I didn't. She had this guy with her. He was nice-looking, a classy dresser with a smooth voice, and very polite, but something about the guy gave me the creeps. She didn't tell me a lot about him, just that she had met him at another club and talked him into coming to Cinderella's." She paused, her lips unfolding in a small smile at the memory. "I think she wanted to show him off."

Jackson reached for the legal tablet and pen that lay in the center of the table, pulled it in front of him, and quickly jotted down her brief description of the guy. "Did she bring men into your club a lot?"

"He was the first. The guys she usually dates are, well, slime balls." Her cheeks turned pink as if it embarrassed her to reveal what she really thought about the men her friend had dated. "Most of the time they are older men she's met at Stardust. Creeps only looking to get laid and figuring a stripper is a sure bet for that. I've met a few of them, most of the time outside of Stardust when I would stop by to give her a lift. With every one, I've told her she can do better."

"Is that what you told her about this guy?" Cooper asked, his tone even and interrogational.

"I didn't get the chance. I haven't seen her since that night." She shrugged. Her gaze momentarily dropped to the table again where she toyed with the ring on the middle finger of her right hand. "I don't know what I would've said. He was an improvement, in appearance and age at least, and he definitely seemed to treat her better, but..."

"Your gut was telling you something different," Jackson finished for her.

"I'm a psychology major, Agent Graham. My education was telling me something different. I can read people, detect when they're holding something back, when they're hiding something. Like the other night with you. You weren't scared even when I was holding a gun to your back. You went with me, but it was more out of curiosity than fear." The corners of her lips twitched. "It almost seemed as if you thought I was a girlfriend playing around or something."

"Or something," Jackson muttered, unable to hide the sourness in his tone.

"You would make a good agent," Mallory said, a trace of amusement in her tone as she worked her way deeper into the other woman's confidence.

Jennifer's smile was laden with sadness. "My brother said that, too, that I would make a good cop. It only took me a few seconds to know Jim was a dangerous guy. I couldn't put my finger on exactly how. I just knew."

Jackson heard Mallory's quick intake of breath and saw her stiffen. She propped her elbows on the table and leaned in closer. "Jim?"

Jennifer nodded. "That was his name. I didn't get his last name. If she told me, I forgot. Honestly, I didn't want to know it. The guy freaked me out that bad."

"Mid to late twenties, chestnut hair, bright green eyes, flawless complexion, built like a swimmer?"

Mallory rattled off descriptive details that sent a bone-deep chill racing through Jackson's system. She knew this guy? She had been close enough to him to see he didn't have so much as a pimple marring his face?

"Handsome"—Mallory continued, drawing her perfect eyebrows together in obvious recollection—"casual dresser, at least he was dressed that way when I met him. A smooth talker, polite, polished, but oddly intimidating."

"That sounds like the same guy."

Jennifer confirmed at the same time Cooper asked, "When did you meet him?"

"The night Jennifer kidnapped Jackson," Mallory answered Cooper. "I was at Cinderella's when he called me to pick him up. I stopped by there for a drink after I left here. Jim came up to me, introduced himself, and we talked for a while."

Talked? Jackson suspected that talking had everything to do with the guy trying to pick her up and very little to do with casual conversation. Jealously, white-hot and fierce, surged through his bloodstream. It wasn't an alien feeling when it came to Mallory. The green-eyed demon had been growing stronger inside him for years. He had fought against it, kept it behind an almost-impenetrable lock and key, knowing he had only to give in and he would be the man touching her, tasting her, feeling the sweet recesses of her amazing body.

You gave in last night.

Yeah, he had, and look where it had gotten him this morning.

"What did he say to you?" Cooper asked.

Jackson shoved the demon back in its cage, knowing it wouldn't stay there for long now, and focused on the conversation.

"He talked mostly about how beautiful I was and how he was surprised I was there alone. I told him I only planned to stay for one drink. He tried to convince me to have another, to dance with him, that sort of stuff."

Jackson's mind flashed back to the ride in the car after she had picked him up, to the brief conversation they'd had about Cinderella's.

I was considering leaving when you called.

Considering? Was there something that might have kept you there if I hadn't called?

She had told him she had thought about staying for another drink, maybe a dance or two. With this guy Jim, no doubt.

Jesus, God. If this Jim guy was responsible for Lexie Stratus's disappearance, Mallory could've been next.

Mallory paused thoughtfully. "He asked a lot of questions about friends, how many people I knew in the club, how often I came there. I didn't think much about it at the time, but…"

"He was digging," Jackson said.

Christ. They'd had the guy right under their noses. Fishing for information was a classic move of human traffickers. Find a lonely, beautiful woman, make her feel like she's above all the rest, gain her trust, slip a drug in her drink, and she was theirs for the taking.

And the bastard nearly had Mallory.

No, Mallory was too smart for that. She wouldn't have left with the guy, likely wouldn't have even allowed him to buy her a drink unless she watched every step of that drink being made until it landed in her hand.

"You were on the phone with me when you walked out of the club." He remembered hearing the blaring music fade in the background. "Were you paying attention? Did he follow you?"

Mallory narrowed her eyes at him. "I always pay attention. No, he didn't follow me. He listened to the first part of our conversation, though. I know that. Well, my end of the conversation at least. I called you something. I don't remember what it was now, but the instant the word left my mouth he turned away, and I walked out. No good-bye. No nothing." She shrugged. "I left him sitting at the bar, and no one walked out after me."

"You called me handsome," Jackson remembered. She had called him that right after she had asked him what kind of position he had thought she would be in. And his mind had boarded an instant flight to do-her island, where he had envisioned her in a number of poses that all included her naked and writhing while he fucked her.

The memory of her last night, beneath him when he had first laid her on his bed, surfaced in his mind. He could still feel her pliant body giving against his harder torso, still feel her hands on his flesh, her thighs clamping his body between them. He saw a flash of how she had looked sitting on top of him, her hair falling like a curtain around her face, teasing the swells of her breasts, and his dick swelled in his slacks.

"That was enough for him to know she wasn't an easy target," Cameron commented behind him. "He has to know Jennifer isn't either. Lexie took him to meet her, proving she has at least one friend in this big ole city."

"Proving *both* women have at least one friend in this big ole city," Mallory corrected. "Jennifer and Lexie at least had each other, but that still didn't stop him from taking Lexie."

"He's been following me," Jennifer cut in. "Him or someone he's connected to. Someone has been keeping tabs on me. I think they've been watching to see if I would go to the cops when I realized Lexie was missing."

"Did you?" Jackson lifted a questioning brow. "You told me that night to find Lexie, that no one else would. Who else did you go to for help? We've checked with the Waterston PD and the task force that frequents Stardust. They were unaware Lexie did anything beyond quitting her job."

"I know. Their apparent ignorance is why I came to you." Jennifer pushed strands of her dyed black hair behind one ear and returned to her recollection of the last time she had seen her friend. "I called Lexie when my shift ended the night she brought Jim into Cinderella's. They had left about an hour before that."

"Did you see her when she left?" Cooper jumped in. "Did she appear to be intoxicated or coerced at all?"

"No. She had one rum and coke. He drank a Heineken. They hung around for about forty-five minutes and then she told me good-bye and walked out the door with him, holding his hand."

"And that's the last time you saw her, the last time you spoke to her?" Jackson asked. If the guy had done something to Lexie, he had apparently waited until he got her alone before he made the move.

Jennifer nodded. "Like I said, I called her after my shift. When she didn't answer, I stopped by her apartment. I wanted to make sure she had made it home okay, but she wasn't there. The next day I tried again, called her repeatedly, and went by her place. I went into Stardust Sunday night and was told she'd quit. I knew something was really wrong then. Lexie needed that job. It might have been less than respectable in the eyes of most people, but she made good money. She was sticking with it because she was finally making enough to enroll at the community college to get her degree. She always talked about being a counselor, helping out girls who'd had the same rough life she'd had. Classes started that Monday. I checked with the college, but she hadn't showed up there either. That's when I called the Waterston PD to report her missing."

"You did call the police?" Jackson asked. And yet their guys at the department had no record of the call. "Who did you talk to?"

"I asked for Detective Reese. He's in the narcotics division, but I knew my brother worked with him before"—Jennifer paused and took a deep breath—"before he was killed. I was told Detective Reese was on vacation, so I got transferred to missing persons. The officer who answered didn't give his name and, when I tried to ask for it after I gave him the information on Lexie, he hung up. I waited, and when I didn't hear anything, I called again. I talked with an Officer Evans that time, who informed me there was no record of the report even being filed.

"I'm not delusional, Agent Graham. I filed that report. Someone at the Waterston PD, most likely the first officer I talked to who wouldn't give me his name, made it disappear. After that first phone call, I realized I was being followed. Most of the time it's a white, four-door sedan with tinted windows. A couple of times, I've noticed a beat-up black Chevy van. Neither has gotten close enough for me to get a look at the driver or the license plate, but I've seen one of them at the university, outside our apartment building, and places I've gone to shop. They're watching me. The sedan even tried to follow me to Meridian. I ditched them about twenty miles out of town."

"Your brother taught you well," Jackson said and watched the saddened smile return to her lips.

"Yes, he did."

"You're sure no one followed you here this morning?"

She nodded vehemently. "Positive."

Jackson exchanged a wordless glance with Cooper. Should they tell her about the body found in the abandoned warehouse that morning? They still didn't have a clue if it was Lexie Stratus or anyone even remotely connected to the girl's disappearance. However, if it had been Jennifer who had made the call, they would know they didn't need to continue looking for the informant.

"The bureau received an anonymous tip this morning that may be connected," Cooper told her, keeping the information vague. "Was it from you?"

"No. What was the tip? Was it about Lexie?" The hope in her voice twisted a knot in Jackson's chest.

"Not directly." Jackson followed his boss's lead, not giving away too much, not wanting to crush the woman's hopes that they might still find Lexie alive.

"We're currently investigating the whereabouts of four other women who have quit Stardust in the last six months," Cooper said. "Do you know anything about these other women?"

"Lexie went to work there about three or four months ago. I know she was hired to take someone's place, but I don't know the details. You think they're connected." Jennifer's tone made her words more of a statement than a question.

"We don't like coincidences," Cooper told her. "Is there anything else you can tell us about this Jim you met or the people who have been following you?"

Jennifer shook her head, frowning. "I wish there was. Lexie is a good person. I've known her over a year. She's been trying hard to turn her life around. She wouldn't have just run off. I'm certain of that. Something has happened to her." She closed her eyes and whispered, "And I've got a sinking feeling it's something really horrible. She's been missing too long already."

Mallory reached across the table and covered one of Jennifer's hands with hers. "Don't give up hope. We're going to find her."

Jennifer opened her eyes, and gratitude swam in the tears she held back. "What happens next?" She shifted her attention to Jackson and then Cooper.

Jackson knew the question she left unspoken. What did they plan to do with her?

"I'm going to assign an agent to watch over you," Cooper answered. "Unless you want to be put into protective custody."

Surprise sliced through the tears and gratitude in her eyes as she stared at the team leader. "I expected you to take me into custody but not for protection. I know I broke several laws. I—"

"You did," Cooper cut her off. "You're also the best informant we have on a case that appears to go deeper than any of us first believed." He pulled his cell from his pocket, checked the screen, and got to his feet. "I want you to tell Agent Stone—Mallory—everything you know personally about Lexie Stratus. I also want the two of you to get with our sketch artist. I want a picture of this Jim guy to run through our databases." He swept a glance across the other agents in the room. "The rest of you come with me."

Jackson followed Cooper, Cameron, and Kell out of the interrogation room, closing the door behind him. Cooper stopped in the hallway and turned to Jackson.

"Do you think I made the wrong call in there?"

"No, sir." Jackson agreed with Cooper's decision to let Jennifer walk as opposed to arresting her. "We make deals with informants when necessary, allowing them to slide on misdemeanors in return for valuable information. What you just did was exactly that, only in an unspoken way."

"Good, then we're on the same page." Cooper glanced down at his cell phone still in his hand. "Tarantino is with the medical examiner now. The body found this morning wasn't Lexie Stratus. Dental records have identified her as Erin Griffin."

"One of the four missing strippers we've been looking for?" Kell asked.

Cooper shook his head. "As of two o'clock this morning she was an employee at Stardust. My guess is she was abducted right after her shift."

"Why kill her?" Jackson voiced the first thought that came to his mind. "If this is a trafficking ring like we think, why not save her and auction her off to the highest bidder?"

Cooper shoved his cell into his inner coat pocket. "That's what I want you to find out."

* * * *

"I'm no longer a little intimidated." Terri moved away from the sign-in table, her gaze sweeping the gathered crowd of firefighters and spectators, her eyes the size of saucers.

"That's good." Thaddeus waited for her to start walking, wishing he could say the same. They had over an hour to kill before the first event, plenty of time to get his nerves in check. Or throw up, which was exactly what he felt like doing at that moment.

"No, it's not, because now I'm a *lot* intimidated. Did you see the names on that list? There were hundreds of them!"

Yeah, Thaddeus had seen, hence his stomach's suddenly overwhelming desire to rid itself of the breakfast he had eaten that morning. "We knew there would be." Firefighters, retired and active, representing departments across the state had traveled to Waterston for the event, each of them hoping right along with Thaddeus and Terri that they could win the title of state champion.

"True, but seeing it certainly doesn't make it any easier to swallow." She puffed out a breath and planted her hands on her hips. "What now, Vegister? Do we head back to the staging area and our gear or do you want to walk around a bit, maybe see if we can find your parents?"

"I doubt they're here yet." Finding them would be easy. His father had used his influence to secure front-row seats to the event.

"Or we could look for Cameron." Terri's eyes glinted with mischief as she looked at him. "I know that's why you asked Jackson about his work day back at the apartment."

"Then you also picked up on the fact that it's highly unlikely Cameron will show." Had he really expected the man to?

Yes. After their date last night, the promise in Cameron's gaze coupled with his declaration that he would see what he could do, the freaking kiss Thaddeus could still feel on his lips, he'd firmly believed Cameron would show.

"Yeah." Terri sighed. "I got that, too."

"Hey. Terri."

Thaddeus watched Terri's eyes return to saucer-state before she closed them and heaved a deep breath. Over her shoulder, he spotted the firefighter she had met yesterday at the restaurant headed their way. He had to work not to grin. "Looks like your man is here."

"He is so not my man," Terri grumbled and painted on a truly fake smile as she turned.

"Wow, I can't believe I found you with all these people hanging around."

"Me either." Terri's tone clearly said she wished he hadn't.

Thaddeus dropped his head and stifled a chuckle as the guy started to ramble. Terri had filled him in on her date over breakfast, a date she expressly stated she had no intentions of repeating. He shoved his hands in his pockets, making a mental note to empty them before he suited up in the staging area, and waited to hear what creative brush-off line Terri would use this time. His attention got diverted when his cell in his pocket started to vibrate.

Unknown the screen read, and he rolled his eyes. *Mental note number two, get a new phone as soon as you get back to Silver Springs.* Every call, whether it was one he had saved to his contacts or not, had been registering as unknown for weeks. Not that he needed his phone to tell him who was on the other end of the cellular waves this time. No doubt it was one of his parents calling to let him know they had arrived.

"Good morning. I take it you made it," he said in lieu of hello.

A soft male sigh followed by, "I wish, sweetie," sent his gut into a riot of tingling surprise.

"Wow, sorry, I was expecting it to be Mom or Dad."

"I take it your phone still isn't acting right." Adrien Bingham's too-sexy voice flowed through Thaddeus's ear and sent embers of familiar heated longing raining through his system. "I hope I didn't disappoint you."

"Of course not! God, it's—" Good to hear your voice, he started to say except, *Jesus*, talking to Adrien after the date he'd had last night with Cameron was far weirder than he had expected. "I'm glad you called."

Was he?

Yes, because even those incredible hours he had spent with Cameron last night hadn't gotten him over his desire for Adrien.

"I would rather be there with you. I wanted to come and, you know, show my support, but I figured it was probably best that I didn't. Things here at the office have gotten all wonky on me."

Concern cut through the longing first, and Thaddeus stiffened. He worried about Adrien. The man was a top-level DEA agent. How could he not? Adrien put himself in a world of danger on an everyday basis chasing down bad guys and hoping those would lead him to worse ones.

Cameron is FBI.

Thaddeus shut off his mind. He so wasn't going to think about those similarities right now. He certainly wasn't going to travel down comparison lane where Adrien stood on one side of the street and Cameron the other, with himself right there in the middle.

Talk about living life on the edge.

Forget the street. He was teetering on a cliff with both men at the bottom, not knowing which direction to fall, and there came the confusion with a trace of skepticism on the heels of his concern. Adrien had always been up-front with him about everything. So why did he get the feeling Adrien's decision not to come to Waterston had nothing to do with work?

"Tough case?" Thaddeus asked. He glanced at Terri, saw she had already ditched last night's date and was now watching him, and briefly met her gaze. Her mouth dropped and he knew whatever she saw in his eyes had been enough for her to deduce who he was talking to.

"It has potential. I didn't call to talk shop, though. I wanted to wish you luck. Your first event starts soon, doesn't it?"

"In about an hour." Thaddeus realized his nerves had settled, at least where the challenge was concerned. Talking with Adrien did that. It calmed him even as it heightened his desire for the man. "You should see the people here. It's crazy!"

"Nervous?" Amusement slid into Adrien's tone, and Thaddeus couldn't help but grin.

"I'm shaking out of my boots."

"You'll do great. Treat it like you would a real fire scene. Give it your all and I know you'll come out on top."

"Your confidence is inspiring, baby."

"I'm confident because I know how good you are. What about the rest of your trip? Have you had any time to get out, see what's changed in your hometown?"

Adrien's question had Thaddeus's mind reeling back to last night, to his walk with Cameron to the Chinese restaurant and back. "Not much. We got here too late Wednesday to do anything. Then Jackson wasn't home and we had to chase him down." He paused, considered whether or not to even mention Cameron, and decided to go for broke. "Cameron, I think you know him. I've heard you mention his name a time or ten."

In front of him, Terri shifted and lifted her brows.

Thaddeus averted his gaze and waited through a beat of thick silence. His heart pounded. Maybe he imagined the weight of that moment, but it sure didn't feel like it.

"Cameron Stone," Adrien finally said. "Yes, I know him."

How well do you know him? "I thought he was the same guy. Anyway, he had to swing by and let us into Jackson's apartment. They, he and Jackson, are working on some case. Apparently they got a pretty big break in it that night or something. Terri and I haven't seen much of Jackson at all."

"So you haven't had much time to talk?"

Adrien's tone sounded conversational enough, but Thaddeus swore he heard more there, almost as if he were afraid Thaddeus and Jackson had found plenty of time to talk. It wasn't jealously. Adrien knew Jackson wasn't gay. But what else did he know about Jackson? More to the point, what did Jackson know about Adrien?

"Not yet. He's hoping to squeeze in some free time before Terri and I head back to Silver Springs."

"This probably isn't the best time to ask, but maybe you can squeeze in some free time for me when you get back. There are some things that, well, we need to talk about, things I should have told you a long time ago."

Thaddeus swallowed, his heart in his throat. Should he tell Adrien he already knew, that he had figured it out? Should he tell Adrien about last night, about his date with Cameron, about the freaking kiss he couldn't get out of his mind?

"I'll call you as soon as I get back to town," he said instead. "We'll meet somewhere, have a drink, and you can spill everything."

Adrien took a deep breath and let it out slowly. "Something is telling me I don't really have to."

Thaddeus closed his eyes. "That would be your agent senses tingling, baby."

He had been right. Cameron *was* the other guy. Trouble came in realizing that having his suspicions confirmed didn't do a thing in washing away his confusion because, damnit, Cameron was now the other guy in his life, too.

Chapter Six

It didn't take long for Mallory to discover working the crowd at Stardust for one night apparently established the norm for any night to follow. The biggest difference her second night on the job presented was that the regulars, who made up more than seventy-five percent of the clientele, knew her by name. The slimy Leroy Platt, who once again sat at the same table drinking the same drink, even continued his attempts to know her by feel.

"You sure have a sweet ass, darlin'." His drunken slur and the feel of his hand cupping her left cheek had bile rising in her throat.

Mallory swallowed it, determined not to puke on the bastard, and gave him her most dazzling smile. "I believe you said something to that effect last night."

"Seems I did, but you threatened to have me kicked out last night. You planning on having Bruno over there come and drag me out tonight?"

"No, I'm planning on serving you this drink and telling you to watch the stage just like I did last night. It's about time for the next lovely beauty to start dancing for you." Though, she would rather toss him out on his ass herself. Unfortunately, the check she had ran on him at HQ that morning revealed so many shady secrets in his closet that she had been forced to put him at the top of her list of people around Stardust to watch, least of which was the substantial withdrawal from his bank account mere days after Lexie Stratus disappeared.

"The beauty I like to watch most won't be working tonight." He scowled and shot a glance at the stage. "Seems like every time I get a favorite in this place the bitch quits."

If it hadn't been the surefire way to blow a cover she desperately needed for this case, Mallory would have jerked the slime bucket out of his chair and demanded he tell her everything he knew about Erin Griffin. How did he know she wouldn't be dancing tonight? Did he have something to do with her murder? Had he killed the girl himself?

"I'd tell you to get up there and dance for me, but then you might quit, too."

Or she might end up wherever the other missing girls had gone. Damn, it was looking more and more like she might have to strip before she got the break she needed in this case.

Leroy squeezed her ass painfully hard, and she tightened her grip on her tray to keep from decking him. "I wouldn't want that to happen. You're the prettiest thing this place has got to look at now."

"I'm sure you'll find another beauty to capture your attention soon enough." Mallory reached her free hand behind her, closed it over his, and firmly, but oh so politely, peeled it from her ass. "I've got other customers to serve. Enjoy the show."

She left his table quickly, off-loading the other drinks on her tray, gathering more orders, and gritting her teeth as she bore more pawing on her way back to the bar.

Sasha met her at the waitress station. "What can I get for you, honey?"

"A barf bag would be lovely," Mallory told her as she set her tray on the bar.

Sasha's lips twitched. "Leroy seems to forget from night to night that he's not supposed to put his hands on the staff."

"Him and every other guy in this place." Mallory shot a glance over her shoulder as Candy took the stage. "He's ill because his favorite dancer quit. Who was he talking about?" she asked, pretending not to know.

"Erin." Sasha propped her elbows on the bar and leaned closer to Mallory as the beat of the music increased the volume of the song. "I didn't expect her to last long. The really pretty ones never do."

"I talked to her last night before I left. She was in the back counting her tips and talking about how much money she made. She didn't say anything about quitting. If anything, I thought she was looking forward to doing it again tonight."

"They all brag about the tips they make. Even in this joint, the strippers make more than you and I do combined. Of course, they're taking off a lot more than we do, too." Sasha shrugged. "All I know is Betty said she got a call from Erin just before lunch. The girl quit. End of story."

Not end of story. Erin couldn't have called Betty because the girl's body had already been lying in the medical examiner's freezer by lunchtime.

"Don't let it worry you, sweetheart. The turn-around rate here is out of sight. Women—or should I say girls because most of them are barely even old enough to be on that stage—take a job here, keep it for a few days, maybe a few weeks or months, and then quit. Being a stripper is not a glamorous job. Some girls actually think it is. Then they get a taste of reality and they're gone."

Gone where was the question Mallory wanted answered. Erin Griffin had ended up in a body bag. Were the other missing girls dead, too, and their bodies just hadn't surfaced yet? Or were they being held captive by some sick, sadistic son of a bitch like the FBI believed, being forced to do heinous sexual acts?

Mallory looked over her shoulder again as Sasha started filling the new drink orders, her gaze landing on the employee door to the right of the stage. Beyond that door was the club office. She needed to find a way into that office tonight. If she could copy the hard drive on the club's computer, they might find something in the club records that would give them more leads to follow.

"Here you go." Sasha placed the drinks on Mallory's tray.

"Thanks." Mallory picked up the tray but hesitated. "I haven't seen Betty tonight. Is she in the office? I thought I would take my break before business picks up and talk to her for a minute."

Sasha lifted a brow. "Interest in taking Erin's place on the stage?"

Mallory pursed her lips thoughtfully. "I might. I mean, I know it isn't glamorous by any means, but the money sure would be. I was hoping she might let me do both, you know, waitress most of the time but pull a few stage shifts now and then."

"She probably will." Sasha's tone was laced with disapproval. "She left about a half hour ago. I don't know when she will be back. You should go ahead and take your break, though. I can handle things out here while you're gone."

Mallory nodded and wove her way through the scattering of tables to deliver the drinks. She walked through the employee door to the back and heard voices from the employee room at the end of the hall on the right. There would be at least two other strippers in there getting ready for their time on the stage. She tried the knob of the door on her left and found it locked. No biggie. The knob was the old-fashioned kind and took her all of five seconds to pick. With a quick glance behind her and another at the doorway down the hall, she twisted the knob and eased the door open.

The office was dark save for the blue glow coming from the screensaver on the computer on the desktop. It provided her enough light to see the office was also empty. She stepped inside, quietly closing the door behind her, and quickly looked around. Hopefully the door on the far side of the room led to a closet where she could hide if someone came in.

She balanced her weight on one foot and pulled the tiny USB device from her anklet. In seconds, she had it plugged into the computer port, copying the information on the hard drive. She ignored the sensations prickling her spine, like centipedes crawling up her flesh. If she got caught, her cover would be toast and the entire operation would be compromised.

She scanned the room around her more slowly as she waited for the download to complete. There were no cameras, at least not in obvious positions. If she were being caught on tape, hopefully no one would see a cause to view it until long after the FBI discovered what had happened to the missing women.

The light on the end of the USB device went out, alerting her that the download was complete. *Thank you, speedy technology.* She pulled the device from the computer port, replaced it in the space in her anklet, and tiptoed back to the office door.

She stopped with her hand on the knob and put her ear to the door. Hearing no sounds from the hallway, she slowly turned the knob, eased the door open, and walked out. Her hand was still on the knob, though the door was now closed, when the voices she had heard from the employee room got louder as the women moved into the hall.

"Hey, Jacqueline, isn't it?"

Mallory sucked in a breath and jerked back. Recovering quickly, she put her palm over her pounding heart as she turned to face the strippers, Natalie and Sabrina. She didn't know which one had spoken.

"That's right. Gosh, you nearly scared the life out of me." She let out a short, shaky laugh. *Think, Mallory. Think!*

"What are you doing?" the stripper named Sabrina asked. Her eyes, which were far too blue to be real and not colored contacts, narrowed suspiciously.

"I was looking for Betty. Have you seen her?"

"I don't think she's in there," Natalie said, her tone far friendlier and without a trace of the distrust she read in Sabrina's expression.

"Yeah, I don't think she is either. I knocked and, well, you know, habit of knocking at the same time you open the door, or attempt to, anyway. It's a bad habit. My mother gets on to me for doing it all the time." She slid a glance at the office door. "But it's locked and it doesn't sound like Betty is in there."

Christ, did I remember to lock it back?

Yes, she had thumbed the lock into place as she closed the door.
Thank God.

"She'll probably be back soon. Brina and I were headed out to
peek on the side of the stage and watch Candy. She's awesome up
there. Are you on break? You can come with us."

"Sure." Mallory stayed where she stood until the strippers passed
her in the narrow hallway and then fell in behind them, wanting
nothing more than to run the opposite direction, straight to HQ to see
what she could pull off the USB device once again securely in its
home on her anklet.

* * * *

Mallory's stomach growled as if it intended to go AWOL on her if
she didn't get food in it fast. She ached from her feet to her back to
her head. Though a part of her couldn't wait to get to the office and
start clicking through the files on the USB device, she knew if she
didn't get something to eat followed by at least a couple hours of
sleep, she would likely miss any key bits of information she found
even if they were highlighted in bright pink fill.

She rested her forehead on her apartment door as she stuck her
key in the lock and turned it. The fact that she didn't feel the tumblers
inside it fall into place had her lifting her head, drawing her Beretta
from her purse, and thumbing off the safety.

All thoughts of aches, food, and information drowned in the river
of adrenaline that flooded her system. She never left her apartment
unlocked. Who did in this day and age? Holding her Beretta in a
secure grip, one finger at the ready on the trigger, she eased her
apartment door open.

Loopy, her black-and-white cat, meowed softly and wound herself
around Mallory's foot. She ignored the cat, steadying her gun as her
gaze did a quick sweep of the interior of her apartment. A flickering

glow illuminated a figure on her sofa. She leveled her gun and started to speak when he beat her to it.

"It's me. Don't shoot."

Relief moved through her so fast it made her light-headed. She slumped against the doorframe, lowered her gun, and waited for her heartbeat to return to some semblance of normalcy. "I should shoot you anyway just for spite. Christ, Jackson! What are you doing sitting in the dark in my apartment at three in the freaking morning?"

"Waiting for you." He got to his feet and walked closer. "And it's not dark. Close the door and you'll be able to see."

Mallory closed the door, realizing it had been blocking the flames of the candles she kept lined on top of the half wall separating her living room and kitchen. A few more steps brought him farther into that light, and all ideas of her heartbeat slowing down disintegrated. No man had the right to be so devastatingly handsome all the time. It simply wasn't fair.

They spent so much time at the office that she rarely saw him in anything besides tailored suits, crisp white shirts, and ties. Tonight, he wore jeans and a pullover shirt with tennis shoes. The effect in the flickering candlelight nearly did her in. He looked ten times more dangerous, more forceful, and God help her, more appealing than ever.

Get a grip, Mallory.

Yeah, that was precisely what she wanted to do, and considering she was finding it difficult to tear her gaze off of him, she knew exactly what she wanted to grip. Those broad shoulders would be a start. Her hands burned to feel the dense muscles flex at her touch. Her fingers tingled with the need to close around his biceps, to dance over the square pecs his shirt clearly defined, to graze lower until she found his rigid cock and could hold it in her fist.

Careful. Get your head right or you're toast.

He had caught her off guard. That had no doubt been his intention. She could handle it, though. She had to. The memories of last night with him, of how close he had come to penetrating parts of her she didn't want to face, were still too clear in her mind. He had left her feeling vulnerable, and damn it, now that she'd had time to realize that, to stew on it, it really pissed her off. Last night had been all about breaking the sexual tension that had been building between them for far too long. It was supposed to lessen the fire burning in her soul, not stoke it to an out-of-control burn.

"I paid my power bill this month." She thumbed on the safety of her Beretta, shoved it back in her purse, and tossed the bag in a nearby chair as she headed for the kitchen. "I'm sure the electricity works fine."

"I'm sure it does, too. The candles work better for my purposes tonight." His long strides brought him to the kitchen light switch at the same time she reached for it. He closed his hand over hers, stopping her from turning it on.

His body heat overwhelmed her. Being this close to him again, knowing what that hand felt like on other parts of her flesh, sent tingles of acute desire dancing through her system.

"And what, exactly, are your purposes?" Something told her she really didn't want to know. Was he looking for a repeat of last night? Every insane, out-of-control part of her was ready for a redo. The single ounce of rational brains she had left knew beyond a shadow of a doubt she couldn't take it, not yet, not again so soon. Being with him again tonight, having him inside her again tonight would destroy her.

"Why did you leave last night?"

She had hurt him. She saw the evidence of that clouding his eyes. She had hurt herself, too. Everything about last night had hurt despite how incredibly fantastic it had been.

"I had to," she admitted in a whisper. "I needed space, my own place." She had needed her comfort zone, a zone he had thoroughly invaded tonight.

"Fair enough. Are you hungry?"

She blinked at him, surprised he let it go so easily. Had he really come to her apartment at three a.m. to cook for her? She started to say no despite the fact that her hunger had returned with a vengeance once the adrenaline of finding someone in her apartment had worn off. Cooking would lead to other activities she needed to steer clear of until she got her scruples back in line. She needed time. She needed sleep. Both would rejuvenate her resolve. She had gotten what she wanted last night, what she had been after from him for years. She had won the battle. Wasn't she supposed to feel victorious instead of confused out of her mind?

Her stomach, of course, picked that moment to growl its loudest yet and prevented her from telling the lie.

Jackson's oh-so-kissable lips spread in a small smile that ruined any idea of a cover-up she might have thought of. "I'll take that as a yes. Go change, get comfortable, and give me a few minutes. I'll fix something to eat."

Pompous ass.

She knew Jackson. She didn't stand a chance right now of getting him out of her apartment. Apparently, he had slipped into take-care-of-her mode. It wasn't the first time she had come home from an assignment to find him in her apartment ready to play the doting friend.

The idea of watching him move about her kitchen coupled with the knowledge that the man could cook better than anyone she knew was far too appealing.

So, okay, she would get comfortable. Somewhere in her remained the part that knew how to goad this man, how to turn the tables of discomfort around on him.

She dropped her hand from the light switch and shrugged off the trench coat she wore. Unlike last night, she still wore her Stardust uniform beneath it. It was probably a bad idea since the last place she needed to land was in her own bed with him tonight. Still, seeing the heat, white-hot and full of desire, that darkened his stormy eyes as his gaze fell down her body in a leisurely slide was pretty rewarding.

"Damn." That single whispered word dripped with male appreciation and unadulterated lust. "You look almost as amazing in that as you do naked."

"I might as well be naked wearing this, Slick. I'm guessing that's why you want me to go change."

"No, I just figured you would want to get out of your work clothes. You're welcome to stay that way if you like."

There had been a time, not so long ago, when he would have told her to put something on, when he would have fought to hide the desire clouding his eyes. Not so anymore. It made it harder to poke at him, harder to get all her synapses firing in the right direction again.

"I noticed you got out of your work clothes." *And did a damn fine job doing it.*

She let her gaze skim down the solid gray T-shirt that matched his eyes and accented every stupendous ridge and plane of his torso to pristine perfection. His jeans looked slightly worn, rode low on his narrow hips, and hugged powerful thighs that made her own burn to feel them flexing between her legs as he thrust his body forward, plunging his cock into her pussy.

She wrenched her gaze back up to meet his. "It's not often I see you dressed down. You lost the tie. It looks good."

The intensity and seriousness in his stare had her heart pounding fiercely against her breastbone. "You took the tie off last night. I don't intend to put it back on."

Shit. He wasn't talking about the material tie now. She remembered thinking in Cooper's office that morning that last night had been enough for him. The way he had acted, how he had appeared unfazed, as if it were just another day, business as usual, had made her wonder.

She had been way wrong, horribly, fantastically, frighteningly wrong.

"Jackson, I—"

"Am going to sit down and relax while I cook us dinner," he finished for her and glanced at the digital clock on the microwave. "Or breakfast. Which would you like?"

Mallory shook her head. He had done a complete one-eighty on her again. She couldn't keep up.

Cooking. Food. Yes, she was hungry, starving actually. Okay, she could do this.

"Have you looked in my refrigerator?" She gave him an incredulous look. "Because, the last time I opened it, there was a half gallon of expired milk, a pack of molded cheese, and a bottle of water."

"All of which is now in your trashcan, replaced by fresh milk, cheese, eggs, steaks, fresh vegetables, and a few other things. There's also potatoes and pasta in your cabinets and a loaf of bread in the bread box."

Mallory laughed, a hot burst of disbelieving air. "You brought groceries when you came over?" She shouldn't be surprised. He knew her, probably better than she knew herself.

And therein lies your biggest problem with this man. He's figured out how to get to you, how to work his way inside.

"I knew better than to come here thinking I was going to cook with anything you would have on hand. Your idea of a full, balanced meal comes from whatever takeout restaurant you can find on speed dial."

He had a point, so she didn't bother disputing it. "Breakfast, please. Steak, medium-well, and scrambled eggs with cheese and whatever else you can find to throw in them, toast, and a glass of milk." Her stomach grumbled again as she rattled off food that sounded scrumptious enough to die for.

His lips twitched as he turned his back on her and got to work. "Easy enough. Give me a half an hour. Take a shower. Take a nap if you want to. Whatever you want to do to pass the time."

"I could help?" The look he shot her over his shoulder was so comical she couldn't help but laugh. "I know. I know. I'm useless in the kitchen, but I had to offer. And since I got that response, I'll leave you to it. I think I will go change after all. Honestly, this uniform really makes me uncomfortable."

"Me, too."

* * * *

Jackson watched her until she disappeared down the hall. The way her hair fell in waves down the center of her back to flirt her trim waist made his fingers tingle. The way her amazing hips swayed when she walked, her ass cheeks flexing and beckoning his hands to touch, had him fisting said hands at his sides.

Uncomfortable didn't begin to describe the way seeing her in that uniform made him feel. The denim of his jeans wasn't pliant enough for the raging hard-on pressing demandingly against his zipper.

He raked his hands down his face in an attempt to rid himself of the image so he could concentrate on what he had come here to do. He had spent the day and much of the night with Cameron, Kell, and other agents at the bureau, combing through information. They worked their butts off looking for leads and evaluating those they already had, attempting to determine if Lexie Stratus's disappearance really tied in with the on-going Operation Water Down or if they had landed into something entirely different. At midnight, they had called it a day. He had gone home and taken one step into his bedroom when the memories he had been fighting all day to keep in the back of his mind swamped him.

He had seen Mallory on his bed, on top of him, riding his cock and allowing every ounce of pleasure she felt to show on her angelic face. He had felt the guard that surrounded that ecstasy, the wall she had been able to maintain around it all even in those erotically charged moments. He had heard the crack in that foundation he knew he had finally managed to create when he felt that single tear hit his chest.

He had let her take control last night, allowed her do it her way, but he had made progress toward his own goal in the process. If he backed off now, he knew she would repair that cracked foundation and come back at him with a will more determined and a heart harder to penetrate than ever.

Tonight, they would play another game. His game. His way. Cooking for her was the easy part. He liked to cook. He had been whipping up meals before he grew tall enough to reach the stove.

He set to that task now, pulling the ingredients he would need from the fridge and finding the necessary pots and pans in the lower cabinets. He knew his way around Mallory's kitchen. She had lived in the same apartment for years and rarely rearranged anything.

Rarely cleaned or organized anything either, he mused as he shuffled through drawers of utensils for cooking spoons and spatulas. One thing about it, Mallory Stone was far from the domestic type.

He lightly seasoned two New York strips and placed them in a pan before moving to chop up the vegetables for the omelets he intended to prepare. Soft sounds drifted down the hallway as he worked. He could hear Mallory in her bedroom opening drawers and shuffling about. He heard the light flick on in the bathroom, heard the water run in the sink, heard both turn off again and felt the awareness move over him as she returned to the kitchen.

"Are you sure you don't want some help? I'm not a total dweeb in the kitchen. I can chop vegetables and boil water and beat eggs." Her pause sounded thoughtful. "There are probably some other things I can do, too, but I can't put my finger on them just now."

Jackson kept his back to her to hide the smile he couldn't keep from his lips as he reached for the egg carton. "You can sit at the table." He cracked four eggs into a bowl, pulled a metal fork from the utensil drawer amongst all the plastic disposable ones, and turned as he whisked them. "And you can talk."

She drew her eyebrows together and frowned. "I gather we're not playing the silent game tonight."

"Nope." Inspiration struck and Jackson rolled with it, remembering something he had read and putting it to use. He set the bowl of whisked eggs on the countertop by the stove and moved to her. Anticipation did an excited boogie with the suspicion in her eyes. He lifted a brow as he raked his gaze over her, noting she had changed into a white button-down shirt with the sleeves rolled to her elbows. The shirttails stopped at midthigh, leaving her delectable legs exposed to torment him. Her feet were bare, her toes painted a sexy siren red.

The shirt belonged to him. He didn't know how she had gotten it, but he saw the confirmation in the teasing smile she failed to hide.

"You're in Chef Jackson's kitchen tonight." He stopped close enough to feel her breasts lightly brush his ribs. His body caressed hers as he stepped around her, and he heard her suck in a breath that quivered when she exhaled. He pushed her hair to one side, leaned in, and spoke softly in her ear. "In my restaurant, silence is frowned upon. Conversation is a required if one expects to be served."

He let the double entendre hang in the air, deciding she could define served however she wanted to. He intended to show her, one baby step at a time.

He eased back, turned slightly, and pulled out a chair at the small kitchen table. She turned her head to watch him, a trace of amusement mingling with the puzzlement in her expression.

He gestured to the chair with a flourish of his arm. "Please have a seat, madam. Your order will be ready shortly."

She made a soft sound of disbelief, shook her head, and sat, turning sideways in her chair to look at him.

Jackson could almost see the wheels turning in her beautiful head. *Good.* He had her on edge, uncertain of his next move, wondering how he intended to play this out. It was exactly where he wanted her.

Giving her time to settle, to find an answer to her current confusion, would return the power to her. He wouldn't let her have it tonight.

He walked back to the stove, flipped the steaks, and added a teaspoon of butter to a skillet for the eggs. A loud meow briefly drew his attention back to Mallory and down to the cat at her feet.

"She went nuts when I walked into the apartment."

"She likes you." Mallory scooped up the cat and cuddled it in her lap. "Don't you, Sloopsy?" she said, cupping the cat's face in her hands and kissing the top of its head. Cameron had rescued the cat outside his own apartment when it was a kitten.

Jackson remembered the sheer delight in Mallory's eyes when her brother pawned it off on her. Once in Mallory's arms, the kitten had put its paws on either side of Mallory's face and started playfully nibbling on her chin. Silly things the kitten did after had gifted her with the name Silly Loopy, which Mallory often shortened to Sloopsy or some variation.

"You're the only person she doesn't attack when they come over." Mallory patted the top of the cat's head and set it back on the floor.

"She meowed at me until I followed her in here. Her food dish was empty."

"Crap." Mallory slapped her forehead. "I forgot to fill it when I stopped by here this morning."

"Yeah, she had a few choice things to say about that, too."

Mallory laughed then took a dramatic breath. "Mmm, whatever you're doing over there is starting to smell yummy. Wouldn't it be easier to see what you're doing if you turned on the light, though?"

"I hate to break it to you, but Chef Jackson's is a fledgling restaurant. Unlike our customers, we can't afford to pay the power bill, so we operate under the guise of romanticism to hide our financial troubles."

Mallory laughed again. "Good one, except don't you need power to run the appliances?"

"Details. Details." And, of course, she never missed any of them. "Stay in character, guest Mallory, and don't think so much."

About anything. If the woman had a single flaw, it was that she thought way too much.

She stifled her laughter but couldn't wipe the smile from her lips. It was entertaining to watch her try, though.

She gave him a regal nod. "My apologies, Chef Jackson."

"Apologies accepted." He turned to the breadbox where he had stashed the loaf he had brought and took out four slices. "I don't need more light. The candles are providing enough. I know what I'm doing."

"I don't doubt that. I often wondered why you don't open your own restaurant. You know, like a business venture on the side, a place where you can go to cook for people when the bureau isn't demanding all of your time."

Jackson shrugged as he scraped the chopped vegetables from the plate into the egg skillet. "I've thought about it. Maybe it will be something I do when I retire."

"Make the whole Chef Jackson thing for real, huh?"

"It's real enough tonight."

That comment brought the uncomfortable silence back. Last night had definitely changed things between them. They had done this before, him cooking for her in her own kitchen, his, or even Cameron's, while she sat at the table and they talked. Despite the sexual tension that had grown thicker between them over the years, they had always managed to keep the solidity of their friendship, the close bond that had built long before adult hormones and emotions had taken over.

He firmly believed the best, long-lasting relationships were built first on friendships. They would get it back. He had only to get her through her fears.

"I stopped by my apartment before I came over tonight." He took the steaks from the pan as he talked and placed them on two of the paper plates he had found in the cabinet. "You know what I'm buying you for Christmas?"

"Probably the same thing you've been threatening to get me for a decade."

"Glass serving dishes," they said at the same time.

Jackson didn't look at her, but he heard the smile in her voice. "It's the thought that counts, of course, but stock in whichever company owns Dixie would be a more useful gift for me. Glass dishes are too much trouble. Use a paper plate or a plastic cup and toss it in the trash when you're done. Cleanup finished. If you wanted glass dishes for tonight you should have brought them with you like you did everything else. You just said you stopped by your apartment before coming over."

"I did." Jackson nodded as he slid the omelets onto the plates with the steaks. "I was about to tell you that my temporary roommates were still awake. I didn't expect that after the grueling day I'm sure they had."

"Oh, yeah. Today was their first day of the firefighter challenge. How did they do?"

"Terri won the women's single event."

"No shit! That's awesome. I bet she was ecstatic."

"She was funny as hell." He chuckled, remembering the jig she had done around his living room while she pumped her fist in the air and chanted, "Go, Terri. Go, Terri." "She's got this spunk that doesn't quit. I haven't spent much time with her since they got here, but it's been enough to see the woman's energy is off the charts."

"What about the guy?" Mallory asked as Jackson set the plates on the table. "Thaddeus, isn't it? Poor guy. What a name. I'm guessing it's the whole carry-down-the-male-name-in-the-family-thing because I know his father is a Thaddeus, too, but jeez, could you imagine being stuck with a name like that?"

"Jason said he got the middle name, too. Leopold, a nice, sturdy, distinguished name." Jackson poured two glasses of milk, snagged two forks and knives from the drawer, and returned to the table. At least the woman had real utensils to eat and cook with. "He's doing a pretty good job and making it known in his own way. He got third in the men's single event."

"Impressive." Mallory picked up her fork and dug into her omelet. She took the first bite, chewed it slowly, and her eyes rolled back in her head. "Sweet heaven," she moaned. "Talk about impressive. If I knew I would be coming home to this, I would never stay out so late."

That can be easily arranged.

Jackson bit into his steak and the words, saying instead, "Then Chef Jackson's is a hit?"

"Are you kidding?" Mallory cut off a bite of steak, closing her eyes once again as she chewed.

The woman was sinfully sexy, even when she ate, and Jackson was so riveted watching her that he momentarily forgot his own food.

"I think I'm in love." Her eyes flew opened and her gaze slammed into his. Shock, horror, and self-damnation battled for paramount emotion in her eyes.

I know you are.

Now, if he could only get her to admit it about more than a piece of steak.

"There's nothing more satisfying to a cook than seeing the person he cooked for enjoy it."

Gratitude that he didn't comment on her statement flickered in her eyes before she dropped her gaze to her plate.

"There's also nothing more embarrassing to a cook than to realize he forgot part of the meal." He got to his feet and quickly toasted the four slices of bread he had set aside in the midst of preparing the rest of the meal.

Mallory smiled up at him as he put her toast on the side of her plate and returned to his seat. "I hadn't noticed."

"You would have. Unless you've gone on a diet I don't know about, I'm expecting what is left of that steak and omelet to be polished off in the next thirty seconds."

"Diet?" She tapped her lips with the handle of her fork and looked at the ceiling. "That word doesn't compute." She shrugged and shoved the last bit of her omelet into her mouth. "I like to eat. And, you should know by now, if you're expecting me to shy off from that because I'm doing it in front of a man, it's not going to happen."

Jackson chuckled. "I wouldn't have you any other way."

"I got the hard drive of the Stardust computer copied tonight."

Tiny thorns of anxiety poked Jackson in the gut. He ignored them as he always did when it came to Mallory. Knowing she was one of the best damn agents in the bureau helped, but it never obliterated his concern for her.

"I thought Tarantino was supposed to do that."

"It was easier for me to get to it. His cover is that of a customer, not an employee. If he had been spotted in the back, he would have had a lot more explaining to do. As it was, I got caught leaving the office."

Jackson's blood turned to ice in his veins. "Who saw you?"

"A couple of the strippers. I played it off, made up a line about needing to talk to Betty, the club manager who I already knew had left for a while. It was no big deal."

"We'll take the USB to Mason in the morning." Mason Sharp was the bureau's self-proclaimed geek and tech-analyst genius. "If there is anything on it to find, he'll be the one to see it."

"You were wrong, you know? It took me more than thirty seconds to finish, and if I eat the last bite of that toast I'm going to pop."

"Then finish your milk while I clean up."

"Uh-uh, you cooked. I'll clean. Even on Chef Jackson's scarce budget, they have to be able to afford someone to do the dishes." She stacked their plates, downed the rest of her milk, put her plastic cup on top, and gathered their silverware in her other hand.

Jackson watched, both amazed and amused, as the plates and cups fell into the trashcan and the silverware went into the dishwasher. A quick rinse to the pans and utensils he had used to cook with, and they followed the silverware.

Mallory closed the dishwasher and dusted her hands as she turned to face him, a wide grin spreading her luscious lips. "See there, so much easier. Cleaning is done in less than a minute."

Jackson chuckled as he got to his feet and walked to her. "And I wonder why I love you."

She froze. It was astonishing to watch. Jackson had never seen a body go as completely still as hers did in that moment. Nothing about her moved, not a muscle, not even her chest to take a breath. He hadn't meant to say it, but he didn't regret the slip. He did love her. He had been in love with her for years. He simply never told her until now.

"Get used to hearing it, Mal. You don't have to say it back. I don't expect you to, not yet." He cupped the side of her face and stared down at her, letting her see the truth of his words and the depth of them in his eyes. "When you took that tie off last night, you released everything I've been holding back. I can't pull it back in now. I won't."

"Jackson, I—"

"Am going to give me dessert now." He cut off her argument as he had done when she walked in the door, dipped his head, and brushed his lips to the tip of her nose. Confessing he loved her had apparently been a good thing. Her being this close to speechlessness would make it easier to continue his game.

"At Chef Jackson's dessert is served by the guests to the cook." He let his hand fall from her face, found the buttons of her shirt, and freed them slowly, one by one. She averted her gaze, bowing her head. He hooked a finger beneath her chin and lifted her face. "Look at me. Last night was yours. Tonight is mine. My game. My rules."

He continued to unbutton the shirt until it fell open, knowing how difficult it had to be for her to look at him right now. She couldn't hide from what he had said to her, couldn't hide from the turmoil it made her feel, not with him being this close to her, with him touching her. It was exactly what he wanted.

"Don't think, Mal." He pushed the shirt from her shoulders and let it fall in a pool of material at her feet. "Listen, react, feel."

He stepped back a fraction, putting just enough room between them so he could see her. The flickering candlelight danced over her flesh, providing him just enough light to see every delectable inch of her body. She hadn't put on panties. His cock pulsed at the realization. They had sat through dinner making idle conversation, and the whole time she had been across from him wearing absolutely nothing but his shirt.

"I can't do this, Jackson."

Her whispered words, the conflict and pain in them, sliced at his heart. He pulled his gaze back up, praying he wouldn't find tears in her eyes. The single tear last night had been bad enough. Watching her cry now would destroy him.

He didn't see any tears, though. *Thank God.* But he had a feeling they weren't too far away. Tough-as-nails Mallory could only be strong for so long before she would break, and what he was doing to her tonight had to be hitting her at the weakest possible level.

"Yes, you can," he said soothingly. "It's sex. It's you. It's me. It's what we've been dancing around for years, what we took the first steps in exploring last night."

"It's not just sex anymore." Her voice broke, and she took a ragged breath, reining herself in.

No, it wasn't, and the fact that she realized that, that she put voice to it, told him he was one step closer to his ultimate goal.

"Let yourself go, Mal. Touch yourself for me. I can't tell you how many times I've fantasized about watching you pleasure yourself."

She angled her head and drew her eyebrows together. "Really?"

His lips twitched. "Really."

She took another ragged breath, let it out slowly, and lifted her hands. She started at her chest, flattening her hands above her breasts, and dragging them down. She cupped her ample breasts in her palms, ran her thumbs over her hardened nipples, and—*Oh holy Jesus*—the sight sent whips of lust slashing at his tortured cock and balls.

"Is that what you've fantasized about?" She caught her nipples between her thumbs and forefingers, rolled the beaded points then pinched, her head falling back as she moaned from the pleasure she gave herself.

"Christ, yes." It was better because this was reality.

"How about this?" One hand moved from her breast to glide down her abdomen, her stomach, then disappeared between her legs.

Entranced, Jackson's gaze, along with every ounce of lust inside him, followed her hand. She parted her legs slowly and turned her hips slightly toward the cabinets on her right. Balancing her weight on her left foot, she raised her right to rest on the handle of the nearby cabinet, opening her pussy to his view and her questing fingers.

"Damn, that's amazing." He tore his gaze away long enough to glance up. Her other hand had stayed on her breast where she continued to massage and toy with her nipple. Her gaze was fixated on him. Shadows of her conflicting emotions remained in her heavy-lidded eyes, but they sparked with the vixen challenge he had seen in them all too often.

How far would he take this? How far did he want her to go? He saw those questions in her gaze even as her lips formed an *O* of pleasure that had his attention plummeting to her hand once more. She used her index and ring finger to part her pussy lips, massaging her clit with her middle finger until the bud became engorged and utterly torturous to his throbbing cock.

Jackson nearly came right then and there, without so much as a touch to his own body from her, his dick still safely enclosed in his jeans. Watching her drove him that close to the edge. He found himself fighting to think about details at the bureau, about cooking, about anything that would divert his mind and body from blowing his wad in his jeans.

"Mmm, so that's what you've really fantasized about." A teasing lilt added a wicked tone to her voice, telling him she was truly enjoying herself now. Getting off on driving him to the brink of insanity was more like it.

"Yes." The word came out rough, breathless, and just short of sounding like a growl. He wanted to close the distance between them, replace her hands with his own, but first he wanted to taste her. "Stop."

Her hands stilled and he glanced up again to find a wicked smile tilting her succulent lips. "What's the matter, handsome, too much?"

Jackson shook his head as he reached for her right hand. "It's not enough."

He brought her fingers to his mouth, took a deep breath, and closed his eyes as the sweet scent of her arousal permeated his senses. He licked her fingers, opening his eyes and locking his gaze with hers as he sucked the digits into his mouth and reveled at the salty warm taste of her feminine juices.

Her free hand snaked around him to cup his nape. He eased her fingers from his mouth, took a half step toward her, and captured her lips with his. Hers parted on a sweet sigh, her tongue immediately darting into his mouth to tangle with his.

God save him. Watching her, smelling her, tasting her, kissing her was driving him to the edge of a nuclear explosion.

She gripped his bicep with her free hand and nipped his bottom lip. Incensed, he clasped her trim waist and lifted her onto the countertop, her hands moving to delve in his hair, her fingers fisting the strands. He felt her legs start to rap around him and barely managed to catch them before they clamped him in place.

"Damn, Mal, you're so fucking hot." Head spinning, cock aching so badly he thought it might kill him, he pulled back and stepped out of her embrace. "I think you need to cool off a bit."

Her eyes narrowed as suspicion and a keen warning raced through her expression. "I thought you wanted me hot."

Yeah, that warning was telling him he damn well better not walk away. He didn't have the first intention of doing that yet.

"Close your eyes." He reached blindly behind him for the handle of the freezer door. He continued to watch her as he reached in, grabbed a piece of ice from the ice bin and returned to her, leaving the freezer to close of its own accord. When he brushed the ice cube over her already taut nipple, her eyes popped open in surprise and she gasped.

It was then that he finally allowed himself another taste, this time a quick one to her bare flesh. He leaned down, grazed his tongue over her nipple then brushed it again with the cube of ice. He alternated a lick and then a brush of the ice, on first one nipple and then the other, until she was panting with her back arched and her breasts pushed out for him.

"Jackson, *please*."

He smiled, pushing her knees farther apart as he trailed the ice cube down her abdomen, watching her shiver from the chill and anticipation. When he touched her pussy with the ice, he thought she would vault off of the countertop. She was so unbelievably hot, and the ice so cold, he wouldn't have been surprised to see steam coming off her body.

Satisfied that he had her teetering close enough to the edge, he tossed the ice cube in the sink and kneeled to bury his face in her pussy. He licked her smooth lips, drove his tongue in the warm, sopping wet opening of her vagina, and her hands tangled in his hair, pulling him to her, driving him deeper. The mere taste of her arousal had his body whirling in wickedly delicious torment.

He reached up and grabbed her wrists, pulled her hands from his hair, and held them as he withdrew to lick and suck her clit. She groaned loudly, her breath so rapid he was almost afraid she would hyperventilate.

"Jackson. Oh, God, Jackson, please."

He knew what she wanted, knew what was about to happen. He could feel her inner muscles tightening around his tongue. He drove his tongue as deep as he could, licking the walls of her channel, thrusting in and out of her until he felt her explode around him. Cum rushed from her pussy in a delectable wave that he fervently lapped up, not wanting to waste a single drop.

Slowly, he stood between her legs and lifted his gaze to hers. She looked worn-out, satisfied, and thoroughly amused.

"That wasn't fair," she whispered.

"What you did to me last night wasn't fair," he countered, and watched as the memory coupled with puzzlement moved through her expression. What part of last night wasn't fair? He could see that question in her eyes.

Was it the part about her sucking his cock but not allowing him a taste.

Yes.

Was it her taking free rein to touch but only allowing him a little here and there?

Definitely.

Was it the way she had sneaked out of his bed and out of his apartment without so much as a good-bye?

Hell. Fucking. Yes.

He would let her decide the appropriate question and figure out the answer.

"That's what I've fantasized about." He skimmed his hands down her sides, loving the feel of her curves, of her heated flesh against his. "At Chef Jackson's we would rate a dessert like that off the charts." He kissed the smile playing at her lips. "You're fucking amazing."

"I could say the same about you." She turned her head, leaned forward, and rested her cheek on his chest. "Take me to bed, Jack. Carry me. I don't think I could walk right now if my life depended on it."

Jackson scooped her into his arms. She snuggled closer against him as he carried her to her room and slowly lowered her onto her bed. Already half asleep, she curled onto her side and moaned softly.

Jackson pulled the sheet over her, tucking it around her, and smiled. He could have told her in one simple word what he really fantasized about. Her. No matter the setting, no matter the scene, it was always her in his dreams.

It always will be.

"I love you, Mal." He leaned down, brushed his lips to her temple, and walked out of the room.

Chapter Seven

Mallory awoke seething. She rode on that tide of anger as she dressed, fixed a cup of coffee, and headed for FBI HQ. The weather outside was picturesque, the sky radiant with the vibrant pink and orange hues of the rising sun. Light traffic moved easily through the streets. No angry horns blasted, no strings of cursing broke the serenity. It was a peaceful, early Saturday morning in Waterston, giving the city time to breathe after the hustle-and-bustle grind that came with every day of the workweek. That tranquility came in total contrast to her current mood and only made it worse. It should have been storming with traffic at a gridlock and road rage running amok. That would have suited her today just fine.

Topping off her morning of fun, the elevator jerked as it reached her floor at HQ. The sudden jolt jostled the coffee cup in her hand and splashed the java on the pale blue breast jacket she wore with her chocolate-brown skirt. She growled as she stepped off the elevator, the sound gaining her curious looks from a couple of agents walking by. Neither agent spoke as their gazes locked on the new stain on her jacket. Smartly, they chose to ignore it and continued on about their business. Yes, when she was in a bad mood, everyone at HQ picked up on it quick and they scurried to find a way out of the line of fire.

She stopped by the blessedly empty employee lounge, snatched a handful of paper towels, and blotted at the coffee spot the best she could as she continued down the hall to find Mason Sharp. He sat in front of a monitor viewing codes in a room he and the other self-proclaimed geeks used as their office.

"I've got something for you, Sharp."

He turned, a slight frown of irritation marring his movie-star handsome face as he looked up through stark hazel eyes and spotted her. He looked less like the stereotypical geek than anyone she had ever met. He was also the best, and he absolutely hated having his concentration broken.

Too bad, so sad. You can swim in the angry sea right along with me today.

"You and everyone else at this bureau." He turned back to his monitor. "You'll find what I'm working on now very interesting."

Somehow Mallory doubted that. The jumble of letters and numbers she saw on the screen didn't mean jack to her. "I might if you tell me what the hell it is."

"Encryption."

"Duh, I know that much." Her sarcasm earned her a sideways look. Yeah, she was a being a bitch. He would get over it. "From what, where, and who?"

"Cooper has the answers to all of that. What I can tell you is that it pertains to Alec McIntyre."

Centipedes of hopefulness and apprehension crawled up her spine. "Alec? He's alive?"

Alec McIntyre had been labeled MIA at the bureau since the op that had taken out Ving Kim Phay in Cambodia six months back.

"Don't know. Cooper dropped this off to me yesterday with the instructions to decode and keep my lips sealed. Highly confidential. I probably shouldn't have even told you it has anything to do with Alec, but I know he's a good friend of yours and Cameron's."

Everything about Alec's last undercover op had been highly confidential. She knew only that it had taken him years to infiltrate Phay's Cartel as deeply as he had before he disappeared.

"Cooper won't stop looking for him." She admired her boss for that. Adam Cooper was a pit bull when it came to his agents. It didn't matter what order came down from above, if he had an agent missing, he would move heaven and earth to bring that agent home.

"I'll tell you two things. One, this shit here is some of the best damn encrypting I've ever run across. I'm having a hell of a time trying to crack it. Two, and it's just a guess, McIntyre is triple-D status. He's out there somewhere. It's going to take more than a big bad drug lord and his team of goons to take that man out."

Triple-D status—dedicated, dangerous, and deadly. It's what they called agents like Alec in the bureau, and if anyone deserved the tag, Alec was the man.

"Is this top priority or…" She let her question trail off, hating to ask but knowing she had a job to do of her own. She had wanted to go through the information on the hard drive herself, but she knew, if there was anything to find, Sharp would be better at discovering it than her.

"Cooper didn't label it as such, but it was heavily implied. Why? What do you have?"

Mallory placed the USB device on Sharp's desk next to his keyboard. "I need you to see what you can get me off of this, and I want you to do it. I don't want it passed down."

Mason Sharp wasn't the only technological analyst and hacker they had. He was simply the best one.

He picked up the device and turned it between his fingers as he leaned back in his chair. "Anything in particular I'm searching for?"

"Auction information, odd transactions, anything that might pertain to the missing women on this list." She pulled a printout from her handbag with the names of the strippers they believed had gone missing before Lexie Stratus's disappearance and placed it on his desk.

Sharp studied the list. "Sex trafficking?"

"We believe so. That's a copy of the hard drive from the computer at Stardust." Mallory sighed. "I don't know if it will turn up anything, but we need all the leads we can get."

"Sure thing. I'll see what I can do."

"Thanks, Sharp."

"Hey." He turned full around in his chair as she started to walk out. "Ditch the pissiness next time you come into my room." His voice sounded stern, but the teasing glint in his eyes gave him away.

"Next time I come to see you, I'll make sure I'm packing a whole a lot more."

His chuckle followed her out of the room.

* * * *

"The guy is in on it." Cameron propped his right ankle on his left knee and leaned back in the chair in front of Jackson's desk. "Which explains why we haven't gotten wind of anything outside of the normal misdemeanors going on at Stardust."

The extensive background check on the Stardust stripper found dead in the abandoned warehouse had revealed a relationship between Erin Griffin and Officer Kenneth Reese, part of Waterston PD's undercover task force that frequented the premises of Stardust and other clubs in the area.

"Ten to one, he's our informant now." Jackson absently tapped a pen on his desk. "Question is who fucked up, Griffin or Reese."

"Did Reese kill Griffin himself, or the people he's working for?" Tarantino took the question further. The agent took the vacant seat in front of Jackson's desk and propped his elbows on his knees.

"Whoever he's working for would be my guess," Jackson said.

"He was getting out of line, maybe threatening to pull out or demanding a bigger cut of the profits," Cameron speculated. "So they killed his girlfriend to get to him, show him they mean business."

"Looks to me like they should've killed him," Tarantino commented.

Jackson shook his head. "They need him. He's keeping the heat off their backs, keeping their operation a secret."

"They hit him where it hurts and it backfired," Cameron said. "He turned on them anyway. Instead of keep him straight, they pissed him off."

"Why not turn himself in?" Tarantino asked with a sideways look at Cameron. "He had to know we would make the connection between him and Griffin. He gives us the body, but it doesn't put us one step closer to finding who killed her. If he came in, told us everything he knows, we would have the fuckers."

"And we would have him," Jackson pointed out. "A BOLO has been issued. He's gone into hiding now, likely from us as well as whoever is behind this."

"He hasn't been at Stardust," Tarantino said. "I've been there every time Mallory has worked. I know the guy. I would've seen him."

"Which is why Cooper wants to continue operating under the assumption that yours and Mallory's covers are safe." Jackson didn't like the idea. It didn't matter that Kenneth Reese hadn't been seen in the club since Mallory took the undercover assignment. Erin Griffin had been.

"Everyone associated with Stardust is coming up clean or missing. Background checks are pulling up drug charges, shoplifting, petty shit, but nothing to tie any of them to a trafficking ring." Cameron raked a frustrated hand through his hair. "And there's still no match on the facial recognition of that Jim guy Mallory and Jennifer turned over to forensics. Either the guy is an angel or he's damn good at hiding his dirty laundry."

Jackson would put his bets on damn good. He simply couldn't fathom an armature hiding his tracks so well. Then again… "We've only been at this a few days. He or whoever is behind this has slipped up twice already. First with Lexie Stratus, which involved Jennifer Moss and put us on the case in the first place. Now with Erin Griffin and Kenneth Reese. The connections are there. We've just got to put two and two together."

"Cooper's got Kell tailing Leroy Platt." Tarantino's expression turned to one of complete disgust. "The guy is a real loser, but a connected one. He skipped town late last night, but it doesn't look like it was for good. I say we stir the pot with Jennifer Moss, send her back in at Cinderella's. She wants to go back anyway."

"Nothing has turned up to connect the clubs," Cameron said.

"Except Lexie Stratus, Jennifer Moss, and Mallory," Tarantino countered. "This Jim guy is the best lead we have so far even if we haven't turned up jack on the bastard yet."

"I think—" Jackson broke off as his office door burst open. The thought sprinted out of his head as Mallory stomped inside. The woman was pissed. He got that in an instant. She hadn't knocked and didn't seem to realize he wasn't alone. Her tunnel vision was cocked and loaded on him. If eyes could shoot bullets, he would have a hole right between his own eyes.

The angry clack of her heels carried her around his desk. She stopped inches from where he sat, tossed her handbag on his desk, crossed her arms under her breasts, and leveled a glare on him that would have made a lesser man run for cover.

Damn, she's gorgeous.

The woman was arresting even with fumes coming out of her ears, a mouth that looked ready to chew him up and spit him out, and a coffee stain on her pale blue jacket. He knew why she was mad and it pleased the hell out of him. He masterfully hid a smile as he turned toward her and waited.

She stared at him for a full three seconds before she let him have it. "You left." The accusation in her tone burned in a fire of rage and pain.

"You did, too," he said calmly. Leaving her apartment last night had been the hardest thing he had ever done. He hadn't thought he was strong enough to do it, not when he had waited so long to be with her. He had sat in her kitchen for nearly an hour while a fierce battle raged inside him. It would have been so easy to crawl into her bed, to pull her close and fall asleep knowing when he woke she would still be there in his arms.

But what would it have solved? His gut had told him nothing. She still hadn't admitted to herself that she wanted him for anything more than sex. She was close. He had gotten that when she had told him their time together the night before had been more than sex. Yet, she still fought him at every turn, still wouldn't allow herself to love him. He had finally walked out in the hope that waking without him this morning when he figured she fully expected him to be there would put another crack in that steel wall she had constructed around her heart.

Apparently, it worked. *Thank you, sweet baby Jesus.*

"So that was payback?" She all but squeaked, her eyes widening with shock.

"It was giving you space," he said evenly.

"You come to my apartment, cook for me, get me off in my kitchen, carry me to bed, and then you walk out? What if I wasn't done with you?" Cameron cleared his throat and her head snapped his direction. "Shut up."

Cameron held up his hands, palms out, and chuckled. "I didn't say a word."

"You wanted me to stay, Mal?" If she had given him the choice, he would have preferred to have this conversation in private. It shocked him that she apparently didn't care that Cameron and Tarantino were getting a kick out of the scene. "Why?"

Say it, Mal. Say you wanted to wake in my arms this morning and every morning for the rest of our lives. Say you wanted me to stay because you love me.

She stared at him and the bullets in her eyes disintegrated. He saw every answer he wanted to hear in her expression. She simply wouldn't say them.

"Looks like he finally got to her," he heard Tarantino whisper to Cameron and saw Mallory's gaze slide to the man. Her lips parted, but a song jingling from her handbag interrupted whatever she intended to say.

She dug in the bag, pulled out a cell phone, and glanced at the screen. Jackson recognized the phone and knew it wasn't her personal cell. It was the one she was using for the assignment, and only one place should have the number.

"Hello?" In a finger snap, she went from stunningly gorgeous, angry, confused Mallory to hard-core agent. Her gaze swept across him, Cameron, and Tarantino, and she dragged a finger across her neck.

Cut the conversation. Yeah, they had all gathered that.

Jackson saw Cameron stiffen and saw Tarantino sit straighter as they listened to Mallory's end of the conversation.

"I was. I had something I wanted to talk to you about." She paused, then nodded though whoever was on the other end of the cellular waves couldn't see. "I can do that. Okay, good-bye."

"You can do what?" Jackson asked as she snapped the phone shut.

"That was Betty. She wants me to come to the club."

"Now?" Cameron asked, suspicion heavy in his tone.

Mallory nodded. "She heard I wanted to talk to her. I used that excuse last night when I worked my way into her office."

"I don't like this, Mal." Cameron got to his feet, shoved his hands in his pockets, and started pacing the floor.

"Neither do I." Mallory put the phone away and lifted her handbag. "That's why I'm going home to change first. I'll go in wearing my uniform. Stardust opens at noon on Saturdays. I'm not scheduled to go in until seven, but if she asks, I'll tell her I wanted to be prepared in case she wanted me to start early. That way I'll have the excuse to wear the anklet and earrings. You and Tarantino can follow me. You'll know where I am, and if anything gets sticky, I'll alert you and you'll be right outside."

"Use the earrings," Jackson said sternly. He didn't like this anymore than the rest of them. Alarm pricked at his spine and punctured it way up his neck. "At the first inkling of trouble. We still can't get a good bead on what we're dealing with here. Don't wait like last time."

"Don't worry." She reached for him, skimming the backs of her fingers down the side of his face. "I know what happens to people who lose someone they love." Her hand dropped from his face to his shoulder and she slapped it hard enough to sting. "Damn you for making me think about that now."

* * * *

Cameron wanted to damn Jackson, too, just about as much as he wanted to congratulate the man for penetrating Mallory's shields. He understood his sister and couldn't imagine the turmoil wreaking havoc on her soul right about now.

Can't you?

He knew it had been easier for her when it had all been fun and games between her and Jackson. She would flirt, lay it on thick in her attempts to get the man in bed, and had convinced herself it would end there. Except it hadn't. It likely would have if Jackson had given in easily, if he had allowed her what she wanted when she had first made her desires clear.

Instead, Jackson had bided his time, waited for her to weaken, waited for his chance to get in deeper, and then made his move.

Mallory was losing control. Stupid as it might be, the only love she and Cameron had ever allowed themselves was for each other and their mother. They had grown up watching how true love could destroy a person once that true love was taken away. He didn't doubt that if Mallory lost Jackson, she would end up exactly like their mother, living a life alone in wait for the day she would be reunited with the man she loved. The thought of his sister ending up that way terrified him.

He stared out the windshield of the SUV. A block away, the front door of Stardust was closed, the parking lot empty save for Mallory's car and the red Nissan Altima the team had traced to Betty Carlisle. One street over, Tarantino was parked, watching the back door. Mallory had been inside no more than five minutes.

Cameron hadn't wanted to let her go in at all. Back in Jackson's office, he had wanted to grab her by the shoulders and shake some sense back into her. How could she let her guard down, even with Jackson? Despite what he had told Jackson about him being the best man for her, and he had meant every word, the part of him that grew up with the same fears she did wanted to smack her for allowing herself to get in so deep.

Now, he only hoped he got the chance. He wanted to walk into that club and drag her ass back out. She might be armed with a GPS device, alarm trigger, and two agents watching her, but that didn't settle the boiling in his gut that told him something was about to go down.

The Bluetooth in his left ear beeped, and he pushed the button to answer the call. "Stone," he said curtly.

"Tarantino, are you still there, too?" Jackson asked as he conferenced the calls.

"I'm all ears," Tarantino replied.

"We finally got an ID on Jim, otherwise known as Wade Forbes. It took Mason Sharp some serious digging on this one."

"Why didn't the run on the sketch pull it up?" Tarantino wanted to know.

"Reconstructive surgery," Jackson answered. "Forbes has been through a ton of it."

"Did Sharp find a link between Forbes and Stardust?" Cameron asked.

"A solid one. Forbes owns the damn place."

"What's his connection to Carl Jordan?" They had investigated every nook and cranny they could find about the listed owner of Stardust.

"Cell buddy. Forbes has done time for embezzlement, robbery, and possession, but his last stint coincides with Carl Jordan's six months in the state pen."

"What was Forbes in for the last time?" Tarantino asked.

"Numerous counts of rape and prostituting women."

"Son of a bitch." Cameron smacked the steering wheel. "I don't want to know how the bastard ended up back on the streets."

"That's not important right now. The fact that he knows Mallory's face is."

"Not Mallory's, Jacqueline's," Cameron corrected, grasping at hopeful straws. "The names aren't connected by anything but her face."

"A face Kenneth Reese knows," Jackson pointed out, and a death chill raced down Cameron's spine.

* * * *

The interior of Stardust looked far worse by the light of day. Mallory raked her gaze over the scattering of tables, the cluttered floor, the stage riddled with articles of clothing, and wondered if there had been an afterhours party she hadn't been invited to last night. Sasha, who Mallory knew put in extra hours cleaning the club, greeted her with a bright smile when she walked inside.

"Check you out. You came dressed for work."

Mallory glanced down at her uniform and shrugged. "Betty asked me to come in to talk. I was hoping when we're finished I could convince her to let me start early, maybe pick up a few extra hours."

Sasha nodded. "I bet she will. I hope you don't mind, but she called you because of me. I told her you were looking for her last night. If you were serious about taking up a few shifts on stage, now would be the perfect time to ask for it. We lost another one last night. Natalie quit."

Mallory's jaw dropped. Shock and a trickle of apprehension surged through her bloodstream. "Really, she quit, too?"

"You just don't know how hard it is to keep a good employee these days."

Mallory turned at the voice behind her and found Betty walking out of the back rooms. "I would think it would be easy with so many people out of work and all." *Easier if you didn't keep kidnapping and killing them.* "Jobs are hard to find, especially one that pays good money."

"These girls just don't get the value of the position Stardust offers them." Betty angled her head. "But I'm getting that you do. Sasha tells me you're thinking of taking me up on the offer I made when I hired you about hitting the stage instead of carrying a tray."

Mallory shifted and wrinkled her face indecisively. "Yes, ma'am. I could really use some extra money."

"Why don't we continue this conversation in my office so we won't be in Sasha's way." Betty turned slightly, gestured toward the employee door, and followed Mallory through it. "How much money did you make last night?"

"A hundred and twelve dollars." Mallory shot the older woman a grin over her shoulder. "It's double what I made the first night."

"You'll make four times that working the stage," Betty predicated as she reached a hand past Mallory to open the office door, taking Mallory's purse with the other. "Go on in and have a seat."

Mallory started to object as she stepped into the office but stopped abruptly when she realized the room wasn't empty.

Game on.

Her instincts screamed as her gaze landed on a tall man with a linebacker build and a handsome face she knew she had seen before but couldn't quite place. Another man she instantly recognized as Carl Jordan, the club owner, lounged on the sofa. Bruno, who was also in the room, greeted her with an almost imperceptible nod. She started to tell the bouncer hello when her gaze landed next on the desk, on the man standing stiffly next to it, and the other who got to his feet behind it.

"Jacqueline, I thought I would never see you again." Jim moved from behind the desk and covered the distance between them in four long strides.

Hit the button. Hit the button.

Mallory lifted a hand and cast a cursory glance at Kenneth Reese. She saw recognition in the man's hardened eyes. Had he blown her cover? Did he know all she had to do was brush her right earring under the guise of pushing her hair behind her ear and Cameron and Tarantino would come running?

Jim caught both her hands in his before she got the chance. "Imagine my surprise when I discovered the most arresting woman I've met in my life has come to work in my club."

His club?

Oh, shit.

Mallory forced a sultry smile to her lips. *Stay in character. You don't know if the shit has really hit the fan yet.*

Yeah, right. She still believed in the Easter Bunny, too.

"Wow, really? I thought Mr. Jordan owned this place."

"Let's just say I'm a silent partner." Jim's grip tightened on her hands, and he spun her around, guiding her right arm to rest at her waist and pulling her left behind her back as he held her against his front. He nuzzled his face in the bend of her neck. "It's easier to keep my involvement in my businesses a secret if no one knows I own them." His breath fanned her flesh as he spoke, and she coughed at the heavy scent of mint.

Had he just finished eating an entire box of Altoids before she walked into the office?

She angled her head back and looked up at him, hoping the expression on her face looked impressed rather than revolted. "You own more than one club?"

His lips unfolded in a smile that chilled her to the bone. "Wouldn't you like to know, Jacqueline? Or should I say Mallory? Mallory Stone. *FBI Agent* Mallory Stone."

Yep, the jig was up. No need to pretend anymore. "Did you know that when you approached me at Cinderella's?"

"I had different plans for you that night." His expression hardened and his eyes turned devastatingly dangerous. "Although, my plans for you haven't changed much in the last few days."

She didn't dare ask what those plans were. A sickening feeling twisted in her gut that if she didn't get her hands free of his soon so she could reach her earring, she was about to find out.

"You have me at a disadvantage, Jim. You know my real name, but I don't know yours."

His lips spread in a satisfied smile that turned the blood in her veins to ice. "That's not the only disadvantage you're in, sweetheart. I would have thought the FBI had figured that out by now."

Shit. Now he knew they were still searching. If he managed to get her out of this club, the team wouldn't know where to look for her.

Jim had pulled her off balance when he spun her around, and she shifted her foot to steady her stance. No way did she want to lean on this bastard anymore than she had to. The movement reminded her of the anklet she wore and the tracking device it concealed. Okay, the team would know where to find her, but would they get to her in time?

"I suppose there's no point in continuing our charade now that I have you. Allow me to formally introduce myself. I'm Wade Forbes." He pulled the hand he held at her waist to his lips and kissed it.

Mallory suppressed a shudder of revulsion. To think she had actually found this guy attractive, even considered having a fling with him. Would she have done it if Jackson hadn't called that night?

No, for the same reason she hadn't indulged in a night with any man in too long to remember. Jackson was the only man she wanted, the only one she burned for. She had known, just like she did now, that no other man could ever satisfy her. No man could ever take his place.

"Where are Lexie Stratus and the others?" She pushed her thoughts of Jackson aside and channeled all her concentration on the here and now. A part of her mind probed for the information they had been looking for, while another part weeded through ways to get her the fuck out of this. "What have you done to them?"

"They're alive. Well, all of them except Erin Griffin, but you know that already."

Mallory couldn't keep her gaze from flicking to Kenneth Reese. A muscle ticked in the man's jaw, the only outward sign that hearing his dead girlfriend's name affected him at all. The team was certain he had been the one to call with the tip that led them to Erin's body. Why was he here now? Was he biding his time, waiting for an opening to help her? Or had killing off his girlfriend done the trick and made him more loyal to Forbes?

"They've completed their jobs for me. They have new masters now."

He had sold them to some pervert, turned them into sex slaves. Her stomach clenched at what those women must be going through, at the thought of what their "masters" might be doing to them. Some of them had been gone for months.

"They're here in Waterston right under your nose." Forbes laughed, and Mallory knew she was face-to-face with the devil himself. "You'll never find them, of course."

She would if it was the last thing she did. And that was not a good thought to have right about now, given her current situation. She switched it off, latching her mind on the list of options she had been subconsciously making. She could take him. He stood behind her with his legs slightly spread. A lift of one heel with all the strength her leg possessed and she would send his balls to his throat.

And the instant she did, one or all of the other men in the room would pounce on her. One on one, she stood a chance. Four on one, against men who were likely armed and definitely stronger, she was so screwed.

Scream.

Sasha was still somewhere in the club. So was Betty, but she knew she wouldn't get any help there. The older woman had led her back here knowing what awaited her in this office. Was Sasha part of it, too?

"Get the van while I get our beauty here ready to transport."

Van? Likely the one Jennifer Moss had informed them she had seen tailing her. Mallory hadn't spotted a van out front when she arrived. That meant it had to be parked out back.

Tarantino, you better not be sleeping on the job.

Bruno and the brute she didn't know stepped out of her line of sight but not toward the office door. She heard a click, the faint sound of hinges creaking, and the unmistakable sound of a door closing. She remembered the door she had spotted last night. Obviously, it led to some kind of passage rather than a closet like she had thought.

Not good.

With two men out—thankfully, the largest of the five—that still left three. That was better odds than before but not by much. Forbes had yet to loosen his hold on her. Carl Jordan hadn't moved from his relaxed spot on the sofa. Kenneth Reese remained in his spot near the desk.

Forbes spun her around to face him, still not letting go of her hands. The movement opened his jacket, revealing the gun he wore in a shoulder holster beneath. If she could just get to that gun...

"When I found out who you really were, I thought about killing you." His gaze slid down her front, sending a repulsed shiver through her she couldn't hide. "You'll be happy to know I've reconsidered.

With a body like yours, I think you will turn out to be my highest-selling merchandise yet."

Mallory narrowed her eyes and scowled at him. "I'm nobody's merchandise."

"Oh, but you are. You belong to me now. At least until I can find an appropriate buyer. I have one in mind already. He likes you, says you've got great spirit. Perhaps he'll be the one. He's been waiting for me to get another girl to his liking. I think he's itching for some girl on girl action. He wanted Erin, but she got out of hand."

Mallory looked at Kenneth Reese. His blank expression was completely unreadable. The muscle continued to tick in his jaw, though. Had he loved Erin Griffin? Surely his feelings for her on some level had been what had prompted him to lead the FBI to her body.

"He has Lexie, you know?"

"Who?"

"That's right, you don't know. Your little investigation hasn't uncovered that bit of information. She's been right under your nose the whole time. They all are. It's good to know I've found my forte with my newest business venture. I've got the FBI looking under rocks and not finding a thing."

"They will. It's only a matter of time."

"Time you don't have. I've covered my tracks well and will conceal them even better now that I have you." He released her right hand and slowly brought his fingers to her ear. "I wonder what accessories you're wearing that are designed to lead them to you. These, perhaps?" His fingers closed on the hoop of her earring and pulled it from her ear. He reached for the other one and removed it as well. "They suited you, accented your face. It's a shame I can't let you keep them." The earrings made a soft thud as they hit the wall across the room.

Mallory's heart raced as his fingers danced over the jeweled choker of her bustier. She fought to keep her breathing steady. Fear wound its way through her system, threatening to overpower her senses. She couldn't allow that. She had to keep her mind clear, had to focus, had to think.

He slid his hand beneath her hair, blindly finding the choker's clasp. "I'm afraid anything you're wearing could have been tampered with. Kenneth tells me the feds have a way of concealing all sorts of gadgets to aid their agents."

Mallory shot Reese a heated look and wished it was enough to make him burst into flames.

"We'll leave all of this stuff here." Forbes removed the choker, slid the connecting straps down her arms, and reached around her to unzip the back.

Dear God, he was undressing her. His hand glided over her flesh, caressing her like a lover would as he removed the bustier and let it fall to the floor.

Think, Mallory. Think!

He released her left hand, skimming both his palms down her sides to the waistband of the skirt. "I imagined doing this when I first met you," he said as he peeled the skirt down her hips. "We would have had fun that night. We still might. Undressing you this way is making me hot. I'll have to sample you for myself before I allow you to be bought."

No. No fucking way.

He kneeled to unfasten her anklet. "I like this look, leather strapped around your ankle. It will look better on both your ankles when I strap you down and fuck you."

Mallory felt the anklet fall away, and his hands left her. She took that split moment of opportunity to act. She might not live through this, but she damn sure had to try. She fisted her fingers in his hair as he started to rise, brought her right knee up with all the force she had in her, and jammed it into his jaw.

"You bitch!" He bolted upright. Blood poured from his mouth.

Mallory didn't waste a second. She lifted her knee again, going for his balls. At the same time, she reached for the gun inside his coat. The knee shot connected right where she wanted, but he doubled over before she could get a grip on the gun.

Forbes recovered quickly, too quickly. He caught her ankles and yanked her feet out from under her.

Mallory's teeth clinked as her head hit the floor, the breath left her lungs in a whoosh. She rolled, knowing she needed to be back on her feet. He would overpower her if he pinned her down.

He got to his feet first. Mallory made it to her hands and knees before he delivered the first blow. The powerful kick to her stomach lifted her an inch off the floor. The next kick landed in her solar plexus and she choked as the little bit of air she had managed to inhale burst from her lungs.

She tried to block out the pain and attempted to get to her feet. She sensed him bend over her and saw the hand come for her face. He closed his hand around her throat and lifted her by the neck. She struggled to breathe as black spots danced in her vision. Her hands instinctively closed around his wrist, her nails digging into his flesh. His grip tightened, his fingers squeezing off her air. She rose to her tiptoes in a futile attempt to ease the pressure.

He's going to kill me.

The black spots joined, threatening to overtake her vision. Dizziness swept through her head. She knew she had only a short time before she would pass out. She released his wrist, balled her fist, and lashed out at him, not caring what part of him she hit as long as she did some kind of damage. Her fist collided with his already injured jaw, and she heard his cry of pain a split second before the faint sound of a bullet readying itself in the chamber of a gun.

"Let her go," a voice said, both calm and forceful. "She's worth more to us alive than dead."

Forbes let her go, and she stumbled back into the owner of the voice. If not for the body behind her, she would have crumpled to the floor. She gasped, taking in breath after blessed breath, sweet oxygen filling her lungs. She fought against her body's reflexive action to take in as much air as possible as quickly as it could, knowing she could hyperventilate. The man at her back stood rigid, acting like a wall to hold her up. He didn't touch her. Dimly, she realized the cocking of the gun she had heard had not been aimed at Forbes but at her own head. The man at her back might have saved her from being strangled, but he wouldn't be any help in saving her from whatever would come next.

Mallory's vision cleared and she looked at Forbes. Blood covered his mouth and jaw, and she saw a bruise already starting to form on the right side where she had punched him. He stared back at her with a truckload of promised torture plain in his eyes.

"As amusing as I find it to watch the two of you go to blows, you will have to finish this in a more private setting later." Carl Jordan gripped her upper arm and pushed her off of him. "It's time to go."

The office door swung open and Betty walked inside. "It's done," she told Forbes in a calm, cold voice that sent a dart of alarm straight to Mallory's belly.

"What's done?" Jordan rounded on her, but he didn't lower the gun trained on Mallory's head.

"Sasha is dead." Forbes said it as if it meant nothing more to him than the color of the paint on the walls. He grabbed Mallory by the arm and yanked her toward the door Bruno and his goon had used to leave the office.

Mallory stumbled and struggled to get her balance in her four-inch heels.

"Take off those damn shoes." Forbes jerked her around as he opened the door. "There's no telling what you've got hidden inside them."

Mallory slipped her feet out of the heels. They were no use to her anyway. She didn't have time to be embarrassed about the fact that Forbes had stripped her naked. Her sole attention was on the gun in

Jordan's hand, still pointed at her head, and the fury the news of Sasha's murder had ignited in the man's eyes.

"What the hell are you doing?" Jordan demanded. "Sasha had no part in this."

"You should have sent her home when she got here this morning." Forbes turned his focus on Kenneth Reese and pointed inside the doorway with his free hand. "Torch it."

"Are you fucking crazy?" Jordan bellowed, stepping closer.

Mallory was starting to wonder the same thing. What the hell was going on? Forbes had obviously made plans he hadn't told Jordan anything about.

Betty apparently knew. The woman leered at Mallory as she pushed past her and Forbes and stepped through the doorway, stopping to rake a cold gaze down Mallory's naked body. "We're going to make a ton of money off you."

"This is my club." Jordan had moved within arm's reach, the gun in his hand now barely an inch from Mallory's temple.

Surely he didn't still see her as the biggest threat here. Except, maybe she was. His fury aimed at Forbes didn't distract him enough to lower that gun, but if she picked just the right moment, she could catch him off guard. A quick duck coupled with a blow to his arm and the gun would go flying.

But then what?

If she could get a sense of which direction the gun would land, she could go for it and gain the upper hand.

She waited, her gaze dancing from one man to the other, her heart pounding in a chest that ached from Forbes's earlier kick. Her belly clenched from the first powerful kick, and she wondered she hadn't thrown up everywhere. She still might, but she had more important things to concentrate on right now.

"This is my fucking club, my fucking business," Forbes seethed through gritted teeth.

For the first time, Mallory saw true insanity in the man's eyes. The gun in Jordan's hand wavered. She saw it move, but Jordan wasn't fast enough for Forbes. In a blink of an eye, Forbes wrenched his own gun from beneath his jacket and backhanded Jordan with the butt of it hard enough to knock Jordan out cold.

Forbes locked a steely, crazed stare on Kenneth Reese. "Leave him. He gets up before you're through, shoot him. Torch the place and meet us at the van."

Chapter Eight

Thaddeus glanced at his Rolex, noted the time was barely ten a.m., and scowled anyway. "Are you going to be ready anytime soon?"

"Cool your heels, Road Runner," Terri called from the hallway bathroom. "I'll be done in a jiffy."

A jiffy? Yeah, he would believe that when he saw it. Terri's idea of a jiffy could be anywhere from thirty minutes to four hours.

Women. How long did it really take to throw on some clothes, run a brush through the hair, dab on a bit of makeup, and step into a pair of shoes? He supposed he should be used to it. He had grown up with three younger sisters, after all. And, okay, in all fairness, he knew a handful of men who could take just as long, if not longer, to get ready in the morning.

"So where are we going?"

Thaddeus barely heard her question over the sound of the water running in the bathroom sink and the occasional conversation coming from the police scanner on the nearby bar. He had turned on Jackson's scanner a few minutes before, listening to the radio communication between the various police and fire departments in the city. So far, it had been a relatively quiet morning.

"I don't know. I thought we would swing by the challenge, see who is in the lead for today's events, grab some lunch, maybe take you around and let you see some of the sights."

He paced the living room floor as he talked, stopping in front of Jackson's bookshelf to scan the spine of the books. Legal thrillers, nonfiction crime texts, and—*Oh, hel*-lo. His gaze locked on one title that certainly caught his attention.

Sex Games. "Seriously, Jackson?"

"Didn't you tell your parents you would try to come by their place for lunch today?"

Thaddeus shot a glance toward the hallway and heard the water shut off in the bathroom. "Yeah, I guess we should do that, too."

He wasn't avoiding his parents, but the short time he had spent with them after the challenge yesterday had confirmed his suspicions. He had introduced them to Terri and hadn't missed the hope swirling in his mother's eyes or the stark approval in his father's expression. Taking Terri to the family home to have lunch would be a bad idea, but he couldn't leave her to entertain herself all day.

Okay, he could. He just didn't want to. Terri would be fine and would likely find a mountain of things to get into without him.

"I like your mother," Terri said. "She seems sweet."

"She likes you, too." *And therein lies the problem.*

"Everybody likes me, Vegister."

He chuckled as the sound of a blow dryer ended their conversation, telling him Terri's jiffy would be at least another five minutes. He pulled the *Sex Games* book from the shelf, opened the front cover, and saw the note written in perfect cursive on the title page.

Jackson, I thought you might like to have a copy of your own. You know, in case you decide you want to play again. Page sixty-two worked out really great last time. Angelina.

Angelina? Jackson's sister-in-law had given him a book titled *Sex Games.*

Play again? Last time? Jackson had sex with Angelina.

"And the surprises just keep on coming," Thaddeus said in a quiet, singsong voice as he flipped to page sixty-two.

Sex with a stranger can be the most arousing of erotic fantasies. Show up at your partner's house and sneak up on him or her. Pretend you have a gun. Be careful he or she doesn't think it's a real gun. A toy water pistol or banana works well. Blindfold your partner and take him or her back to your place where you've set the stage for a night of bed-burning sex.

"Holy smokes, Batman." Thaddeus started to close the book but found another dog-eared page closer to the front. Curiously, he read that one, too.

Setting the mood can be vitally important. Light several candles and scatter them through the house. Set the table and have some sort of menu ready. When you greet your partner, pretend you are in your own restaurant and that you are his or her servant. Spark up a light conversation over the tasty dinner you cook and see what stupendous dessert ignites in the kitchen.

"Hmm, planning something, Jackson?"

"Talking to yourself now?" Amusement laced Terri's voice as she came up behind him. She put a hand on his hip, pressed her front to his back, and rested her chin on his shoulder as she peered down at the book in his hands. "Jiminy Cricket, you found that on stuffy man's bookshelf?"

Thaddeus closed the book and put it back on the shelf. "Don't tease him about it, Ter."

"Shit. I want to borrow it if it's any good."

"Ask Angelina where she bought it when we get back home. She's the one who gave it to him."

"Seriously?" Terri squeaked, turning her chin on his shoulder to look at him. "Damn, no wonder she and Jason have a marriage to die for." She frowned. "Ever notice how almost everyone around us is so happily married they're about to burst? Jason and Angelina, Dean and Veronica, Ryan and Tina, Cory and Rayne..."

"Cory and Rayne aren't married."

Terri rolled her eyes. "Only because Ford is in the picture, too, and women aren't allowed to marry more than one man at a time in the state of Mississippi. Jeez, Rayne's really got it made."

Thaddeus chuckled. "You have enough problems handling one man. You would never be able to devote yourself to two."

He felt Terri shrug against his back. "I might if it meant I would be happy. Look at them." Her gaze flicked to the framed photo of Jackson, Mallory, and Cameron on top of the bookshelf. "Tell me they don't look happy."

Thaddeus had been working not to look at that photo, not to look at Cameron's too-handsome smiling face. That face had smiled like that at him the other night, those lips had kissed him and left him wanting more.

Thaddeus sighed. Terri lifted her chin, her hand falling from his hip as he turned. "They're friends. She's Cameron's sister."

"I know, but doesn't it make you wonder?"

No. No it didn't. He knew exactly where she was going with this, and he wouldn't let her put that wonderment in his mind.

Except, it was already there. No Terri implications necessary. Yeah, he could easily see himself standing there with his head resting on Adrien's shoulder and Cameron smiling down at him.

"Are you finally ready?"

"Yep, I'm all spruced up and ready to hit the town." She crossed her ankles and did a full one-eighty. "What do you think?"

"Smashing as always."

An alarm tone blasted through the apartment, and they both whipped their heads toward the scanner on the bar.

"Rescue 14, Engine 14." The dispatcher's voice followed the alarm. "We have reports of a structure fire at 2300 Lynch Street. Possible people trapped inside. Proceed with caution. Time out 1024."

"Sounds like a good one." Thaddeus felt the all-too-familiar adrenaline kick up in his system.

"2300 Lynch Street, do you know where that is?"

He looked at Terri and saw the same excitement he felt echoing in her expression. "Yeah, it's on the east side of town."

Terri rocked back on her heels, a slow grin unfolding on her lips. "Want to check it out?"

Thaddeus grinned back at her. They were both itching for some real action. They probably wouldn't be able to get involved, likely wouldn't even be able to get close, but they could stand back and watch as Waterston's smoke eaters did what they did best.

"Bet your sweet ass I do." He snatched up his keys and they bolted for the door.

* * * *

"I don't like this, man." Tarantino's voice sounded concerned through Cameron's Bluetooth. "She's been in there too long."

"I don't like it either." Cameron glanced at the dashboard clock. Mallory had been inside Stardust for nearly an hour. "Any sign of movement back there?" he asked Tarantino as he scanned the parking lot and the street out front. Betty Carlisle's red Altima and Mallory's Lexus remained the only cars in the lot. The front door hadn't opened, no one else had arrived, and barely any traffic had been down the street since Mallory stepped into the building.

"Nada."

"Patch through to Toshie, make sure he still has her on his radar." They had left Toshie back at HQ, monitoring the signal from the GPS device hidden in the anklet Mallory wore. If she moved from that building they would know about it.

He listened as Tarantino connected the calls, as Toshie confirmed Mallory's signal was still strong inside the building.

"I want to know the instant that signal moves," he told Toshie, and Tarantino cut the connection. "She's good," he said, more to comfort himself than Tarantino. It didn't work. The niggling in his gut that something was about to go down got worse instead of better.

"If we walk in there, we'll blow it," Tarantino reminded him.

"If I walk in there, I'll blow it. Your face is known in there. You've become a regular customer."

"True, but the place doesn't open for another hour and some odd minutes."

Also true. Damnit, should they wait that long?

You don't have a choice.

True words number three. If they moved and it turned out to be unnecessary, they would blow Mallory's cover and the entire operation.

"Even if they had managed to get her out of that building somehow without us seeing, she wouldn't have taken off the anklet and left it behind," Tarantino said, breaking into Cameron's thoughts. "She promised Jackson, in not so many words, that she would play this one by the book." He let out a half chuckle. "After that scene in his office this morning, I doubt she would go against her word."

Yeah, Cameron doubted it, too. He also knew there was no way anyone could get her out of that building without them seeing. Only two doors led in or out of the place, and they had their eyes on both.

"She and that Betty chick are probably talking shop. Mallory will draw it out as long as she can, ask every question she can think of that won't raise suspicion trying to find out what happened to those women. All we can do is sit here and wait."

Fuck. Cameron hated waiting. Patience had never been one of his virtues, though he was forced to utilize it all the time on the job.

"All right," he reluctantly agreed. "But if she's not out by noon, you're going in."

"Damn right I am."

They fell silent, watching, freaking waiting. Cameron forced himself not to look at the clock, keeping his gaze trained on the building door, scanning the area for activity as the minutes ticked by.

"Son of a bitch." Tarantino broke the silence, alarm heavy in his tone. "Are you seeing this?"

Cameron spotted it at the same time Tarantino did. He gripped the steering wheel and leaned forward, angling his head to see the top of the building through the windshield. Smoke, stark black and thick, had started seeping through the roof.

"Fuck, the damn place is on fire." Tarantino swore again, and Cameron heard a rustling sound through the cellular waves.

Cameron bolted out of the SUV and started running across the street. "Call the fire department," he ordered Tarantino. "I'm going in."

Heart pounding out of his chest, fear for Mallory surging through his veins, he reached the front door of Stardust, wrenched it open...

And found himself face-to-face with a wall of flames.

* * * *

Mallory gritted her teeth against the pain shooting through her shoulder blades. She stiffened reflexively as the van hit a pothole and her body bounced on the unforgiving metal floor. Forbes had taken her out of the club via some sort of underground passage that ended in the field where she had picked up Jackson a few nights ago. Bruno and the other goon had been waiting there for them with the van.

Forbes had shoved her in the back of the van, pushed her to the floor, and tied her hands and ankles together. Naked, cold, and scared out of her wits, though she would never let them know it, she lay there now, her mind reeling.

Forbes had ordered the goon to wait until they saw the first signs of smoke coming from the club before they sped away. Betty had argued about leaving Kenneth Reese behind and had gotten smacked hard enough for it to be heard for her trouble.

Mallory couldn't see where the van had come out of the field, but she suspected it was somewhere out of sight of where Cameron and Tarantino were parked. Without the GPS on her ankle, they wouldn't know she had been taken from the building until the fire was put out.

"That was probably the stupidest thing you could've done." It hurt to talk, but she did it anyway. She swallowed, wincing at the pain in her throat. It felt scratchy, bruised, but she didn't think Forbes had done any permanent damage when he had choked her. "You murdered at least two people back there."

"Kenneth will take the fall for it." Forbes sat on the bench seat lining the sidewall of the van, his elbows on his knees as he hovered over her, a larger menace than the devil himself. He smiled, a devious tilt to his lips that sent an evil fear down her spine. "If he managed to make it out alive."

"You set him up. No one is going to believe that fire started accidentally."

"Of course they won't. But they will believe a jilted cop went crazy after learning about the death of his girlfriend and sought revenge. Did you know Carl Jordan was fucking Erin Griffin, too? They're both getting what they had coming. They should have kept their hands off of her. She belonged to me."

"Is that why you killed her?" Mallory's head spun as she tried to piece it together. Had Forbes been in love with Erin Griffin, too? Why was Kenneth Reese still following his orders? None of it made any sense.

"Kenneth Reese killed her." His smile turned sardonic. "Although, I did hold a gun to his head while he tortured her. She screamed and pleaded for her life. It was a truly classic sight. I wish you had been there to see it."

Bile rose in Mallory's throat. Forbes talked about Erin's death as if it had been something fun, a spectator sport where he had been the victor. The changes in him were almost instantaneous. The night she met him, she had somehow known he was dangerous, but she hadn't suspected for a second that he was insane. Back in the office, he had seemed in control. He still did, but something inside him had obviously snapped somewhere along the line. Had ordering Erin's death, watching as she had been tortured beyond recognition, done that to him? Had it lit a fuse that waited until now to detonate?

"Where are you taking me?" Mallory shifted and tried to sit up, but the van picked that moment to make a sharp turn and she fell onto her back again. She briefly closed her eyes on the pain that shot through her head, solar plexus, and belly. Forbes had done some damage with his powerful kicks, though she didn't know how much. He hadn't broken a rib. She was sure of that, but he had definitely bruised a few.

"Somewhere private where you and I can finish what you started in the office." He reached for her. She attempted to scoot away from his touch, but the floor of the van didn't offer enough space. He circled her right breast with a fingertip.

Please, God, no.

"I told you I have plans for you." His finger trailed down her abdomen, her stomach, lower.

"Don't touch me, you bastard." She tried to buck away, lifting her bent knees both to shield her pussy and in hopes of somehow hitting him. She had to fight back. She couldn't simply lie here while he pawed at her, while he... *Oh, God.* She didn't want to think what he might do next.

She saw the back of his hand flying toward her face right before he backhanded her. Stars exploded in her vision. Her cheek screamed. Her teeth bit into her tongue at the blow, and the sweet, metallic taste of blood filled her mouth. She spit it in his face.

Fury filled his eyes as he wiped the spit from his face. "You bitch." He caught her nipple, pinched and twisted it until she cried out from the sharp pain. "You're in no position to make demands." He reached for her other nipple and delivered the same punishing pinch.

Involuntary tears leaked from Mallory's eyes. Her back lifted off the floor of the van and she bit back the pleas she knew would only give him satisfaction.

"You spit at me again, you try to hit me again, and what I do to you in just a little while will be far worse than anything you can imagine."

"You can't harm her, Wade." Betty's stern voice came from the front of the van where she sat between Bruno and the goon. "Our buyers don't want damaged girls."

"She will heal, just like Lexie did. Then we'll put her up in a private auction."

He released Mallory's nipples and her chest heaved. The fire in her breasts made it hard to control her breathing.

"I've decided not to let Lexie's master have her." One hand flattened between her breasts, and he slid it down between her legs to cup her pussy. "We'll get more for this body than he has in any bank account."

"That body belongs to an FBI agent," Betty reminded him crossly. "We need to get rid of her as fast as possible. She's right about one thing, you fucked up back there. You handed Kenneth Reese to the damn feds on a red-hot platter."

"They won't find her." The confidence in Forbes's tone was almost enough to send a death-nail through Mallory's hopes.

They *would* find her. She believed that in her soul. But would they find her before it was too late?

* * * *

"Where is she, Toshie?" Cooper punched the gas pedal of his SUV and flew through a stale yellow light at top-notch speed. He weaved through traffic, narrowly missing the rear bumper of a car as he swerved into the opposite lane to go around.

"She's still in Stardust, sir." Toshie's voice filled the SUV through Cooper's phone set on speaker mode. "She hasn't left that building."

Fear, red-hot and all consuming, tightened around Jackson's heart. He exchanged a worried glance with Cooper then leaned forward in his seat for a better view of the sky. He immediately wished he hadn't. They were less than a mile from Stardust and he could already see the billowing smoke filling the sky.

"Don't move from that monitor," Cooper ordered. "If that signal so much as budges, I want to know about it."

"Yes, sir." Toshie disconnected the call, and a heavy, worried silence enveloped the air of the SUV.

"I know the lieutenant on duty," Cooper said, his attention not leaving the road. "He and his crew are some of the best Waterston FD has to offer."

It was an inane attempt to ease their concern and they both knew it. The best firefighters in the world didn't stand a chance at saving someone's life if they were trapped in the kind of seemingly instant blaze Cameron had described to them on the phone. Stone had tried to get into the building the moment he had noticed the smoke and had gotten burned for his efforts. Jackson didn't know how badly. He only knew all signs indicated that Mallory was somewhere inside those flames.

"She didn't follow protocol the last time I put her on an assignment like this. I chewed her ass for it, and now I'm praying she disobeyed me again."

Jackson remembered the last thing she said to him before leaving his office that morning. *Don't worry. I know what happens to people who lose someone they love. Damn you for making me think about that now.*

He wouldn't think about the ramifications. He couldn't. Those words had been a promise to him that she would follow protocol this time, if for no other reason than to keep him from worrying.

And he damned himself for asking her to make that promise.

* * * *

Flames licked the smoke-filled sky. Thaddeus had smelled it even before the building came into view. He parked a block away from the scene and slid out of the car, sheer adrenaline pumping through his veins. A scattering of onlookers stood on the sidewalks, watching the action from a safe distance. Uniformed officers had set up a perimeter around the scene. Rescue 14 and Engine 14 had set up a stage at the front of the building, hoses pulled and firefighters already battling the raging beast. One firefighter stood at the deck gun above the pump panel on Engine 14, spraying gallons of water a minute on the flames.

"It took us, what, ten minutes tops to get here, and that place is already fully involved." Terri jogged to catch up with him as he walked toward the closest officers. "Thad, if there are people trapped inside, there is no way the firefighters will get to them in time."

Yeah, the realization of that had already hit Thaddeus's mind. He had been on more fire scenes than he bothered to count in his career, and the sight before him ranked at the top of his personal holy shit list.

"They're trying to surround and drown it," Thaddeus said, noting the position of the firefighters he could see. "They're going to need more men than they obviously have to pull that off." He heard the wailing sirens growing louder in the distance, no doubt trucks from a neighboring department attempting to make the scene.

"Hey, get back on the sidewalk."

Thaddeus ignored the officer, walking instead straight to the man. "We're firefighters. I'm Thaddeus Carter. Who is incident command on scene?"

"Thaddeus Carter?"

He saw the name register with the officer in an instant. His family was heavy supporters of the Waterston PD. He didn't like using the connections that came with the family name, hadn't intended to today, but one look at the fire and the lack of men struggling to get it under control changed his decision.

"Lieutenant Tommy Vance." The officer turned, pointing to a tall, beefy man a few feet away. "Go on through. They need all the help they can get on this one."

"Thank you." Thaddeus weaved his way through other officers and personnel to the lieutenant in charge of the scene. His step faltered when the lieutenant shifted slightly and Thaddeus saw the man the lieutenant was speaking to.

"Isn't that..." Terri let her question trail off.

Cameron. Yes, it was.

"We're doing all we can," the lieutenant was telling Cameron. "That building is a fireball. Both entrances are blocked. I can't get a man close to that place, let alone inside the damn thing. It's just not safe. I can't endanger the lives of my men more than I have to. I radioed for help as soon as we got here. Two more trucks have already taken up position in the back, and there are more on the way. All the fucking firefighters in this city right now, and I'm shorthanded on a monster like this. I—"

"Excuse me, Lieutenant Vance?" The lieutenant's head snapped Thaddeus's direction, and he saw surprise move through Cameron's expression when he spotted him. Thaddeus extended a hand to the lieutenant. "Thaddeus Carter, firefighter engineer with Silver Springs FD. This is Terri Vega, firefighter/EMT."

The lieutenant gave both of them a once-over gaze as he quickly shook Thaddeus's hand. "Today you're both Waterston FD, son, if you're here to help."

"We are, sir. Just tell us where you want us."

"I've already got men manning the trucks. What I need is another on the nozzle. You got turnouts?"

"Yes, sir, back in the trunk of the car."

"Suit up." The lieutenant shifted his attention to Terri. "EMT, right? Medical equipment is in the rescue. I've got both my men from there fighting this fire. See if you can get Agent Stone to let you have a look at his burns."

Thaddeus started to turn when he heard the lieutenant's words. His gaze flicked to Cameron, raked over him, and halted on his right arm. A four-inch patch of flesh on his forearm was red and shiny, with white areas already starting to blister. "Oh my God, baby, you're hurt."

"I'm fine. Thaddeus, Mallory is inside there."

A chill unlike anything Thaddeus had ever felt washed through him. He shot a glance at the building and raced to his car, digging his keys out of his pocket as he ran. He wrenched the trunk open, yanked the zipper of his gear bag, and pulled out his turnouts.

Methodical movements carried him through the process of suiting up. Each routine step of pulling on the turnout pants, coat, and waterproof boots, sliding the Nomax hood over his head and covering that with his helmet and connected face shield was habit more than thought. Good thing, too, because his thoughts were on Cameron's last words.

Cameron's sister was inside that building. *Dear God, there's no way she's still alive.*

Thaddeus double-timed it back to the lieutenant, delving his hands in his thick, fire-retardant gloves as he ran. He shut off the thoughts of Cameron's sister, buried the fear for her rising inside him, and focused his mind on the job. Despite the habitualness of it, the act of battling this fire would demand his full attention.

He halted in front of the lieutenant. "Where do you want me, sir?"

"Grab the extra crosslay and find a point of attack. We need to surround this thing if we're going to get it under control. There's a spare SCBA on the engine. Grab it, too."

"Yes, sir." Thaddeus followed the command, finding the self-contained breathing apparatus and sliding the face mask over his mouth and nose before snagging the already-charging crosslay hose. Clean, cool oxygen filled his nostrils as he headed for the flames.

* * * *

Jackson stood on the sidelines with Cooper and Waterston PD task force leader, Jerry Blanchard, watching as more than twenty firefighters fought to put out the fire in front of them. There was nothing he could do, and the knowledge of that cut into his soul. Nothing he could do and no way Mallory could have made it out of there alive.

Toshie had called them back seconds after they reached the scene with the news that the signal from Mallory's GPS had gone off radar. It hadn't moved. It had simply gone out.

It had been burnt out, Jackson knew. Toshie had designed the GPS to be waterproof but not fireproof. The loss of that signal had brought with it a loss of hope Jackson fought desperately not to feel, hope he knew deep down to be futile as he looked at what remained of the building that was once the Stardust Club.

He and Cooper had been at the scene now for nearly a half hour. The firefighters had skillfully gotten the fire under control. The front half of the building looked to be out, leaving nothing but a charred frame.

"I've got my men combing the area," Jerry Blanchard said. "Damn near every cop on duty in this town is out here somewhere right now."

"I've got an agent inside that building." Cooper sounded livid. "And one of the bastards we're looking for is one of your guys."

"I'm aware of that," Blanchard said hotly. "My guys won't hesitate to bring Kenneth Reese in when he's found. We don't tolerate traitors in this department."

Jackson stopped listening to Cooper and Blanchard's conversation and focused on the reports coming through the firefighter radios he could hear.

"Still some hot spots in here."

"Nothing left but debris."

"Structure is compromised…be lucky if what's left of this place doesn't collapse on our heads."

"Cut the chatter!" One forceful voice came through above the others, silencing the radio waves. "Lieutenant, I've got a body in here. It's, oh, God, it's—" The firefighter stopped talking, and all Jackson heard was the sound of retching.

Jackson stumbled backward, slamming into the fender of a nearby car as his world spun.

* * * *

Mallory's head ached, but not from banging against the van floor this time. It couldn't be. This pain was internal, a sharp dagger stabbing incessantly across her forehead from temple to temple, and rather than the cold, metal floor, she felt something soft beneath her. She forced herself to open eyes that felt glued together, and the pain worsened as light penetrated the foggy darkness.

"You're awake." The female voice, sweet, young, and gushing with relief came from somewhere beside her.

Mallory turned her head slowly to her right, groaning as the pain skated down her neck, and struggled to focus on the voice and her surroundings. The light came from a fluorescent bulb overhead. The softness beneath her was a bed in an otherwise seemingly empty room, empty but for the voice.

"Here. Drink some of this." The bed dipped and she turned her head left. A girl, eighteen at most, sat beside her, holding a plastic cup. "It's safe. No drugs. I promise. I drank half of it myself to make sure first."

Drugs? Mallory grappled to make sense of the girl's words. It hurt to concentrate, but somehow she knew she must.

"What happened?" It hurt to talk, too. Her throat felt scratchy, dry, and bruised. She lifted a shaking hand and took the cup of water.

"I don't know exactly what he did to you," the girl answered. "Careful. Don't drink it too fast or you'll throw up."

Mallory drank the water slowly, her eyes closing as the room-temperature liquid soothed her aching throat. "Who?" She strained to remember. Her last clear thought was being in Jackson's office, going off on him for leaving her last night.

No, she remembered more after that. She remembered promising him, in not so many words, she wouldn't remove the anklet and that she would use the alert device in her earrings at the first sign of trouble.

"Jim," the girl told her. "I don't know if that's really his name, but that's what he calls himself."

Jim. The name jarred Mallory's memory further with a painful clarity that nearly made her eyes explode. She remembered arriving at Stardust, talking with Sasha, and Betty leading her to the office where "Jim" and the other men had been waiting.

"His real name is Wade Forbes," she said softly, handing the cup back to the girl. She paused when the girl reached to take the cup and didn't let go of it. "You drank half of that first. Why?"

"To make sure it wasn't drugged." The girl pulled the cup from Mallory's fingers and set it on the floor by the bed. "He does that, puts drugs in the food and drink he gives us."

"You were trying to keep me from being drugged?" It was getting easier to focus, though only marginally. She studied the girl with long dark hair, blue eyes, a slender face, and an equally slender build. A dark bruise on her left cheek and another on the right side of her jaw marred her otherwise-pretty face. Mallory saw other bruises, too, on the girl's wrists and the top of her thighs the plain T-shirt she wore failed to hide. Despite her red-rimmed eyes and the puffy bags beneath them, she didn't look like someone who would have wanted the drugs for herself.

"I'm weak, tired, and still woozy from all the drugs he's been pumping into me. I knew the food and drink was drugged and held out for as long as I could, but I had to eat, had to drink. You just got here. I was hoping you would be stronger." Her eyes filled with tears she didn't attempt to hold back. "I was hoping you could help me."

Mallory pushed herself up and pulled the girl into her arms. What had Forbes done to this girl? He had obviously beaten her, and the marks around her wrists were telltale signs of being tied down. Though she didn't want to think about the implications of that, she had to know.

"Has he hurt you?"

The question made the girl cry harder. Sobs racked her body, and she squeezed Mallory so hard it reminded her again of the pain in her solar plexus and belly, the ache that had only dulled a smidgen since the powerful kicks Forbes had given her.

"What's your name?" Mallory tried a different question, softly smoothing her hand down the back of the girl's hair. If felt matted, dirty, as if it hadn't been washed in months.

"Sophie," the girl managed on a ragged breath. "Sophie Reese"

Mallory gasped and drew back to look at the girl. "Sophie *Reese*? Do you know Kenneth Reese?"

Hatred more acute than any Mallory had ever witnessed dried Sophie's tears. "He's the reason Jim, or whatever you called him, took me. Jim said he was using me to keep Kenneth in line. That's why he didn't sell me like the others yet. But he"—she gulped and the tears started to flow again— "he plans to. He said there are a lot of men dying to get hold of a child like me."

Dear God. Mallory didn't ask Sophie her age. She had first thought she was eighteen, but it didn't really matter. Sixteen or twenty, the girl was too young to be mixed up in something like this. Any woman of any age was.

"He's wrong." Sophie viciously swiped at her tears. "Jim, he's wrong. Kenneth doesn't give a shit about me. Money makes his world go around. That's all he's ever cared about, and he's never given a damn about who gets hurt in the process of him getting it, even people who love him."

"I think you're wrong." Mallory remembered the constant ticking she had seen in Kenneth's jaw, the tip he had given the bureau that led them to Erin Griffin's body, the haunted look in his eyes. She understood it now. It all made sense. "Kenneth has done some terrible things, probably a lot that I don't even know about, but I believe he's done them to protect you."

"How do you know my brother?" Sophie's tone rang with fear and suspicion now. She backed away, quickly moving off the bed to stand next to it. "How do you know Jim's real name?"

"I'm Mallory. Mallory Stone. I'm a special agent with the Waterston branch of the FBI."

Sophie's eyes widened to the size of saucers. "You're an FBI agent?"

"Yes, my team has been investigating a string of missing women, young women between the ages of twenty-one and twenty-eight. All of them worked as strippers at a club called Stardust. Kenneth is part of a task force the Waterston PD set up to aid us in investigations of human trafficking. Sexual slavery," she clarified. "We didn't find out until this morning that Kenneth was working for Forbes, Jim, too."

"Did Natalie work at Stardust, too? And Lexie?"

"You've seen them?"

Sophie nodded. "They took Natalie out of here early this morning. She wasn't here long, a few hours at most. Lexie was here when they brought me in, but then they took her out to let her go to the bathroom and I never saw her again."

"Yes, they are two of the women we've been looking for."

"How many more are there?"

"At least four that we know of, maybe more." Mallory prayed there weren't more. "Do you know what happened to them? Do you know where he took them?"

Sophie's gaze dropped to the floor. "He sold them. After he took Lexie, I kept demanding to know what happened to her, and he said she was with her new master now."

"He didn't use any names or tell you anything more?"

Sophie shook her head and looked up at Mallory apologetically. "I lost it when he told me that. If he did, I don't remember. I was so drugged up at the time I could hardly think straight. Then, when he started telling me the things a master does to his slave, things that would happen to me when he finally decided to sell me I...I lost it." Her face crumpled again, and she sank back down on the side of the bed.

"It's okay. I probably would have lost it, too." Mallory stroked Sophie's back and waited a beat, until Sophie's breathing steadied once more. "Sophie, you have to tell me what he's done to you. You said he's been drugging you. What else has he done? Has he hurt you?"

"He took pictures of me." Sophie's voice shook. She took a deep breath, but it didn't help to steady her words. "Naked pictures he said he would use when he got ready to find me a new m-master. And he r–raped me."

Mallory felt the blood drain from her face as Sophie put voice to her worst fears.

"I don't know how many times," Sophie whispered. "I lost count. I think he let others do it, too. One night I was so drugged I can barely remember anything, but I have these nightmares of at least two other men touching me, doing t–things to me that seem too vivid to be dreams." Her entire body stiffened and she whirled on Mallory. "I don't want to talk about that. I don't want to think about it."

"Okay," Mallory said quickly, gently. "We don't have talk about that anymore. You aren't drugged now, at least you don't seem to be."

"Because I haven't eaten anything he's brought me in days, haven't drank anything either until I had some of the water he left for you. I told you he puts stuff in it. That's how he got me. I was at a party. My friends talked me into going to a rave. I didn't want to go. I heard about all the drugs, ecstasy and roofies and special K and stuff that goes around at those kinds of parties. My friends swore it wasn't that kind of rave."

What other kind of rave is there? Mallory kept quiet and let Sophie continue her story.

"I wasn't having any fun at first." She laughed, but there was no humor in the tone. "I was too scared to be there. Then one of my friends started in on me about loosening up, getting out on the dance floor. She handed me a glass of punch." She closed her eyes and bowed her head. "There must have been something in that first drink. I've thought about it over and over since that night, and I realized it didn't really make me feel funny, but it made me feel happy. I started to have fun."

"Ecstasy," Mallory said softly. "That's what it does to you."

Sophie shrugged. "Maybe. I don't know. All I know is I wasn't afraid anymore. Then Jim started dancing with me and he gave me another glass of punch. That one tasted funny, but for some reason, I drank it anyway. I was so stupid," she said through gritted teeth. "Almost immediately, I started to hyperventilate. He wrapped his arm around me and walked me outside where there was a van waiting. I knew not to get into that van, but by that point, I couldn't do anything. I was so out of it. I passed out in the back of that van and woke up here."

"How long have you been here?" If Lexie had been here when they brought Sophie in, the girl had to have been here for several weeks, maybe even a month.

"I don't know. The days get all jumbled together." Sophie narrowed her eyes and angled her head at Mallory. "You said you're an FBI agent. Surely you weren't as stupid as I was to let Jim buy you a drink."

"No." Though he had tried the first night she met him. Damnit, if only she had known that night. She could have saved this girl at least a few days of horror. "I was working undercover at Stardust. Kenneth—at least I'm pretty certain it was Kenneth—blew my cover." The only explanation she could come up with was that Kenneth purposely gave her away so she would be brought here where he knew his sister was being held. "The manager called me in this morning to talk before the club opened. When I got there, Jim, Wade Forbes, was waiting for me."

"You're here because of my brother, too," Sophie said on a scornful laugh. "If I ever get out of here, he better hope he's nowhere to be found because I will rip off his balls and feed them to him through a straw."

Mallory didn't tell her about the fire at Stardust or about the possibility Kenneth hadn't made it out alive. He might be their only hope of being found. God, wasn't that a horrible place to put her hopes?

"I think he did it on purpose. I think he knew Forbes would bring me here to you."

"You were asleep for hours. He drugged you."

Mallory nodded. "In the van, right before he brought me inside, I guess." She looked down at her arm and saw the tiny hole the needle had left in her flesh. "I don't know what was in the syringe. All I know is one minute I was struggling to fight back and the next I was in la-la land."

"I'm sorry I don't have anything for you to wear. Some woman brought this shirt to me. I don't know when. It feels like years ago, but I'm sure it couldn't have been that long. I hope not, at least. I know it probably stinks. It's been forever since they've allowed me a bath."

Betty had to be the woman Sophie spoke of. Mallory looked down at herself for the first time since she woke. A faded blue blanket covered her naked flesh. She forced a smile as she looked back at Sophie. "A blanket is better than nothing. Where are we? Do you have any idea at all?"

"A room in a cellar or basement or something." Sophie shrugged. "There's a long hallway outside that door and a bathroom somewhere. He's made sure I was too wacked out to notice anything the few times he's taken me out of here. He left that pan over there for me to, um, relieve myself the rest of the time. That's why it smells so bad in here."

Mallory hadn't noticed the stench until Sophie drew her attention to it. Funny how the senses could block out unimportant things when the mind was focused on primary details.

"Sometimes I hear music," Sophie continued. "Club music, but it's very faint, almost like it's next door or across the street or something."

Mallory's mind reeled. They weren't close to Stardust. She knew that much because the ride in the van had been too long. She tried to think back to that trip and attempted to gauge how much time had passed before Forbes injected her with whatever had been in that syringe. Had it been ten minutes, fifteen, twenty? She wasn't exactly sure.

"You're an FBI agent," Sophie said again. "That means you'll have a butt load of big bad guys with guns looking for you, right?"

Mallory had to laugh at that. "My team will be looking for me, yes." But she wasn't going to stack all her cards in one pile on them finding her before Forbes returned. She could find a way out of this herself. All she needed to do was think.

Chapter Nine

"It can't be Mallory." Jackson said it more to convince himself than anyone else in Cooper's office. They were all listening, though, and Tarantino and Cameron shook their heads as they watched him pace the tiled floor. Cooper sat behind his desk talking quietly on the phone, to whom Jackson didn't know and frankly didn't give a shit unless it was Mallory. It obviously wasn't, so he continued his pacing.

It had been hours since the fire, since the discovery of not one but two bodies. The second hadn't been as badly charred as the first. The medical examiner had quickly determined it to be male due to the frame build and other indicators, though a conclusive identification had yet to be made. Firefighters were still at the scene, making sure the fire was indeed out, and wetting down hot spots. Fire investigators had been called in, but so far, nothing had been found to give them any further leads.

"You may not want to hear this," Cameron started, then sighed. "Hell, I know you don't want to hear it, but I'm not sure if we should hope it is or it isn't."

Jackson saw red. He whirled on Cameron, fisting his hands at his sides. For the first time in years, he wanted to beat the holy living shit out of his best friend. He maintained enough control to keep his distance, to keep his voice low when he spoke out of respect for his boss's phone call, but he knew his tone was cold as ice with an expression on his face to match. "How in the *fuck* can you say that? She's your sister."

"Yeah." Cameron's voice cracked on the calmly spoken word. "And I don't want to think about what that bastard is doing to her right now if that's not her lying in the ME's office."

Forbes would torture her. None of them had a doubt about that. Knowing she was an FBI agent, that she had penetrated one of his businesses enough to get inside in an effort to take him down, would lead him to do things to her Jackson didn't want to think about. Forbes would try to get her to reveal whatever information the bureau had managed to gather on him.

Which isn't a whole hell of a fucking lot.

"She's alive," he said through gritted teeth. "Forbes took her out of that passageway the firefighters found. He got her out through the woods."

He wouldn't believe anything else. He couldn't. Tough-as-nails Mallory could get through anything as long as she lived to try. Whatever Forbes did to her before they found her didn't matter. He would see that she got whatever help she needed to cope. "That's not her, damnit. That's not Mallory."

Please, God, don't let it be Mallory. Don't take her from me now.

He understood. After all the years of dancing around one another, all the years of her fighting her love for him, he finally, truly understood why. If he had lost her, his life would never be the same. No one could ever replace her. He wouldn't even try. He would live the rest of his days waiting for his time to come, waiting for the moment when he would be reunited with her again.

"No, it's not."

Jackson stopped in his tracks and spun to face his boss, half certain the intense hope inside him had caused him to hear what he wanted to hear rather than what Cooper actually said. His pulse pounded so loudly in his ears that he barely heard Cooper's next words.

"No positive identification has been made yet. However, our ME is ninety-nine percent certain that is not Mallory's body."

A heavy, thankful silence blanketed the office. Jackson wanted to move, he wanted to sit, he wanted to rush out of the office and find Mallory, but shock and sheer elation froze him in his spot.

Tarantino was the first to speak. "What about the second body, sir? Has the ME identified it yet?"

The second body had been found in the rear of the building where the office had been.

Cooper nodded. "It was Carl Jordan, the club owner. Or at least the one on record, in any case."

"When is the last time Kell checked in, sir?" Jackson actually felt his mind switch gears. Mallory was alive...for now. They had to find her, and fast.

"I talked to him about an hour ago. Leroy Platt is bouncing around the surrounding cities alone. If he has one of the missing girls, she isn't with him. We were hoping he would lead us to where he's stashed the girl, or girls, but so far he isn't doing anything to draw any real attention to himself, isn't leaving any indication that he's out for more than a simple vacation."

"We can't wait for him to decide to come back to town," Cameron said. "Mallory may not have that much time."

"I want a warrant to search his house." Jackson didn't ask his boss. He told him.

"I'm already a step ahead of you, Graham. We'll have the warrant by morning."

"That's not soon enough." Mallory could truly be dead by morning. If the information they had gathered on Platt was as solid as they believed, then he might be able to lead them straight to Mallory.

Cooper lifted a brow and steadied his gaze on Jackson. "It's the best I can do."

"Have Kell bring him in, sir." Jackson added the "sir" as an afterthought, knowing he was skirting a thin line by giving his boss orders.

"Mallory's life isn't the only one on the line here, Graham," Cooper reminded him sternly. "If we bring Platt in before we know what he's done with the girl, we may never find what he's done with her. Searching his house will be risky enough. If he's tipped off that we're on to him, he and his connections in this town will be all over this bureau. We'll be in a fight to prove his guilt with little more than circumstantial evidence, wasting valuable time we could be using to find these missing girls."

"Platt isn't the only fucker in this city paying top dollar for a sex slave," Tarantino reminded them. "There must be others or we wouldn't have so many missing girls."

"Sharp is working around the clock to analyze the data from the Stardust computer hard drive," Cooper told him. "It's taking longer than anticipated to pinpoint and decipher the cash transactions he's finding. Forbes is apparently good with computers."

"Sharp is about to get some help," Jackson decided.

Cooper's lips twitched. "He won't like that. He prefers to work alone."

"I don't give a damn what he likes, sir." What Jackson liked was Mallory by his side, and right now, that computer hard drive was his best link to her.

Cooper gave him an almost imperceptible nod. "Good enough." His gaze switched to Tarantino and Cameron. "I've got men watching Platt's house. If so much as a rat scurries outside that place, we'll know about it. If he hasn't returned by morning, we'll move in as soon as I get confirmation of the warrant. Cameron, I want you to go home and take care of that arm. I need you in top shape when this goes down."

Cooper got to his feet, walked to his private closet, and took out a casual shirt and another pair of pants. "Jennifer Moss returned to work at Cinderella's tonight. I'm not crazy about that, but she hasn't spotted a tail on her in days and hasn't noticed anything unusual."

"Are you thinking her going back will cause Forbes to resurface tonight?" Jackson asked doubtfully. If he wanted Jennifer Moss, he would've taken her a long time ago.

"No, but I've been wrong before. Forbes felt threatened enough by her association with Lexie Stratus to have her watched for a while. As far as we know, he isn't aware she's been talking to us. I want to make sure that hasn't changed."

* * * *

He shouldn't be here.

Thaddeus leaned against the front bumper of Cameron's SUV, tipped his head back, and stared at the stars. It was a beautiful night, too pretty after the day it had been. Two people had died today, one of them possibly Cameron's sister. God, what the man must be going through right now.

He lifted his head, glanced at the door to the building, and sighed. He had thought about going inside, but he didn't want to disturb Cameron. The man would be working, feverishly attempting to find his sister's killer, if she were truly dead. And if that wasn't her body found today, he would no doubt be turning over every rock and leaf in Waterston to find her.

Which means he could be in there all night.

And that would leave Thaddeus standing out here waiting like an idiot. He should go. He hadn't talked to Cameron, not *really* talked to him, since their date. It was bad enough that he had slipped at the fire scene today and called the man *baby* in front of the lieutenant. Now he was waiting outside the man's place of employment and had been for over a half hour.

Jeez, what are you thinking?

He hadn't considered what it would look like if someone saw him out here. Then again, no one here knew him. They didn't know he and Cameron had spent several fantastic hours together mere nights ago.

They were unaware that Thaddeus couldn't seem to get those hours out of his head, couldn't stop thinking about Cameron and how badly he wanted a repeat of that night.

But that's not why you're here.

No, it wasn't. He had come to see if Cameron was all right, to offer a shoulder if the man needed one, to...

Oh, hell, he didn't really know why he had come here. If Cameron needed a shoulder, he had Jackson, his best friend and a man who would need comfort just as badly if the worst had happened today. He should have gone to Jackson's apartment and waited for him to come home with news.

Thaddeus pushed off the bumper to do just that when he spotted a figure walking toward him in his peripheral vision. Cameron looked beat, defeated. Thaddeus couldn't see his face in the darkness, but he saw the man's step falter slightly when he spotted him.

Bad idea. He definitely shouldn't have come here.

Cameron's steps brought him into the light of the nearby street lamp and Thaddeus saw his face, saw his lips curve in a small smile that looked both happy to see him and exhausted as hell. His gaze locked with Thaddeus's, and a world of questions and surprise swirled in his expression.

"How long have you been out here?"

Thaddeus's gut did a decidedly nervous roll. "Not long, about a half an hour maybe."

"You should have come inside." Cameron stopped within arm's reach of him. "The night guard would have called me for you. Or, hell, you could've called me yourself. You've got my number, baby."

Thaddeus grimaced. "I didn't think about it. Well, I did, but I didn't want to bother you. I didn't know..."

Cameron touched him, a soft glide of his fingers down Thaddeus's bicep. "It wasn't Mallory."

"Oh, thank God." Thaddeus released a breath he hadn't realized he had been holding.

"Yeah, but she's out there somewhere and we don't have a fucking clue where to look."

"The fire investigator was still at the scene when I left. I don't know how much more he'll be able to find to help you, though. Whoever set that fire did a damn good job at covering up the evidence."

Cameron nodded. "That's what they intended." He sighed, raked a hand through his hair, then winced when the movement caused obvious pain to his injured arm. "We'll find her. I just hope we get to her before that bastard hurts her."

"How is your arm? From what I saw of the burn, it looked pretty vicious. Terri said it's borderline third degree but you wouldn't let her do more than put some ointment on it and a bandage."

"It stings, but she did a bang-up job treating it. Is she with you?" Cameron cast a cursory glance around the parking lot before meeting Thaddeus's gaze again.

"I dropped her at Jackson's apartment. He gave us a key, you know, so we don't find ourselves locked out again. Of course, if she decides to leave before I get there tonight I'm screwed, but..." He shrugged.

"I could let you in again." Cameron waited a beat, his gaze lingering on Thaddeus's eyes before dropping to his mouth. He took a half step closer and put his hand on Thaddeus's waist. "Or you could come to my place."

Thaddeus swallowed. Being this close to Cameron again, having that simple contact of his hand on his waist, reignited the fire inside him that had been smoldering almost since the first moment they met.

"Is that where you're headed?"

"I've been ordered to go home, change my bandages, and sit around going fucking crazy wondering where Mallory is and how the fuck we're going to find her."

"Aw, baby, I wish there was something I could do."

"There is. You can come home with me, keep me company since I'm not going to get a wink of sleep tonight. Honestly, I don't want to be alone."

Thaddeus's heart skipped a beat, and he slowly nodded. "I'll follow you."

* * * *

"Are you hungry? Want something to drink?" Cameron bent to stick his head inside the refrigerator and laughed. "I can't offer you much. It looks like my grocery fairy has gone on strike." He straightened and looked over the refrigerator door at Thaddeus. The man stood in the kitchen doorway, one shoulder resting against the frame, arms and ankles casually crossed. In that pose, he looked like a *GQ* cover model, and Cameron found himself wanting to rush for his camera, to capture the moment.

"I've got beer and water." Cameron turned his attention back to the fridge and pulled out a beer for himself. The ice-cold bottle of water would probably be better at putting out this fire burning inside him for the man standing a scant few feet away. Thaddeus might be a firefighter, but he was damn good at starting them, too. "On the food side, there's probably a couple of frozen pizzas in the freezer and a box of Twinkies in the cabinet."

"Grocery fairy, huh?" Amusement danced in Thaddeus's voice. "Something tells me she's made sure you have the main essentials ready and waiting."

Cameron glanced back at Thaddeus and grinned. "Yeah, I'm the stereotypical bachelor. Mal's the same way. Jackson stays on both of us about our eating habits."

"Beer. Competing tomorrow with a hangover would be horrible, but one won't hurt. I've seen enough water today to last me a little while."

"I bet." Cameron pulled another can of beer from the fridge, popped the top, and walked closer to Thaddeus to hand it to him. He couldn't stop his gaze from roaming over the man. His hair was charmingly tousled, his return gaze comfortable and mildly flirtatious. His SSFD T-shirt had black smudges on the chest, as did his neck and left cheek. "Did you want to take a shower?"

Thaddeus drew his brows together. "Do I smell that bad?"

Cameron laughed. "No." He lifted a hand to Thaddeus's neck and wiped at the smear there. Thaddeus angled his head at the touch, exposing the corded muscle that ran up the side of his neck. Cameron swallowed. The urge to run his tongue along that muscle made his mouth water.

"You've got black stuff on her neck and your cheek," he said, his voice barely above a whisper. Damn, touching the man drove him friggin' crazy. Electricity zinged up his arm, sizzled in the burn beneath the bandages, and exploded in a blast of desire to touch so much more of this man.

"Maybe in a bit," Thaddeus said huskily.

He licked his lips and Cameron's gaze was instantly there. A craving to kiss, to taste, collided with the need to touch, and he forced himself to drop his hand. He had asked Thaddeus to come over tonight to keep him company, to keep his mind off Mallory, not so he could seduce him, for crying out loud.

"I didn't get a shower after I left the fire scene today."

Because he had gone to HQ to wait for him. Yeah, Cameron knew and, God, walking out of the office to find Thaddeus in the parking lot had offered a ray of sunshine to an otherwise horrifically dark day.

"We should probably take a look at your arm, put more ointment on the burn and change the bandages. I'm not a certified EMT, but we're all trained on basic medical treatment."

"It's okay for now. You were pretty amazing today, you know?" Cameron took a step back and drank a swig of his beer as Thaddeus's lips tilted in a boyish grin that made it almost impossible to keep his distance.

"It was great." Something moved through his eyes that Cameron couldn't quite define, and his smile quickly faded. "I mean, the fact that the place was torched like that wasn't. Knowing that we couldn't get the fire out fast enough to get someone in there to look for survivors, knowing that Mallory was believed to be inside..." He dropped his gaze and shook his head. "God, no it wasn't great."

"I know what you meant." Cameron understood. The danger, the sheer adrenaline rush that came with it was what men like them lived for. "That kind of destruction, knowing that lives are on the line, it's never a good thing, but the job, battling something so out of control, is what you love."

Surprise flashed through Thaddeus's eyes. "Yeah, it is."

"Do you get to do it often?" Cameron leaned a hip against the counter and took another swig from his can. "You're an engineer on the SSFD, right? Which means you stay with the truck on fire scenes. Do you ever get pulled away from it, ever get a chance to be in the rest of the action like you did today?"

"Sometimes. It's not as rare as it used to be. Ryan Magee, he was the engineer before I signed on with the department. He's lead nozzle man for Engine 1 now. We've been swapping out here and there lately."

"I've met Magee." He had been there on his first assignment in Silver Springs when Magee's now stepson had been kidnapped by the Phay cartel. "Former SEAL, definitely a bad ass."

Thaddeus chuckled. "That's Magee." He angled his head and seemed to be choosing his words carefully before he spoke again. "It's a wonder you and I never met before the other night, given how many of the same people we know."

"I've thought about that, too. Jason, Jackson, Magee..."

"Adrien," Thaddeus supplied, and Cameron's heart skipped a beat.

Shit. Why hadn't the possibility occurred to him? Jackson had thought of it. He had even tried to warn Cameron.

I'd be careful though. Thaddeus is from Silver Springs, too. I don't know if it's still happening, but when I was there, the DEA office was crossing paths with the SSFD quite frequently.

Think Thaddeus would be one to go home and gossip to the town?

No, but there's a good chance he and Adrien are acquaintances.

Was it a good chance they were more than acquaintances? Cameron stared at Thaddeus, momentarily speechless. "You know Adrien?"

"Yeah, small world, huh?"

He knew, Cameron realized as he held Thaddeus's unwavering gaze. His mind spun through all the late-night phone calls with Adrien, all the conversations they'd had about people and things going on in Silver Springs. Adrien had never once brought up Thaddeus.

"How well?" he dared to ask because, Jesus, what if he had unknowingly come between them somehow? He had suspected for a long time that he wasn't the only man in Adrien's life, but he hadn't known for sure.

"Very well," Thaddeus said evenly, his tone heavy with insinuation.

Thaddeus didn't sound pissed. He didn't sound hurt. Yet, Cameron knew those two words had been Thaddeus's way of telling him that he and Adrien were, or had been, a whole lot more than mere acquaintances.

"Fuck." Cameron closed his eyes and dragged a hand down his face. "Do I owe you an apology, a plea for mercy while you kick my ass?"

Thaddeus actually laughed. "I have no reason to kick your ass. I mean, I figured out, or was fairly certain at least, right after I met you that you were the reason he's been side-stepping me for years, but that's not your fault."

"It might be," Cameron admitted. "Adrien and I have been doing our own fair amount of side-stepping the last couple of years. It didn't start out that way. We found ourselves working the case against Ving Kim Phay. You know about that fiasco, right?"

"Yeah, he talked to me about the case. Well, he told me as much as he could, anyway."

"We started talking a lot, about the case at first and then one thing led to another, and we got closer." Cameron thought he saw a dart of pain shoot through Thaddeus's eyes. "We were never romantically involved. Hell, I never got close enough to kiss him, much less anything else." He had wanted to, though. Christ on a pogo stick, he was so damn attracted to Adrien he couldn't think about the man without getting a hard-on.

"You wanted to." The certainty in Thaddeus's tone made the words more statement than question.

Cameron nodded anyway. "I'll give it to you straight. I wanted to fuck him. He's hot, sexy, freaking amazing."

Thaddeus's lips actually twitched at that. "Tell me about it."

Cameron chuckled. He couldn't help himself. "When I realized what was happening between us, where things had the potential of going, I shut it down. I was honest with him. I didn't want to lead him on, and I felt like I had been."

"That was the last time you were in Silver Springs, right?"

"Yeah, right before we finally got Ving Kim Phay. Why?"

"It wasn't long after that Adrien started slowly getting closer to me again. Then, a few weeks later, he started backing away…again."

Cameron sighed. "Which means I *do* owe you an apology." He tipped back his beer, downed the remainder of the can, and tossed it in the trash across the kitchen. "I cut off all communication between us for weeks. It drove me fucking nuts. Not talking to him, not hearing his voice, not being able to call him when I needed a ready ear, I felt like I lost a part of myself when I did that."

"Are you in love with him?"

"No," Cameron said quickly. The disbelieving look in Thaddeus's eyes made him say it again, more forcefully this time. "God, no." He shook his head and raked a frustrated hand through his hair. "But I can't seem to stay away from him either."

"Yeah." Thaddeus laughed slightly, but the sound held more irritation than humor. "Neither can I."

"Are *you* in love with him?" Cameron turned the question around and felt his heart plummet when Thaddeus sighed.

"Yes. I tried not to be. It worked for a long time, too. But somewhere down the line the lust morphed into more and I fell anyway."

"Is that what the other night was about?" Cameron dared to ask. "Our date, was that you trying again not to be in love with Adrien?"

"Part of it." Thaddeus shrugged. "Terri has been telling me for months that I need to move on. I was attracted to you. *Am* attracted to you," he corrected. He chuckled and rolled his eyes. "Shit, who am I kidding. Adrien isn't the only one who is hot, Cam."

Cameron grinned. "Tell me about it."

"Touché." Thaddeus stared at him for a long moment. "I went out with you because I wanted to, because I like you, and I had a fantastic time. Tonight has been pretty good so far, too, despite the day that led us to be here now."

The fire. Mallory. Jesus. Cameron had actually managed to push it all from his mind for a few short minutes.

"I had a great time, too," he told Thaddeus, trying desperately to hold onto a few more minutes before the bone-deep worry for his sister took over his sanity. Except, what was happening between him and Thaddeus tonight was completely *in*sane. "I enjoy being with you. Adrien is a dumbass for letting me stand in his way of claiming you."

Thaddeus slanted him a look. "*Claiming* me? Honey, that sounds so barbaric."

"It doesn't change the facts."

Thaddeus nodded thoughtfully. "And our date the other night was, what, about you wanting to fuck me, too?"

His bluntness surprised another laugh out of Cameron. "Oh, I do want to fuck you. It's a bad idea, but my mind seems to be having trouble explaining that to my dick. That isn't why I asked you to follow me home tonight."

"Then why don't we do what you did ask me to come over for? Let's go in the living room, change that bandage on your arm, and find something stupidly hilarious and equally cheesy on television to watch for a while."

"I'm game." Cameron walked to the fridge. "Do you want another beer?" he asked, pulling out another can for himself.

"No, but I will take that bottle of water now."

* * * *

Voices seeped into Mallory's quiet world. Her head spun, the ache between her temples returning with a vengeance. Vaguely, she remembered that pain and the cause, remembered it being the result of whatever had been in the syringe Forbes had stuck in her arm before taking her from the van.

He had done it again, too. That memory slowly swam to the forefront of her mind. He had come into the room where she and Sophie had been, a loaded gun in one hand and another full syringe in the other. Sophie had screamed, pleaded, and even attempted to stop Forbes by begging him to give her the drug instead. She had pretended to be going through withdrawals, crying and apologizing for not eating the food he had left for her that would have given her a quick fix.

Forbes hadn't bought the act, but the girl deserved an Emmy for trying. He had backhanded her for her attempts, sending her flying across the bed, and advanced on Mallory. There hadn't been anything she could do. He had left her with only the options to fight and be shot by a bullet or take the shot from the syringe. She had gritted her teeth as he plunged the needle in her arm, and almost instantly, the world had started to spin.

Another hazy memory had her being dragged down a long hallway. She had tried to pay attention to her surroundings, but the drug had made it impossible to focus. She didn't remember blacking out, but she knew she must have, and she almost wished she had stayed that way.

Something cold and unforgiving was biting into her wrists. *Handcuffs?* An incessant tingling travelled down her arms. Her legs ached from standing too long. But that couldn't be right. How could she be on her feet if she had been knocked out?

It took every ounce of strength she could gather to lift her head and look up. Shock and fear slammed through her system and brought unwanted tears to her eyes. The links of the handcuffs were secured over a huge meat hook attached to a thin chain in the ceiling that didn't look any different than the one of the room she had been in with Sophie. She was naked. The blanket she had used for cover was gone.

Don't think about that. Concentrate of rebuilding your strength, on how you can fight this bastard.

Her legs were far stronger than her arms, and he had left them unrestrained. They ached, but she flexed the muscles in her thighs and calves and knew she could ignore the pain if she could just get a chance to fight.

"Good, you're awake."

Mallory startled at the voice from behind her. She shifted, trying to look back, but couldn't turn sideways enough to see. That was good to know.

Note to self, make sure the fucker is right in front of you before you kick his balls into his throat.

"You are a true sleeping beauty, but my customers like to see the merchandise with their eyes open."

Customers? Oh, shit. Her heart raced, her pulse thumping so loudly in her ears she couldn't hear anything beyond the pounding.

Jackson, baby, please. Cameron, Adam, Nick, anyone, please, help me.

They didn't hear her, of course, because none of them were inside her head. They weren't here. They hadn't found her yet. No one was here to stop this bastard from doing whatever it was he planned to do.

"Don't cry now," Forbes warned as he walked around her and came into view.

Too far away. Damnit, come closer, you son of a bitch.

Tears burned the backs of her eyes, but it wasn't his warning that kept them from falling. Her determination did that all on its own. She couldn't rely on anyone to save her right now. She could do this. Somehow, someway, she could get out of this.

"If you cry, I'll have to give you more drugs. It will have to be something different this time so you don't black out on me again, though. I really do need your eyes open for the pictures."

Pictures? Oh, thank God.

A stupid sense of relief washed through her as she watched him move behind a tripod holding a digital camera, which he had set up several feet in front of where she hung. He planned to take pictures of her, full-body shots he would no doubt use to auction her off. There would be naked pictures of her shown to who knew how many perverts, but it was far better than her first fear, that those perverts were here in this room about to view her firsthand.

"Now, smile for the camera."

Mallory twisted, bobbing her head from side to side and turning her body as much as the cuffs would allow.

"Stay still or you'll make the pictures blurry."

Well, duh! That was the whole point.

She stopped flailing though, realizing she was wasting precious energy, and focused on his finger on top of the camera. She waited a nanosecond before she anticipated the flash and stuck out her tongue.

It was childish and she knew it, but it was the only way she had to fight at that moment.

The bastard actually laughed, the sound one of pure insanity. "Mallory, Mallory, Mallory, you'll have to pay for that later. Let's try it again. Ready? Say cheese."

Mallory pulled her nose up, drew her brows together, and twisted her mouth, making the worst possible face she could.

Forbes sighed, straightened behind the camera, and tsked. "Now, Mallory. The more you do things like that, the more you're going to regret it. I only need one good picture and then we will be done with this part of our evening."

This part? What did he have planned next? Should she continue to push him? She thought about it. She really, *really* wanted to, but the prospect of him taking her down from this damn hook and putting her in a better position to fight won out.

Mallory looked at the camera and painted her best evil grin on her lips as the light flashed.

* * * *

"Got it!"

Jackson jolted at Sharp's shout and raked a hand down his face.

"You might want to wake up for this one, Graham."

Cooper bumped Jackson's leg, and he opened his eyes to find his boss standing over him. He had actually dozed off. How the hell had he managed to do that? He had been sitting in a chair near Sharp's computer table for hours, his feet propped on the edge, his head resting on the back of the chair as he stared at the ceiling and hoped, prayed, and mulled over everything they knew.

And he had fallen asleep in the process.

Good one, dumb shit.

"What did you find?" Cooper asked Sharp.

Jackson straightened, his gaze landing on the digital neon numbers of the clock hanging on a nearby wall. Five a.m. Damn, they had been at this all night.

"Give me a few more minutes, sir," Sharp answered absently, his long fingers flying over his computer keyboard.

"It better be good," Cooper told him. "I need all the good news I can get right now."

Sharp ignored him, continuing to work his magic on the computer screen.

"What happened at Cinderella's tonight?" Jackson flicked a glance at the clock again and corrected himself. "Last night."

Cooper rubbed the back of his neck. "Loud music, *very* loud music, a lot of dancing, and even more drinking."

"In other words, nothing out of the norm."

"Not a thing that I could see or sense. Kell reported in about twenty minutes ago. Leroy Platt is headed back this way. By the time he reaches home, we'll have him and the warrant."

"You're going to need more than one, boss," Sharp informed him, not looking away from his computer screen. He rattled off a list of names as a printer on a separate table kicked to life. "Add those fuckers to your list."

"You're certain?" Two strides took Cooper to the printer, where he snagged the page from the completed tray.

"As a heart attack," Sharp replied confidently.

Cooper shot Jackson a look as he pulled his phone from his inside coat pocket. "Time to move."

* * * *

Cameron stumbled into the kitchen. Coffee. He needed coffee and a giant bottle of ibuprofen because, Jesus, he hurt. His entire body felt as if it had been twisted into a pretzel. He had apparently slept that way, too, for—he glanced at the clock on the microwave—three and a half hours.

The powers that be were having mercy on him, though, he discovered, spotting a full pot of coffee that had just finished brewing. No, not powers. Power, singular, as in Thaddeus. His new, magnificent god. His god who had apparently woke with the same aches and pains he did because the bottle of ibuprofen sat on the counter by the coffee pot.

Cameron smiled as he poured himself a cup, took two pills from the bottle, and knocked them back, listening to the water run in the shower down the hall. Yep, that was next on his own agenda, a long, hot shower to loosen the tight muscles in his neck and back.

He considered joining Thaddeus for a full three seconds before he pushed the notion aside. It was long enough to add a new area to his morning arsenal of aches. His cock stiffened at the image that formed in his mind. He saw Thaddeus standing beneath the showerhead, water streaming down his broad shoulders, hard chest, and ripped abs.

"Get a grip, Stone."

His verbal warning to himself didn't help. It only brought back the memory of last night, of how he had gotten that grip on Thaddeus. Oh, not in the way he truly wanted, and it had really been Thaddeus who had gotten the grip on him. They had found a movie on television and settled on Cameron's sofa where Cameron had eventually curled up in Thaddeus's strong arms and fallen asleep.

An upbeat jingle sliced into his thoughts, and he followed the tune into the living room. Thaddeus's cell phone lay on the end table, the screen illuminating the words "unknown name, unknown number."

Cameron shot a glance down the hallway. He should probably just let it ring and let Thaddeus's voice mail pick up the call. But what if it was something important?

"Aw, to hell with it," he muttered and answered the call. "Hello?"

Silence for a full heartbeat. Cameron thought the caller had hung up, but then he heard a slight, surprised familiar chuckle flow through the cellular waves that made his gut flip-flop.

"Wow, um, sorry sweetie, you're not who I was trying to call. I must have pushed the wrong contact button."

Adrien. Cameron closed his eyes, the sound of the other man's voice giving him one hell of a cardio exercise. How in the hell should he play this one off?

"No, you pushed the right one." Cameron went with the truth. Nothing had happened between him and Thaddeus last night. They had talked and dozed off in one another's arms, yes, but... "He's in the shower."

More silence, this time so thick Cameron could have cut it with a knife.

"Adrien?"

"I'm still here," the other man whispered. "I'm just, well, wow, you know?" He laughed again, the sound so heavy with shock it was almost tangible. "He told me he met you. I knew he would, given how close you are to Jackson. It's just..."

"Nothing happened." Cameron wanted to reassure the man. He had caught Adrien off guard by answering Thaddeus's phone, surprised him, but he had hurt him, too. Cameron could hear the pain Adrien was obviously trying to hide.

"It's none of my business," Adrien said softly.

Cameron raked a hand through his hair and turned toward the hallway. Something tightened in his chest.

Hurt? He had no right to be. He had given up his shot with Adrien, pushed the other man away because he knew he would never, *could* never, give Adrien what he deserved.

Guilt? Yeah, that was probably it. He didn't want to come between Thaddeus and Adrien, but what if he had? Thaddeus was the man for Adrien. Cameron had known that last night. Thaddeus was in love with Adrien. He could, and would, give Adrien everything he deserved and more.

"Yes, it is your business," Cameron told Adrien and then proceeded to come completely clean. Maybe it would help if Adrien knew everything. "I asked him on a date the other night. We went for a walk and had a nice dinner. I kissed him, but it didn't go any further. He came to my apartment last night and we talked, watched a movie, and fell asleep on the couch."

"You kissed him, had him alone in your apartment, and you managed to fall asleep?" The surprise was back in Adrien's voice, this time laced with true amusement.

Between being with Thaddeus and knowing that Mallory was still out there somewhere with Wade Forbes, Cameron couldn't believe he'd gotten a wink of sleep either, much less three and a half hours of it.

"Sweetie, I knew you had a will of steel, but damn, it must be completely impenetrable."

Cameron chuckled. He couldn't help himself. "Yeah, he's pretty amazing." And, *damn*, the man could kiss. He had nearly lost it so many times last night, nearly threw every ounce of his resistance to the wind and said to hell with it all simply for the chance to taste Thaddeus again.

"Adrien, Mal has been kidnapped."

"What?" Horror buried Adrien's amusement in an instant. "Oh my God! When? How? Who?"

"We've been working a case, sex trafficking. She went undercover at a local club. That cover was blown and they got her." Cameron recounted yesterday's events, leaving nothing out.

"Jesus, sweetie," Adrien said, genuinely concerned. "I can't imagine what you're going through."

"It's been a rough eighteen hours." Cameron glanced at the clock on his cable box. It really had been eighteen hours since Mallory had gone missing, and for at least four of those he had thought she was dead.

"I'm glad Thaddeus was there for you."

Adrien meant it. Cameron heard the sincerity of his words in the man's tone. "Honestly, so am I. He—" Cameron broke off when the theme song from *Men In Black* started playing through the living room. His attention landed on his own cell phone dancing feverously on the coffee table. "Jackson is calling. I've got to go, baby. I'll have Thaddeus call you back when he gets out of the shower."

"Tell him not to worry about it. I know he'll be busy with the firefighter challenge today."

"I'm sure he'll make time to call." Cameron hung up Thaddeus's phone with one hand, picking up his own and answering it with the other. "Tell me you've found her."

Jackson didn't miss a beat. "Not yet, but we're one step closer. Platt is headed back to town. Cooper and I are on our way there now. We're going in."

"I'll meet you there." Cameron shoved his cell in the pocket of his shorts and slipped on his tennis shoes. Wearing yesterday's clothes and with his cup of coffee forgotten, he headed for the door. He was reaching for the knob when he heard the shower shut off in the bathroom.

Shit. He needed to tell Thaddeus he was leaving.

He snatched up Thaddeus's cell phone as he hurried down the hall, pushed open the bathroom door, not thinking to knock, and froze. Thaddeus did, too, in his effort to snag the towel off the nearby rack. For a nanosecond, Cameron completely forgot why he had barged into the bathroom as his gaze moved over Thaddeus's bare chest speckled with water drops. His attention followed the springy dark curls that thinned down the man's abdomen, thickening again as it reached his groin.

"Good morning. I decided to take you up on last night's offer of a shower before I left. I've got to get to Jackson's apartment and pick up Terri so we can get to the challenge on time."

Cameron's gaze slammed into Thaddeus's. The man's eyes danced with amusement, heat, and a temptation Cameron knew would knock down his resistance if given enough time. That time was something he blessedly didn't have right now.

"Sorry, baby. That's why I came in here. Jackson just called. We got a break in the case."

"Mallory?"

"Not yet, but we think we're a step closer. God, I hope we're a step closer."

"Go. I can let myself out."

Cameron nodded then, remembering Thaddeus's phone in his hand, he set it on the bathroom counter. "It rang while you were taking a shower. The screen said unknown. I thought it might be important so I answered it. It was Adrien, baby. He recognized my voice. I told him nothing happened between us, but…" He trailed off and shook his head, remembering the hurt he had heard in Adrien's voice. "I don't think he believed me."

A myriad of emotions moved through Thaddeus's expression Cameron couldn't define even if he'd had the time to try.

"Don't worry about it." Thaddeus pulled the towel from the rack and wrapped it around his lean hips. "I'll call him when I get the chance. Thank you."

"Thank *you*, for being here last night. I would've gone nuts without you here to take my mind off of this for a little while."

"Anytime."

Cameron left his apartment with Thaddeus's smile clear in his mind and a world of confusion weighing heavy in his chest.

Chapter Ten

"Five minutes." Cooper tossed his cell phone in the drink holder of his SUV, pulled his Glock from his shoulder holster, and checked the magazine.

Five minutes of fucking torture. Jackson readied his Beretta as he stared out the windshield at the house a block ahead. Agents were in place surrounding Leroy Platt's house, prepared to move in on Cooper's order. In five minutes, less now, Platt would be pulling into the driveway. They would wait for him to approach the house, to unlock the front door, then make their move.

"What's happening with the others, sir?" Scattered around town and back at HQ, other agents were feverously working to pin down the other leads Sharp had uncovered. They didn't believe they would find Mallory at the same place as any of the other missing girls, but surly one of them or their "master" would lead them to where the girls were kept before being sold.

"We've got teams moving in on Roger Fuse and Hank Alvarez. Both appear to be at their residences. Our team at HQ is still trying to track down the others." Cooper looked at Jackson, his expression hard, determined. "We'll get them, Graham, and we'll find Mallory. I want the teams to move as simultaneously as possible. If word somehow gets out we're moving in, these bastards are going to scatter."

And if news of the takedowns got to Forbes first, they might lose any chance they had of finding Mallory. She had been missing for too long already. And the other girls? Jackson didn't want to think about what they had been going through or if they would even find any of them still alive.

The seconds ticked by, and his mind reeled with thoughts of Mallory. He saw her amazing smile, heard her sex-kitten voice, remembered the turmoil twisting with realizations in her eyes the last time he had seen her. Tarantino had been right. Jackson had finally gotten to her. He had shattered the wall she had so carefully built around her heart, worked his way in exactly where he had wanted to be, and now he didn't have a fucking clue one what to do about it.

All these years he had thought he understood her, believed he had only to get her past her fears of loving him and everything would be okay. For the first time ever, he truly doubted his philosophy. Would either of them survive this? Christ, could either of them continue to live if one of them died?

"Move."

Cooper's single, harsh command ripped Jackson from his thoughts. His attention snapped to the driveway where Leroy Platt had just pulled in. From that point, the operation went like clockwork, each agent carrying out his duty with pristine precision. By the time Jackson and Cooper had double-timed it the block down the road, agents had Platt in custody and were entering the house.

The most terrified scream he had ever heard came from inside the house. Jackson saw every agent on the outside freeze, their gazes snapping to the house as he bolted for the front door. He took the stairs two at a time to the second floor, sensing Cooper at his heels. More agents were in the hallway, others blocking an open door, and he scarcely heard a voice attempting to talk through the screams.

Cooper pushed past him, through the agents blocking the door, and raced into the room. Jackson followed, stopping short just inside the doorway.

He immediately recognized the girl on the bed from the grainy driver's-license photo. Lexie Stratus lay spread-eagle, stark naked and chained to the bed. She was jerking, her head lolling wildly in her attempts to get away from the agents surrounding her.

"I can't get her to stop," one of the agents told Cooper helplessly. "She had a ball gag in her mouth when we found her. I took it out and she started screaming. I can't get her to listen."

"Unchain her." Cooper moved slowly across the last few feet to the bed and eased down onto the side.

"We're trying, sir," an agent answered loudly to be heard over Lexie's continued screams. "We've got to get something to break the padlocks."

Jackson stepped closer, noting the wounds on Lexie's ankles and wrists, the blood gushing from the cuts. Not all of that had come from the last few seconds. The girl had obviously been chained to the bed the entire time Platt had been out of town, probably longer. More deep cuts and dark bruises covered her slender body. One of her eyes was swollen shut. Her lips were cracked, and her jaw looked to be broken. That didn't stop her from screaming, though.

"Lexie, I'm FBI agent Adam Cooper." Cooper spoke loudly, sternly, but his tone was full of compassion as he tried to get through to the girl. "We're here to help you. You're safe now." He repeated it all again and again and again until finally his words started to calm her. Her screams turned to whimpers and she stopped thrashing, her one good eye locked on Cooper's face.

"We're here to help you," Cooper said again, softer this time. He didn't try to touch her. None of them did. Jackson knew, as he was certain they all did, that a touch from any man right now would likely send the woman back into hysterics.

"Get me a female agent in here," Cooper demanded to the room at large, not looking away from Lexie.

Mallory. Dear God, if Mallory were here she could calm the girl, comfort her. Of course, Mallory wasn't the only female agent on the bureau, but if she were here, that would mean she wasn't chained to a bed somewhere like Lexie had been, having the same horrid things being done to her.

Bile rose in Jackson's throat and he forced it back down. He didn't want to think they would find Mallory the same way. Lexie had been held hostage here for close to a month. He would be damned if it would take them that long to find Mallory.

Jackson stood back and watched as a female agent he barely knew rushed into the room carrying a blanket. Another agent was close at her heels with tools to bust the padlocks. In minutes, Lexie was free and sat in the bed, with the blanket wrapped around her. The female agent talked to her softly, asking if she could walk or if she would allow one of the men to carry her out.

Minutes stretched as Lexie obviously struggled to calm herself, to absorb the realization that she was being rescued. Cooper sent most of the agents out of the room with orders to continue searching the house, to look for anything that might lead them to where she had been held before being brought here.

"H–how did you find me?"

An instant silence fell in the room at Lexie's softly asked question.

Cooper's lips unfolded in a small, comforting smile. "Jennifer. She came to us and asked for our help. She's been worried about you."

Tears streaked Lexie's face and continued to slide down her cheeks. It obviously hurt her to talk, but she did anyway. "Is she o–okay? They didn't g–get her, too?"

"She's safe. I saw her myself a few hours ago at work."

Lexie's good eye widened and filled with horror. "At Cinderella's? No, you've got to get her out of there. She's not safe there. They'll get her. They'll take her downstairs."

"Is that where they took you?" Cooper asked, alarm in his tone.

"Son of a bitch." Jackson didn't wait for the girl's answer. He spun around and collided with Cameron as he headed for the door. "Cinderella's. That's where he's holding Mallory."

* * * *

Mallory forced herself to sit up, gritting her teeth against the pain that seemed to have become a constant part of her new existence. How long has she been here? A day? A week? A month? Her head didn't feel as scrambled and foggy as it had every other time she had awakened since Forbes had brought her here.

Wherever here is.

This room looked different than the others, save for the bed she sat on being the only furnishing. The walls were painted a pale blue rather than the stark white of the room where she had met Sophie.

Sophie. God, was the girl still in that room? Had Forbes done something to her after he had taken Mallory out? Why hadn't he put Mallory back in that room with her?

The rattle of the doorknob cut off her questions, and her heart leapt to her throat. She slid off the bed, no longer caring that she didn't have anything to cover herself with, as the door opened and Wade Forbes walked into the room. He closed the door, locking it behind him with one hand, a gun aimed steadily at her in the other.

Mallory flicked a glance at each of the four corners in the room. She didn't see any cameras but figured he must have some hidden. He seemed to always know when she woke.

"Where am I?" She fixed her attention back on him, on the gun pointed dead center at her chest. Time was running out. She knew it. She felt it in her bones. He hadn't done more to her so far than rough her up a bit, drug her, and take pictures of her naked body. The unbalanced look in his eyes told her that was about to change.

"In a room." He advanced on her slowly.

Her heart pounded furiously with each step he took. "Where is Sophie? What have you done to her?"

A devious smile tilted his lips. How had she ever thought this man was handsome? "Where she's always been. I haven't done anything to her...yet. Well, other than break the news to her of her brother's death." He wrinkled his brows, perplexed. "She didn't take it as hard as I expected. Surely she hoped he would come to her rescue." He laughed. "He actually thought I would let him have her. Stupid bastard."

"That's what you told him, isn't it? If he did what you told him to do, if he murdered Erin, if he burned Stardust, you told him you would give him Sophie. Instead, you set it up so he would die in the fire."

"He didn't die in that fire, but I made him wish he had. He thought he could hide from me. He was wrong. I'm sure your buddies at the FBI will find him, or what is left of him, eventually."

Mallory's blood turned to ice in her veins. "They will find me, too. It's only a matter of time. You're slipping up, making too many mistakes."

"Shut up." He screamed at her, his expression contorting to one of pure, deranged fury. "I don't make mistakes. I know exactly what I'm doing. Right now, I'm going to do what I've been waiting days to do. You. Now get on the bed."

No. Oh, God, no.

Mallory didn't move. Her gaze locked on the gun, on the fact that it was cocked and loaded and ready to shoot. Her mind scrambled, fighting to think through the fear.

He took another step closer, and she took an involuntary step back. "I won't hesitate to shoot you, bitch. I'll be happy to fuck your brains out while you lay dying beneath me."

Mallory inched away until the backs of her knees hit the mattress. Terror made her whole body shiver as she slowly sat down. There had to be a way out of this. Damnit, she had to do something!

"Lay down," he ordered through gritted teeth, the gun now inches from her chest.

Mallory scooted to the center of the bed, turned, and lay back, her sole focus on the gun. Without that gun, she knew she could take him. If it hadn't been for Carl Jordan back in the office at Stardust, she would have taken Forbes out then.

Forbes moved to the foot of the bed, the gun never wavering from its bead on her chest. He grabbed her right leg with his free hand, somehow managing to hold it down and belt a leather strap around her ankle without ever lowering that gun. He did the same with her left ankle, then returned to the side of the bed.

He would have to put that gun down at some point, wouldn't he? He reached for her left arm next, stretching it above her head and fastening it to the headboard with the same kind of belted strap that was now around both of her ankles. By the time he put the gun down, she would be bound to the bed, unable to move.

Think, Mallory. Dear God, think!

He climbed onto the side of the bed and the gun wavered a fraction, but he still didn't lower it.

She would let him shoot her. It was her only option. She had one hand left free. As soon as he got close enough, she would go for the gun, angle it away from her heart, and pray for the best.

Fear clogged her throat and threatened to cloud her mind as he started to move over her.

"You're going to make a great whore. Did I tell you I found you a new master already? I knew it wouldn't take long. He has big plans for you, too."

Mallory watched him, the world seeming to spin in slow motion now as he reached for her right arm. The knock at the door startled them both.

"Go away." Forbes didn't look away from her, didn't move the gun, didn't stop reaching for her free arm.

"Get the fuck out here," Betty bellowed through the locked door. "We've got to talk now."

"Whatever it is can wait." Forbes yelled back, his fingers a scant inch from Mallory's wrist.

She flexed the muscle in her arm, readying herself to fight.

"The Feds got Leroy," Betty yelled. "They found Lexie Stratus. They got Holder and Marcum, too."

Forbes's eyes widened in shock and he whipped his head toward the door.

Mallory balled her fist and swung. Her forearm connected with the gun, the force behind the blow knocking it out of his hand. A shot fired as the gun hit the floor. She didn't spare a second wondering where the bullet hit. She fisted her hand in Forbes's hair, lifted her head, and head butted him hard enough to make herself see stars. He screamed and she bucked, miraculously hard enough to send him bouncing off the bed. She heard him hit the floor, heard him scrambling to get back up. She fumbled with the strap on her left wrist and managed to get it free just as he got to his feet.

He didn't bother to go for the gun. *And the man said he didn't make mistakes.* He came after her barehanded, and she was ready for him. She lunged at him, going straight for his eyes, and dug her nails into his flesh. She felt the blood start to trickle beneath her fingernails and dimly heard the door to the room slam open over the adrenaline pounding in her ears.

"Christ, get him off of her," someone, she could've sworn it was Cooper's voice, shouted, but she held on tight, determined to claw the bastard's eyes from his skull.

Before she knew what was happening, a pair of arms appeared around Forbes's neck and he was yanked back away from her.

"No!" she screamed as a different pair of arms came around her shoulders from behind her. She twisted away from them, going for the bindings around her ankles. Sheer fury controlled her movements as she jerked the belts free and jumped off the bed.

Tarantino had Forbes in a neck lock, but Mallory lunged for him anyway. "I'll kill you, you fucking cock-sucking bastard."

"Mal, stop." An arm snaked around her waist and yanked her back. She didn't need to see the hard body behind her. The feel of Jackson's body against hers was enough for her to know it was him. "We got him, baby."

"I'll get him, too, if you'll let go of me," she fired back, but she stopped trying to get out of Jackson's embrace. "Damnit, I want to kill him. Please, let me kill him."

Cooper moved into her line of sight, and she could have sworn she saw him actually considering her request before he shook his head. "Get him out of here," he ordered Tarantino. Then he lowered his voice and spoke directly to Mallory. "Are you hurt? Do I need to get medical personnel in here?"

"I'm pissed," Mallory said through gritted teeth.

Cooper's lips actually twitched. "Yeah, I got that."

She felt Jackson shifting behind her. He released her long enough to drape his jacket over her shoulders before enveloping her in an embrace hard enough to crack her already bruised ribs.

"Jesus, Mal," he whispered against the side of her neck. "Please tell me he didn't hurt you."

All the fight left her at the sound of his voice, at the worry and heartbreak that made his words crack. She turned in his arms, lifted her head, and met his gaze. The glimmer of tears in his eyes nearly destroyed her. "He didn't hurt me."

Jackson swallowed, nodded, then kissed her.

Where had the man learned to kiss? She didn't know, but damn if he wasn't a pro at it. She melted in his arms and lost herself in his scent, in the taste of him, in the feel of having his body pressed to hers. She forgot about the other agents in the room, about her boss watching them, and kissed him back.

Several long, breathtaking moments later, someone cleared his throat.

"Sis, we need to get back to HQ."

Cameron. Mallory pulled back from Jackson, turned slightly, and found her brother standing in arm's reach. She threw her arms around him and hugged him tight as emotions clogged her throat.

"I knew you guys would get me out of here."

"From the look of things when we barged in, you were doing a pretty damn good job at getting out of here yourself," Cooper told her, his tone full of pride.

Mallory shot him a grin. "I was working on it." She stepped back from Cameron and pulled Jackson's jacket tighter around her. "There's at least one more girl here. Sophie. She's Kenneth Reese's sister."

Cooper nodded. "We already found her."

Mallory nodded once and turned, meeting first Cameron's gaze and then Jackson's. "Then I'm ready to go now."

* * * *

"Call him." Terri jabbed the top of Thaddeus's cell phone into his chest.

Thaddeus stepped back a fraction but didn't take the phone. "Jeez, when did you become my mother?"

Terri lifted a quizzical brow. "Is that what your mother would tell you to do?"

Thaddeus barked a half laugh. "No, my mother would tell me to marry you."

"Which explains why you've been practically avoiding your parents like the plague since we've been in town. Yeah, I figured as much. I'll duke it out with you later over that one when we have more time." Terri jabbed him with the phone again. "Right now, Vegister, time is running out. Call him before it's too late."

Thaddeus sighed and raked a hand through his hair. "I'll call him tonight, okay?"

"You'll call him now." Terri growled like a pit bull, proving she wouldn't let up until she got her way. "We've got a good ten minutes before this thing starts. If you don't call him now, you're going to go into the challenge with your head wrapping around what you want to say to him when you finally do call him instead of what you're supposed to be doing. Do you really want to deal with me if we lose this thing today because your focus is in the wrong place?"

No, he didn't, any more than he wanted to let his partner down. He knew better than to go into a fire scene with his head in the wrong place. And, okay, today wasn't a fire scene, but the challenge was equally important at this point in time. Terri was right, too. At the moment, his mind *was* wrapped around Adrien and what he would say when he talked to the man, instead of concentrating on the events they were about to endure.

Thaddeus sighed again and took his cell phone from Terri's outstretched hand. He held her gaze, letting his annoyance show as he thumbed through his contact list and found Adrien's number. The man answered on the first ring.

"Shouldn't you be racing against a clock right about now, sweetie?"

Thaddeus closed his eyes at the sound of Adrien's voice. Flashbacks of last night hit him, bringing with them a truckload of guilt he knew deep down he really shouldn't feel. "In about ten minutes."

"Ten minutes you should be using to get in the zone," Adrien countered.

Thaddeus glanced at Terri. "Yeah, so I've been told. Cameron told me you called this morning."

"To wish you luck."

"Adrien, I—"

"Don't have to explain, sweetie," Adrien cut him off. "Actually, I wish you wouldn't. If either of us owes the other an explanation, it should be me giving you one. I thought I would do that when you got back. When I asked if we could get together and talk, that's what I had in mind. Which was stupid of me." He laughed, but there was no humor in the tone. "I should have done that before you left, not after the fact."

"It's okay. I understand. Really, meeting Cameron has made it easier to figure out what has been going on the last few years."

"You mean it's made it easier to figure out why I'm so fucked up?"

Thaddeus chuckled. "Yeah, a guy like Cameron can do that to a man."

"You noticed, huh?" A trace of jealously sounded in Adrien's tone.

Thaddeus thought about Cameron, all six-feet-plus of pure temptation wrapped in nearly irresistible sex appeal. "Yeah, I noticed."

"Well, get him, and me, out of your head," Adrien ordered. "You've got a challenge to win today, sweetie, and I have no doubt you can come out on top."

"Done." Thaddeus smiled as he cut the connection and stashed his phone in his gear bag.

"Better?" Terri lifted a brow, a smile of her own playing with the corner of her lips.

"For now." Talking to Adrien had helped. He raked his gaze over the firefighter course, his attention landing on the five-story tower. He had only to make it to the top of that thing and back down again in the best possible time to hand the rest over to Terri. He could do it. He *would* do it. But deep down he knew that tower wasn't the only obstacle he was battling to win.

Trouble came in also knowing he was no longer certain if the other hurdle he wanted to conquer was Adrien or Cameron.

* * * *

"How are you feeling?" Jackson eased onto the edge of the sofa where Mallory lay with her head on a pillow and her feet propped on the armrest on the opposite end. She looked like shit. Amazingly beautiful shit, but it was obvious the last twenty-four-plus hours had taken their toll.

"Great. Like I'm in Heaven on earth." Her smile reached her incredible eyes as she gazed up at him. "I'm happy and relieved. My head hurts like a bitch. My throat is still a bit scratchy. My solar plexus is bruised and my tummy aches, but all in all, I'm peachy."

Jackson angled his head. "All that isn't peachy, Mal."

"It is when you consider the cause and the fact that it will all go away." She sighed, the sound one of pure contentment. "Those girls are safe now. Sophie is out of that place. Lexie and the others have been found. They'll all get the help they need, both physically and mentally, so they can move on with their lives after what has been done to them. Every ping in my head and pang in my body was well worth it for that."

Five of the six missing girls that they knew of had been found. The pervert whom they believed to have purchased the sixth, Leah Gibbs, one of the first strippers to go missing from Stardust, was in custody, but so far, the bastard wasn't talking.

A shadow moved through Mallory's expression. "Do you think there are others out there we don't know about?"

"If there are, we'll find them. This isn't over. Not until we're certain we have them all."

"It won't be over even then. There will always be some sick bastard out there stealing women, attempting to make them into sex slaves, and sadistic perverts out there willing to pay for them."

"Unfortunately, you're right. And it's our job to catch and stop as many of them as we can."

Mallory lifted a finger and poked Jackson on the tip of his nose. "And you, slick, are right about that." She let her hand fall to her belly. "I'm still having trouble grasping the fact that Cinderella's was a part of this all along."

"You and everyone else. Cooper is pissed that we didn't catch that sooner."

"We've checked the place out before. Of all the clubs in Waterston, we all believed it to be the squeakiest."

"Between Forbes and Kyle Zyler, they did a hell of a job at covering up the club's involvement, making it look like a class-A establishment when, behind the scenes, beneath the club floor, women were being held and tortured."

"I didn't recognize him, you know? Zyler, he was there in the office at Stardust and in the van they put me in when they took me to Cinderella's. I thought he was just some goon Forbes had hired." Mallory rubbed her forehead. "I had only seen him once or twice, but God, you would think I would have recognized him."

"Don't beat yourself up over it. The important thing is we got all of them."

Mallory narrowed her eyes at him. "I still wish you wouldn't have pulled me off Forbes. Doing that bastard some real damage would have really made my day."

Jackson laughed. "I bet it would have."

"So, do you think Cooper is going to ream our asses for not figuring out the Cinderella connection sooner?"

"Not before he reams his own. He went there last night and didn't get a clue himself."

"He went to Cinderella's? Why?"

"To watch after Jennifer Moss. This is going to sound crazy, but I think he's got a thing for her. Did you notice the way he looks at her?"

Mallory barked a surprised laugh. "Are we talking about the same Cooper? Adam Cooper, our big, bad, ferocious boss has the hots for a woman?"

"Shocked me to my toes, too."

"Wow!" Mallory laughed again. "It might be good for him, though, you know, to fall in love with someone?"

Would it? Was falling in love good for anyone, especially those who lived on the edge of danger day in and day out the way they did? Jackson was no longer sure anymore.

"I'm surprised you didn't want to go to your place." Jackson changed the subject. After their debriefing, he had offered to drive her home, but she told him she wanted to come to his apartment instead.

Mallory grinned, her eyes glinting with pure mischief. "Chef Jackson's is closed at my place."

Jackson smiled. "Is that so?"

"Yep, seems the restaurant supplier went on strike or some such nonsense."

Jackson pushed to his feet, turned toward her, and bowed. "Welcome to Chef Jackson's, madam. What can I get for you this afternoon?"

Mallory beamed at him. "Anything hot, tasty, and in *very* large quantities."

"Want some ibuprofen for your headache?"

Mallory shook her head. "No, it will go away on its own. I've had enough drugs to last me a lifetime."

* * * *

Something is up. Mallory rolled onto her stomach, stifling a grunt at the pain in her belly and solar plexus, and watched Jackson walk to the kitchen. Her gaze immediately landed on his perfect ass clad in what she always thought of as his trademark black Armani slacks. Her mouth watered, her belly growling for nourishment that had nothing to do with food or drink and everything to do with the man walking away from her.

Is he walking away? It suddenly felt like it. Oh, she knew he was merely going to the kitchen right now to fix her something to eat, but the sense she had gotten when she had looked into his eyes made her wonder if she might be losing him.

She pushed herself up and slid off the couch as he disappeared into the kitchen. She had been in his apartment numerous times over the years and practically knew the layout, its furnishings, and other contents as well as her own. That didn't stop her from perusing the living room now.

Nothing had changed much. The same photos sat in frames on shelves also occupied by the same books. Her attention paused on one of the photos. She laughed quietly and shook her head.

"Will it ever stop amazing me how you and Jason look exactly alike?" The brothers stood side-by-side in the picture, turned slightly away from each other, the backs of their shoulders touching. She could tell them apart simply by the look in their eyes. Jason's eyes glinted with a boyish mischief. He was always the twin getting into something. Jackson was smiling in the photo, but his eyes were serious, contained.

"We're identical twins, Mal," Jackson said from the kitchen. "We're supposed to look exactly alike."

"Got any plans of seeing him anytime soon?" She shifted her gaze to another picture, this one of an early morning at the docks in Silver Springs. The sun had just begun to rise in the distance, painting the water with streams of pinkish-orange light.

"He's trying to get me to come down for the Fired Up For Kids benefit in a few months. I told him I would make it if I could."

"Fired Up For Kids?" Mallory shot a look over her shoulder and swallowed a groan. Jackson was moving around the kitchen gathering ingredients for whatever he planned to cook. Every move was decisive yet graceful. The muscles in his forearm tightened as he pulled open the refrigerator, and her waist tingled in remembrance of that strong arm wrapped around her. He ducked, leaned into the fridge and—*Holy hormones*—that perfect view of his ass made her panties wet.

He chuckled, the sound muffled by the refrigerator. "It's a benefit the local fire departments are putting together to raise money for area kids." He straightened with what looked like celery stalks and a bag of carrots in his hand and moved to the nearby counter. His shoulder muscles flexed as he situated the celery on a cutting board. She didn't know what he was putting together, but it was certainly entertaining to watch. "Kind of like the calendar they did a few years ago for the hurricane victims, except this will be a strip show."

"A strip show. Wow!"

"That's pretty much what I said." The noise of an electric can opener put a pause in the conversation. "Why were you asking if I planned to see him soon?"

Mallory shrugged and looked back at the photo of the beach. "I don't know. It's been a while since I've seen a beach. I thought I might go with you."

Jackson didn't comment, his attention seemingly snagged by the meal he was preparing. Then again, maybe he didn't want her to go with him.

Stop it, Mallory. You're being ridiculous.

Wasn't she? Something definitely seemed off between them today.

She skimmed the spines of the books on the shelves, attempting to convince herself the out-of-sorts feeling she was getting was her imagination working overtime. They hadn't talked about the scene she made in his office before all the shit had gone down at Stardust. Maybe that had something to do with what was going on now. She had been pissed at him for leaving her, for doing the same thing to her she had done to him the night before. Tarantino had pegged it on the head. Jackson had finally gotten to her. And there wasn't a damn thing she could do about it.

She didn't want to do anything about it. She had come to that realization at some point during all those hours Forbes had held her captive. Though the drugs he had given her had knocked her out most of the time, apparently it hadn't put her mind to sleep. In her efforts to battle the terror of what Forbes might do to her, that he would likely kill her, a fear she had lived with most of her life had diminished.

She loved Jackson with every ounce of her heart and soul. She could admit that now, to herself and to him when the time felt right. She still feared losing him, being left alone in the world as her mother had been, if and when anything happened to him. She also knew no man would ever replace him.

She started to turn when a title among all the crime thrillers caught her eye. Okay, so apparently they weren't all the same books, after all. She lifted a brow as she pulled the book from the shelf. *Sex Games? Nice.* An inscription was written on the title page, and she immediately recognized the name. *Interesting book for a girl to give her brother-in-law.*

Mallory scanned the table of contents. *Escort and Client, Bar Pick-Up, Kidnap Time, Menu for You...* She glanced at Jackson in the kitchen.

Hmm, what exactly is he preparing in there?

She went back to reading. *Adult Twister, See the Mirror, The Bedroom Dance, Truth or Dare...*

Now those could be fun and useful.

She read through several more, flipped to the appropriate pages, and her mind spun with ideas. Grinning to herself, she put the book back on the shelf.

"Do I have time for a quick shower?" She had taken one mere hours ago at HQ, but she still felt grimy. Deep down, she knew it wasn't dirt making her feel that way. It was her body's memory of that sadistic bastard's touch, a recollection her mind was trying desperately to forget.

"Sure, this needs to simmer for at least thirty minutes."

"Got anything I can wear?" The clothes she had on were the spare outfit she kept in her office. While still clean, the dress skirt and blouse wouldn't serve for what she had in mind.

"I'm sure you can find something in my bedroom. Help yourself."

* * * *

Jackson glanced at her as she disappeared down the hall. He figured he had twenty minutes tops to prepare himself for the sight of her amazing body clad only in one of his shirts. He didn't expect her to find anything else in his closet that would fit.

He sighed and dumped two cups of egg noodles into the pot already simmering with onions, celery, carrots, and chicken. They needed to talk. He knew that. How to broach the subject was what he hadn't quite figured out. They were dancing around it again, but this time was different. This time, he understood her more than ever before.

And now you're the one with the fear.

He braced his hands on the edge of the counter, bowed his head, and closed his eyes. *Big mistake.* When he did that, he saw her bound to that bed, naked and more vulnerable than he had ever imagined she could be.

Except, she hadn't been helpless. She had been fighting back and doing a damn good job of it, too. But would she have succeeded if they hadn't gotten to her when they did? The realization that she had come so close to ending up like Lexie, or worse, Erin Griffin, still sent horrified chills down his spine.

He almost lost her. All these years, he had never allowed himself to think about that, to worry about it. It was hitting him now, though, pounding at him until his heart felt like a punching bag, heavy with the knowledge of how close it had been and bruised from the repeated blows that it likely wasn't the last time they would find themselves in a similar situation. Only next time, it might be far worse, and he didn't know the hell to handle it.

She gave him fifteen minutes before he heard her come sashaying back into the living room.

"You okay, Slick?"

"Yeah." Jackson straightened, moved to the stove, and stirred the chicken soup. The pot simmering was far more than the two of them could eat alone, but Terri and Thaddeus would be back at some point, and he fully expected Cameron to show up any minute, too.

"Mind if I turn on some music? It's too quiet in here."

"No, go ahead." He heard the television power on, caught traces of words as she flipped through the channels before settling on the Music Choice station that played modern-day rock. Though he preferred classical or classic rock himself, he recognized the fast beat tempo of Finger Eleven's "Paralyzer" as it streamed through the television speakers.

"I love this song."

Jackson heard her singing along, her voice growing louder as she came up behind him. When he turned, she grabbed his hands and started to pull him into the living room.

"Mal." He used her name as a warning.

She sang along with the song, her body swaying sexily to the beat, her eyes gleaming with wicked temptation a she spun around to face him. "The tie is already gone, handsome."

"So is my rhythm. I can't dance." But, damn, the effect of watching her went straight to his cock. His shaft thickened, his balls tightening as his senses went into overload.

"Everybody can dance." She dropped his hands, pressed her swaying body to his, and gripped his hips. "Follow my lead."

Jackson splayed his hand on the small of her back and moved his hips.

Mallory beamed up at him. "That's it."

Jackson reached his free hand behind her, molding her ass with his palm, and watched as intense lust filled her eyes. She arched her lower body into him, extended a leg around his, and ground her pussy against his thigh.

"Sweet Jesus," he growled as he moved with her, the heat between them building to boiling temperatures.

A wicked smile tilted her lips. "Thought you didn't know how to dance, Slick."

"I'm a fast learner." *At some things.* Apparently, he still hadn't learned this woman had the power to destroy him.

Her hands moved from his hips, skimmed up his back, and sent icy slivers of hunger raining through his body.

Jackson dipped his head, catching her mouth in a kiss that drove him to the brink of insanity. Her tongue tangled with his, dancing, demanding, and he felt himself go over the edge. He dropped his other hand to her ass and squeezed as he pulled her more firmly against him. Whips of heat slashed at his cock. The need to be inside her sopping pussy controlled his movements and mind.

Absently, he heard the song play out, segueing into Nickelback's "Never Gonna Be Alone." He licked the inside of her mouth, dragged his tongue down her pallet, and nipped her bottom lip as he eased back.

She gazed up at him through heavy-lidded eyes filled with so many emotions it took his breath away. "Truth or dare?" she asked softly.

Jackson stared at her, mesmerized by the challenge that took over her eyes. "I don't know." Either one could spell trouble for him right now.

"Then I'll choose for you. Truth." She lifted a hand to the side of his face and skimmed the backs of her fingers down his cheek. "What happened? Why does it seem like you're the one who is running scared now?"

"That's two questions."

"Combine them together as one."

Jackson took a deep breath and briefly closed his eyes. "I nearly lost you," he finally answered through the tightness in his throat.

Her hand slipped to his nape, her fingers toying with the back of his hair. "You could've lost me plenty of times over the years. Maybe not in the same way, but I wouldn't have been yours."

He understood what she meant. She could've given up her game, could've stopped trying to get him in bed, and taken on any number of boyfriends. He knew she had been with other men. She'd had her flings, but none of those men ever got close enough to her to stake a claim.

"You would've still been in this world."

She nodded slowly, her gaze never leaving his. "A world where you would have still wanted me. Your turn."

She was right. He would never stop wanting her. "Truth or dare?"

A sinfully sensuous smile unfolded on her lips. "While I can't wait to get to the dare portion of this game, I'll go for truth this time."

"Where did the fear go?"

"Apparently into you. Here's the question that pushed it out. What is the difference between us loving one another, spending our lives together, then waiting to reunite in Heaven and loving one another, but not being together out of fear we might lose one another? The answer I got is that, either way, we risk ending up alone, but we get time, hopefully many years, to enjoy our lives together before that day comes."

Great answer. It was the one he had always had in his head, too. He simply lost track of it somewhere in the last twenty-four hours. "Do you love me?"

"You didn't ask truth or dare."

"I'm not playing anymore."

"Yes, I love you. I've always loved you."

Her eyes glistened with tears, but he didn't think they were ones of sadness. He sensed they were more from relief, from finally letting go of everything she had fought so hard to keep bottled inside for so many years, from surrendering at last.

"I *will* always love you," she whispered.

* * * *

Jackson kissed her, and for the first time in her life, she felt truly free. Every piece of her life snapped together in a perfect puzzle that predicted a long, happy life with the man she loved. And, okay, that last part might be wishful thinking, but she would wish and think on it gratefully for the rest of her life.

He broke the kiss far too soon, and she nearly protested before she saw the devious glint in his eyes.

"I dare you to strip for me."

Mallory lifted a brow and ran her tongue teasingly over her bottom lip. "Are we playing again?"

"We are, but this game is all about dares. Are you up for it?"

Mallory stepped back, immediately missing the warmth of his body against hers. She waited a beat, listening to the more upbeat song now playing on the television, and felt the tempo move through her. Locking her gaze with his, she let her body go. She swayed in a sensual ripple of her body that began at her feet and traveled up. She hooked her fingers in the hem of the T-shirt she had found in his drawer and slowly pulled it up, purposely revealing a scant inch of flesh at a time.

He gulped, the muscles in his neck tight as his gaze dropped to her hands, climbing up her body as the shirt did. His focus stopped on her breasts, and she smiled as she pulled the shirt over her head and tossed it to the floor. She hadn't bothered to put on her panties after her shower, hoping they would soon end up right here.

"You're so fucking beautiful," he said, his voice husky and thick with arousal.

Mallory covered her breasts with her hands, rolled her nipples gently between her thumbs and forefingers, and bit back a laugh when she saw him take a half step forward before he stopped himself.

Enjoying the fact that he was so obviously on the brink of losing all control, Mallory flattened her hands beneath her breasts and dragged her fingers down her body. She widened her stance, arrowed one hand to her pussy, and used her thumb and middle finger to spread her pussy lips, touching her clit with the tip of her forefinger.

Jackson made a sound of pure torture and intense need. "Christ."

"Want to take over for me?"

He answered by closing the distance between them, catching her waist, and spinning her around. He pulled her back against him, one hand instantly finding her breast while the other cupped her pussy.

"You like teasing me, don't you?" His heated words fanned the sensitized flesh on the side of her neck.

Mallory grinned even though she knew he couldn't see it. "I've always liked teasing you. That's one thing that isn't going to change, my love." She felt his eyelashes flutter on her neck and knew he had closed his eyes on that.

"Say it again," he told her softly.

"What? My love?" Mallory reached a hand behind her and found his nape.

"Yes." His hand on her breast began a gentle, tantalizing massage that had her head falling back on his shoulder.

She angled her head so she could look at him. "How about I say I love you instead?"

"I could hear you say that every second for the rest of our lives."

"I dare you to move that hand."

He squeezed her breast. "It's already moving."

Mallory grinned. "Wrong hand, wise guy."

"Oh, you mean this one?" His hand on her pussy glided up, and then he slipped a finger between her pussy lips, grazed it over her clit, and pressed at her sopping opening with the tip.

"That one," Mallory groaned, rotating her hips in an effort to draw that finger inside her. Her hips bucked at the first thrust of that wide digit into her flaming channel. Her hand fisted in the back of his hair, an uncontrollable shiver racing through her body as he plunged, adding a second finger and stealing her breath. Passion grew razor-sharp claws as he held her tightly against him, finger-fucking her and applying a gentle pressure to her clit with his thumb.

"Jackson." Her head rolled involuntarily on his shoulder as rapturous sensations sizzled through her.

"I dare you to come for me." He pinched her nipple, stretched his arm farther over her chest to reach her other breast, and delivered the same stupendous assault to that nipple. Between her legs, his fingers thrust in and out of her pussy in a rapid rhythm that sent juices streaming down her inner thighs. "I dare you to come apart in my arms."

She couldn't have resisted the challenge if she had wanted to. The third finger he added to the other two did her in. Pleasure tore through her, streamed out of her in waves of cum and sounds of ecstasy that had her body jerking in his arms.

"God, that's amazing. I want to feel you do it again." His fingers eased out of her pussy, smearing her wetness over her upper thigh and hip as he moved both of his hands to her waist. His cock pressed against her lower back, hard, thick and insistent, and she wanted it inside her now.

She reached behind her back, pushing her hands between their bodies, and groped to unfasten his belt. She growled in frustration, narrowing her eyes at him when he had the nerve to laugh at her.

"I dare you to undo those."

He shook his head. "Uh-uh, in this game, I'm the one who gets to issue the dares."

"That's not fair." But she managed on her own anyway, finally releasing the buckle of his belt along with the button beneath and sliding down the zipper. She delved a hand inside his briefs and giggled when his eyes rolled back in his head as she curled her fingers around his stiff shaft. "What's the matter, handsome?"

"I think my game is backfiring on me."

"That's the trouble with daring people." She stroked his cock as she spoke, applying just enough pressure to draw a low-throated groan from his lips. "Sometimes you just don't know how it will turn out."

"I do." He turned her, seemed to hesitate for a nanosecond before making up his mind, then walked her toward the coffee table. "I can't make it to the bedroom, Mal. I've got to be inside you now." One hand moved to her shoulder and slowly slid down her back as he eased her forward.

Mallory released his cock, flattening her hands on the coffee table as he bent her over it. The surprise of the position he was putting her in heightened the anticipation coursing in a white-hot rush of need through her system. He *was* out of control. She had expected him to insist they take this portion of their game to the bedroom, to want to go slow, to need to be face-to-face. He didn't do any of that. Stuffy, restrained Jackson Graham had lost it enough to make love to her right there in the middle of his living room, from behind, and apparently had no intentions of taking it slow.

She bent her head, watching between her wide-spread legs as the head of his cock moved toward the opening of her pussy. The sight taunted a plea out of her. "Jackson, please. I need you inside me."

He didn't make her ask again. With a firm grip on her hips, he guided his cock into her pussy in a single thrust that sank him all the way in.

Pleasure ripped through Mallory, the orgasm from mere moments ago already a thing of the past as he started to pump. He rolled his hips on the inward thrusts, reaching parts of her cunt she hadn't known existed. She slid her hands forward, curling her fingers around the edge of the coffee table and holding on tight.

"Christ, Mal," he growled. "Baby, I'm not going to last. You're too tight. You feel too good."

"Harder. Faster." Who knew Jackson could let go and fuck her this way? It was astounding, fantastic, and exactly what she wanted.

She pushed her hips back, meeting him thrust for thrust. Their bodies slapped together, sweat pooling on their flesh as moans turned to cries of passion and breaths morphed to ragged bursts of air, each of them competing for what little oxygen remained in the room.

Mallory teetered on the edge, her body craving a second release that clawed its way through her core like a razor-sharp, double-sized sword. "Jackson!"

"Come for me, Mallory. Ah, God, come with me."

Mallory didn't have a choice. Just like the first, the orgasm slashed through her and spilled out of her with a force that destroyed her senses. Her body convulsed, her nails digging into the wood of the coffee table as her channel started to spasm. She heard him grunt, felt his cock jerk inside her as his hot seed filled her body…and the doorknob rattled.

"Shit."

Before Mallory could even register what was happening, Jackson had yanked her up by her waist and was half running, half stumbling with her down the hall to his bedroom. He kicked the bedroom door closed just as the front door opened and voices fluttered down the hallway.

"We still get to go to regional. I wonder when that will be. Wow, I wonder—" Terri's voice broke off and they heard a quiet "shush" that had to have come from Thaddeus.

Jackson slowly set Mallory on her feet. His head fell back on his shoulders and he closed his eyes, a smile playing at the corner of his lips.

Mallory covered her mouth to silence her laughter, then gasped when she remembered the evidence they left in the middle of the living room floor. "My shirt is still in there."

Jackson lifted his head, blinked at her, then stopped trying not to smile. "I guess we're busted."

Mallory giggled softly. "Looks like."

He reached for her, pulled her against him, and brushed his lips to hers. "I don't care. Let's get busted all the time. Marry me, Mal."

"I—what?" Her heart skipped a beat as shock slammed through her system. Did he really just ask her to marry him? Now?

"I know this is a crazy time and place to propose, but I—"

"Yes." She didn't give him a chance to explain, didn't give herself time to think. As far as she was concerned, this was the perfect time and place even if they were standing against the door in his bedroom with her naked and his cock hanging out while two firefighters from Silver Springs stood in his living room. "Yes, I'll marry you, and we can get busted making love all over the city."

Jackson chuckled. "I bet Cooper would love that one."

The phone rang on the bedside table, and Mallory glanced at it. "Want me to get that?"

"Please." He kissed her again before letting her go.

"Should I find another shirt, or do you want to bring the other one to me?" she asked as she walked to the phone.

"You should probably find another one and maybe the jogging pants in the bottom right drawer of the dresser." He paused in the act of reaching for the doorknob and shook his head, but pure amusement lit his expression. "I might be awhile coming up with an explanation for this one."

Mallory laughed and answered the phone.

"That sound is music to my ears," Cameron said. "How are you doing, sis?"

"Absolutely fantastic." She caught herself dancing a little jig by the bedside table. "What's happening around HQ?"

"Wrapping up loose ends. Nothing new to report."

"Then come over here when you're done. Jackson made some chicken noodle soup." At least she thought that was what she smelled. She didn't add that it might be burnt by now considering...

"Chicken noodle soup?"

She could all but hear Cameron wrinkling his nose. "Hey, it beats cooking for yourself tonight."

"Very true. I'll be there shortly."

Shortly turned into nearly two hours. The soup hadn't burned after all, though Jackson had to reheat it once Cameron arrived. She and Jackson didn't have to do much explaining, though Terri and Thaddeus obviously knew what they had nearly walked in on. They greeted both her and Jackson with wide, knowing smiles and had left it at that.

They gathered in the living room, bowls of soup in hand. Terri and Thaddeus sat on opposite ends of the sofa. Cameron perched on the coffee table. Jackson sat in the recliner. Mallory sat in the middle of the floor.

"Now that everybody is here," Mallory said, and the conversation halted. She turned her attention to Terri. "I heard you say something about making it to regional."

Terri nodded, her smile so wide it reached her eyes. "Thaddeus and I took second in the coed tandem team competition today. The top three teams get to go on to the regional competition."

"That's awesome. Congratulations!" Cameron said, and they all chimed in.

"Do you want to tell them our news now?" Jackson asked Mallory.

Mallory shrugged. "I'm game."

"What news?" Thaddeus asked, setting his bowl on the end table.

Mallory watched Jackson and saw him lock gazes with Cameron. "I asked Mallory to marry me. She said yes."

Terri squealed, and Thaddeus reached over to pat Jackson on the shoulder. Jackson smiled but didn't look away from Cameron.

The best friends stared at one another for a long moment, and then Cameron slowly nodded. "Congratulations."

Mallory shifted her attention to her brother, found him looking at her now, and saw equal parts happiness and fear swirling in his eyes.

She held his gaze, knowing she didn't need to speak to tell him she understood. She had seen the way he looked at Thaddeus, knew he had something going on with Adrien Bingham back in Silver Springs, and understood why he was running from it all. She had done it for years, but she had stopped now, and she hoped one day soon he would, too.

THE END

ABOUT THE AUTHOR

Tonya Ramagos is a bestselling author of contemporary, fantasy, paranormal, and cowboy novels. She spends most of her time in a fictional world dreaming up hot hunks and headstrong heroines. When she's not writing, she's reading. Her idea of relaxing is curled on the sofa or on her back deck with a book and her favorite beverage. A single mother of two fantastic boys, she enjoys playing games, throwing darts, dancing, and walking the nature trails around her home in Tennessee.

For all titles by Tonya Ramagos, please visit
www.bookstrand.com/tonya-ramagos

Siren Publishing, Inc.
www.SirenPublishing.com

CPSIA information can be obtained at www.ICGtesting.com
Printed in the USA
LVOW131453121012

302647LV00013B/47/P